PRAISE FOR THE NOVELS OF JOHN LANTIGUA

Remember My Face, Private Eye Writers of America 2021 Shamus Awards Nominee in the Best Original Private Eye Paperback category

"Miami private eye Willie Cuesta is sent to central Florida to track down a missing person. Maybe persons. A heartfelt account of the risks Latinos face in modern America whether or not they're undocumented."

—*Kirkus Reviews* on *Remember My Face*

"The rich and varied characters in this intriguingly twisty tale spring organically from the sandy soil of South Florida. This intelligent, timely novel is sure to win Lantigua new fans."

—*Publishers Weekly* on *Remember My Face*

"This thoroughly entertaining crime novel flirts with a number of the genre's central themes—kidnapping for ransom, drug dealing, betrayal, revenge, the silky seductiveness of a whole lot of money—filtering them through the special sensibility of Miami PI Willie Cuesta. A real find for crime-fiction fans."

—*Booklist* starred review of *On Hallowed Ground*

"The fast-paced action is well matched by concise prose, making this a treat for Elmore Leonard devotees."

—*Publishers Weekly* on *On Hallowed Ground*

THE ULTIMATE HAVANA

A WILLIE CUESTA MYSTERY

JOHN LANTIGUA

Arte Público Press
Houston, Texas

Recovering the past, creating the future

Arte Público Press
University of Houston
4902 Gulf Fwy, Bldg 19, Rm 100
Houston, Texas 77204-2004

Cover design by Mora Des!gn

Names: Lantigua, John, author.
Title: The ultimate Havana / John Lantigua.
Description: Houston, Texas : Arte Público Press, [2022] | Series: Willie Cuesta
   mystery series ; 2
Identifiers: LCCN 2021056533 (print) | LCCN 2021056534 (ebook) | ISBN
   9781558859401 (trade paperback ; alk. paper) | ISBN 9781518507045 (epub) |
   ISBN 9781518507052 (kindle edition) | ISBN 9781518507069 (pdf)
Subjects: LCSH: Cuban Americans—Fiction. | Miami (Fla.)—Fiction. |
   LCGFT: Novels.
Classification: LCC PS3562.A57 U48 2022 (print) | LCC PS3562.A57 (ebook) |
   DDC 813/.54—dc23/eng/20211119
LC record available at https://lccn.loc.gov/2021056533
LC ebook record available at https://lccn.loc.gov/2021056534

22 23 24   3 2 1

ACKNOWLEDGMENTS

Thanks to Gordon Mott, managing editor of *Cigar Aficionado* magazine, and Hendrick Kelner, of Davidoff Cigar in the Dominican Republic, for their help and hospitality. Thanks to all the folks at El Credito Cigar in Little Havana and Henry Vilar and the staff at Macabi Cigar in South Miami for putting up with a layman's questions. I'm grateful to Juan Tamayo of *The Miami Herald* for sharing his contacts. Thanks to Jane Bussey and Greg Aunapu for their contributions to the manuscript, to my editors Joseph Pittman and Genny Ostertag at Signet for their support, and to Michelle Urry, again, for her friendship.

For Elise O'Shaughnessy

CHAPTER ONE

Willie Cuesta, private investigator, sat slouched in a wicker chair, his bare feet propped on the windowsill in his Little Havana office. He stared at a small, green lizard that clung to the pane of glass hunting a mosquito in the corner of the casement. That window overlooked the tropical garden that Willie cultivated in his backyard. At the moment, the hibiscus were in bloom.

The gecko stood absolutely still. Every two minutes or so it darted forward an inch and then froze, so that it might take an hour to traverse that one pane of glass. Willie and the lizard had been roommates for several years and Willie had observed this methodical, painstaking and heartless hunting process many a time. It was as transparent as the window but very successful. The mosquito, Willie knew, was toast. The gecko always got his man.

Willie took a swig from a sweating bottle of Presidente beer and wished that he were as efficient as his roommate. The two of them had an unspoken agreement: Willie paid the rent, while the reptile was responsible for the mosquitos and the occasional housefly. The creature was keeping up his end, but Willie was falling behind. The phone wasn't ringing.

He watched as the lizard leapt forward and again went still. Overhead the ceiling fan turned. In the background, Oscar D'Leon, the salsa singer, crooned about taking a trip to Cali, a city in Colombia.

Willie sipped his beer. "Why don't we go to Colombia, lizard? Take a little vacation."

Given all the trouble with drug cartels and guerrillas, Willie could make a good living as a bodyguard in Colombia. With his

1

background as an officer in the Miami Police Intelligence Unit, he could demand top dollar.

Just then the phone rang, and Willie glanced at it expectantly, as if someone were calling from South America. He picked up.

"Willie?"

It was his brother, Tommy, who ran a Latin nightclub called Caliente on the border of Little Havana and Coral Gables. Willie served as chief of security for the business, which earned him a modest retainer.

"What's up with you?" Tommy asked.

"The lizard and I are going to Colombia. We see opportunity there."

A pause ensued.

"What the hell are you talking about? Don't joke like that with Mama if she calls. You tell her you're going to Colombia, she'll kill you."

Not far away, their mother ran a botánica where she sold a large selection of natural medicines and effigies of saints worshiped in the Catholic and Santería religions. Mama covered all her bases.

"Are you working on anything?" Tommy asked.

"Not at this very moment," said Willie. And not at any previous moment in the past two weeks, although Willie didn't mention that.

"Well, Cesar Mendoza called the club a while ago looking for you. He left a message on the machine. He says a woman friend of his may need your services. She has a serious problem. But he wants you to go see him first."

Cesar Mendoza was a legendary figure in Cuban Miami. Blind since birth, he had developed his senses of taste and smell in the tobacco fields of Cuba and had become a world-renowned expert on fine cigars. Willie and Tommy's father, a Cuban musician now deceased, had known Cesar in Cuba in the old days. Eventually they had both made it to Miami. Cesar, now almost seventy, ran his own cigar store, Tabacos El Ciego—The Blindman's Cigar Shop—in the heart of Little Havana. Willie's father had always purchased his cigars from Cesar. Later, when Tommy added a "cigar room" at his club, it was Cesar who acted as a consultant and supplied the stogies. He was an old friend of the family.

"Make sure you go see him," Tommy said.

"I will. Don't worry. Did he say what the serious problem was?"

"Not to me. Listen, you had another call too. From Amy. She said she'd try you later."

Amy was Willie's girlfriend—rather, his estranged girlfriend. He hadn't heard from her in ten days, despite his repeated calls.

"I gotta go," Tommy said. "I'll see you later at the club and forget about going to Colombia."

"We'll see."

Willie hung up, drained his Presidente, slipped on a pair of brown leather sandals, turned off the CD player and headed for the door.

"The trip is on hold," he called to the lizard, who was still stalking his mosquito like a pointer dog.

CHAPTER TWO

Cesar's shop was located about fifteen blocks west of Willie's place, right on Calle Ocho, the main drag in Little Havana. Willie had grown up in the neighborhood and later worked there, first as a Miami Police patrol officer and then as a detective. On almost every block he had either assisted citizens in peril or busted someone. By now he knew everybody in the barrio—good, bad, and in-between.

At the moment he was passing the house of Rui Pelayo, whom Willie had once arrested for running a cockfighting ring in his garage. Rui was a big, round-bellied Cuban man who wore his chestnut hair in a pompadour, so that it resembled the red coxcombs of his fighting birds. He was also renowned for his expertise with a straight razor, which he kept as keen as the blades that he tied to the claws of his roosters. Rui used the razor to collect payments from welchers, which had led to his downfall and landed him in jail. Every time Willie heard a rooster crow, he recalled Rui.

On the next block was the house of Venecia Santamaria, a dowdy Cuban lady who he had never arrested, but who ran a rough brothel on the Miami River, an establishment specializing in the Caribbean maritime trade. No law enforcement type had ever closed Venecia's operation. In fact, at one point she had been obligated to remain open because she had become such a valuable informant against narcotics smugglers along the river.

"It's amazing what some stupid sailors tell hookers in the throes of love, amigo," Willie was told by one of the cops on the case.

A couple of blocks further west sat Cesar Mendoza's place. Cesar was as much a character as the other two, although his activities were all legal, at least as far as Willie knew.

4

Willie parked in front of the shop, which featured gold lettering across the front window, TABACOS EL CIEGO. Cesar had run his business there for three decades, surviving many rough years and then prospering when the cigar boom hit in the nineties.

Just catching sight of the shop transported Willie back to his childhood and the pungent aromas in which his father had always drifted. In fact, whenever he entered the place, Willie felt Papi materialize next to him, like a being composed of smoke.

A slender, elegant man, Willie's father had played horns in Cuban orchestras around Miami. When he didn't have a *trompeta* or sax in his mouth, he was chewing on a dark stogie. Whenever he needed to stock up, he would pile Tommy and Willie into the old, black Buick and drive to Cesar's.

The first thing that hit you as you entered was the aromatic quality of the place. Cesar always had a cigar burning for himself, usually a thick, black *robusto*. He smoked only the best, or at least the best made outside of Cuba. Those aromas had seeped into the walls, which were paneled in mahogany and lined with shelves of open cigar boxes.

The other atmospheric touch was music. Cesar played tapes of Cuban cigar songs. At the moment, Willie heard a tune in Spanish about a witch who broke spells using tobacco and honey.

Ojas de tabaco
mezclado con melao
para curar los males
de envidia y pecao

The place never changed much. For the two boys, Willie and Tommy, cigars had symbolized the mysteries of manhood. The brand names were romantic—Montecristo, Hoyo de Monterrey, Flor de Monte Carlo, Partagas and his father's favorite, Romeo y Julieta. The boxes containing them were works of art, embossed in gold, with colorful illustrations on the lids of beautiful women, dashing and powerful men, coats of arms or exotic tropical settings. When his father finished a box, his sons would fight for it, eventually filling it with baseball cards, marbles and other invaluable holdings. Those cigar boxes had been the treasure chests of Willie's youth.

And the person who had supplied them to the Cuesta family was Cesar Mendoza, part Latin pirate and part wise man. Willie's father once said that Cesar could not only identify any of the dozens of brands of cigars made in Cuba just by taking a few puffs but could also pinpoint exactly where on the island the leaf had been grown, sometimes down to the individual grower. It was impossible to fool him. Cesar was a *mago* according to Willie's father, a magician.

But for young Willie, Cesar had also been the object of scary fascination. Willie knew no other blind people and he could only wonder what it was like to live in perpetual darkness. As an adult, and now a former policeman who'd processed countless crime victims, Willie found Cesar's blindness worrisome. Here was a sightless man running a business by himself, in a city full of violent felons. Miraculously, no one had ever hurt him; there seemed to be an unwritten rule that you didn't mess with Cesar Mendoza. But Willie wished it were a written law and also wished that Cesar would get an assistant with eyes that worked.

The old man, stationed behind his sales counter, was just hanging up the phone and Willie called out his name. Cesar turned in his direction, his sightless eyes hidden behind small, round, opaque glasses. "*Eres tú*, Willie?"

"That's right, Cesar."

The blind man came around the counter, deftly avoiding the display case, and held out his hand. He had owned the shop so long, he navigated it expertly.

Willie shook hands with him. Cesar was a square-shouldered, solidly built man of medium height. If he hadn't been blind, he might have made a good middleweight. His complexion was olive, and Willie had no idea what color his eyes were. He had never seen them. Cesar wore a beard because, as he said, he didn't want to "feel" his ugly face every morning in the mirror. His hair was stylishly long, not because he planned it that way but because he never noticed when he needed a haircut. He wore an umber-colored *guayabera* with a small leather cigar case stuck in the front pocket, big enough to fit about five smokes. In his left hand, he held a burning stogie.

Cesar was a graceful man, but by no means handsome. No one would have suspected on first meeting him that he had a wondrous reputation with women. Willie's father had long ago regaled his son with the blind man's extremely active romantic life, which Cesar himself had later confirmed, although only in general terms.

"There exist women for whom a blind man is irresistible," he told Willie. "It has to do with the sense of touch. I see them through my fingers. And there are women with lovely voices who may not be good-looking to other men, but who to me are classic beauties. I don't look for them, but they always find me."

Over the years, Cesar had alluded to affairs, even shared some reveries about his trysts, although he was always discreet, never mentioning names.

Now he pumped Willie's hand.

"*¿Cómo estás, muchacho?*" he asked in a voice left gravelly from so many cigars.

"I'm doing fine," Willie said. "And from the prices on your merchandise, I think you're doing the same." Willie was inspecting a display case full of carved, wooden humidors. Some of them carried prices that would have purchased a nice coffin.

Cesar turned to the display case and looked down as if he could actually see the merchandise. "It's all because of the big boom in stogies, Willie. It's been incredible these last few years. I keep the cigars affordable, but for some of the big spenders I keep articles like these. I give them a chance to spend their money. What can I say?"

But he didn't want to talk about that now. He took Willie by the elbow and led him to a long, black leather couch at the back of the store. It sat near a steel-doored storage freezer and was flanked by two tables, each equipped with a Havana Club ashtray, a cigar cutter and a lighter. A Persian rug lay before it. This was the tasting area and it was comfortable.

"Can I offer you a smoke, Willie? I have a very nice Macanudo here. A very sweet number." Cesar couldn't see colors, but he spoke in a colorful patois with a bit of an accent.

Willie accepted the gift, and Cesar clipped and lighted it for him.

"Well, now down to business," Cesar said. "Or like the Americans say, let's get down to the *neety greety*."

"What's going on, Cesar?"

The old man turned to him with those two perfectly round, black lenses.

"I'm not sure what's going on, amigo," he said, "but right now I'm afraid."

CHAPTER THREE

Willie frowned, as if something disturbing were written on the old man's opaque lenses.

"Why are you afraid, Cesar? Tell me." In all the years they had known each other, Willie had never before heard the other man express fear.

"Oh, it isn't for me, Willie. I'm scared for a friend of mine, a very old friend named Victoria Espada."

The blind man pointed to a spot high on the wall, above the shelves of open cigar boxes. "Hanging up there somewhere is a poster of a young woman, a painting that once they put on a cigar box. That was her when she was young."

Willie saw it amid other cigar posters. The girl had pearl-white skin, raven-black hair, eyes to match, blood-red lips, bare shoulders and a full bosom above an off-the-shoulder white peasant blouse. She was pure, idealized Cuban exoticism.

"She's very beautiful," Willie said.

"So I've heard. That was Victoria when she was eighteen. In Cuba, when she walked down the street, I could hear men sigh. They fought over the right just to follow her around. Cigar makers competed to put her face on their cigar boxes. That's how beautiful she was. Her father was a well-known tobacco grower in the Pinar del Río region in Cuba, where they grow the best tobacco in the world. Before she was twenty, she married a man named Ernesto Espada, who came from a very old and respected clan of cigar makers."

Willie nodded. He remembered seeing the Espada brand name on cigar boxes in the old days. Cesar puffed and went on.

"Victoria was, in many ways, the crown princess of the Cuban cigar world, Willie. She led a life out of a fairy tale, full of nightclubs

9

and country club balls. She was pursued by young men who were heirs to the big sugar, rum and tobacco fortunes. She had it all."

Willie drew on his Macanudo and exhaled luxuriously. "But the fairy tale didn't last, I take it."

Cesar shook his head. "No, it didn't. The revolution came. Castro took over, and Victoria and her husband left Cuba. Like the other major cigar makers, Ernesto moved from place to place, both in Latin America and in Europe, trying to reestablish his operations. It was bad, Willie, an extremely difficult time, for all of us in the trade. Espada, he wasn't as resourceful as some of the others. Things went very badly for him."

The old man stopped and seemed to study the cigar in his hand.

"The fact is, Ernesto began to drink rum," he continued. "He drank a lot, like a fish, and a few years later he committed suicide like a fish."

"What does that mean?"

"It means the family has a house here in Miami, on the bay, a house called *Bahía Azul*. One day he walked into the water and began to swim until he was too far out to make it back. He left his young wife, Victoria, with two infant children: twins, a boy and a girl. The Espada brand name was finished. One of the great cigar dynasties of all time was dead and Victoria was left to swim on her own."

It was clear, by his tone, that Cesar disapproved of what the late Ernesto Espada had done.

"What happened then?"

The blind man shook his head. "Victoria lived off family money. When it was gone, she rented out their big house and now they live in a smaller residence on the property. She has never remarried and has sunk almost completely into isolation. She isn't a well woman. A few amigos like me stay in touch, but that's all."

"And her children?"

"They both continue to live with her. It is a very close family. The closest I can think of, and you know how close Cuban families are. That's why I called you, because now her son is missing. His name is Carlos. She can't find him. Nobody can."

"How long has he been gone?"

"About two weeks."

Willie puffed his cigar and shrugged. "People take off all the time, Cesar. I saw it when I was on the police force. After a while they come back."

Cesar shook his head brusquely. "This is different, Willie. The kid has been in real bad shape lately. For years he has wanted to revive the Espada cigar brand and to make it the finest cigar around, in honor of his father. But they don't have the money to do that. Since the boom started, many of the old cigar families are doing very well. Even newcomers who don't know the business make money, sometimes buckets of it. But Carlos' family was left behind. He works as a salesman for a cigar company, but he isn't very good at it. He doesn't have that kind of personality. He's serious, like his father was. Nathan Cooler, the manager at Great American Tobacco, keeps him on, but only out of loyalty to the family. Carlos knows this. He feels like a complete failure. He came to see me not long before he disappeared and told me he had to get money and get it now."

"There's nothing wrong with ambition, Cesar."

"It depends what that ambition is. The kid sounded like he was ready to rob a bank, or something else illegal, Willie. He was desperate. Then he disappears without a word to anyone. It's driving his mother to an early death, and I want to help her. I want you to find Carlos. Sometimes I'm psychic, and now I feel that something bad could happen to him."

When a guy like Cesar told you he was psychic, you didn't argue. He looked like one of the old, blind oracles from the Greek plays in high school English.

"I'll go talk to them."

"You should be very careful with the mother, Victoria. She's a woman who has suffered a lot. Any mention that her son may be deeply disturbed or mixed up in something illegal will only drive her farther away from reality. It's better to talk to the daughter when you have a chance."

The phone rang and Cesar shuffled off to answer it. Willie stood up with him. As he waited, Willie saw a white stretch limousine pull up in front of the store. It looked like an ocean liner sailing into view. The chauffeur, a big guy dressed in a black coat with gold buttons, jumped out and opened the rear door. A man emerged—blond, thirties, wearing an aquamarine caftan with gold fringe, sandals and amber-tinted sunglasses. Speaking of Greeks, he looked like an ancient god, wearing shades.

He waited by the car door and two women climbed out. Both wore extremely brief red shorts, even briefer bikini tops and white sandals. One was black, the other a tawny-skinned Latina; both very young, slim hipped and big breasted. They linked arms with the man in the caftan and cruised into the cigar shop. Cesar was just hanging up as the customer called to him.

"Mendoza, it's your lucky day. It's me, Richard."

Cesar turned so that his right ear faced the man. "Is that you, Mr. Knox. I guess it is my lucky day."

"Do you have my special stogies?"

"They came in yesterday." Cesar padded off toward the refrigerated locker at the rear of the store. He came out seconds later pushing a dolly with two large cardboard boxes on it. Knox and his two bookends met him at the front desk. The girls inspected Willie up and down, decided he looked all right, but not worth as much as their boy in the caftan, and they held on that much tighter to their prize.

Knox ripped open one of the cardboard boxes and removed a wooden cigar box. On the lid was engraved, "Richard Knox—Private Collection." He undid a brass hook, looked inside, picked one cigar, passed it under his nose, smiled and put it back. Then he produced a gold credit card from inside the caftan and slapped it down on the counter so Cesar could hear it. Willie was witnessing a phenomenon of the cigar boom. It was quite something.

"There you go, Mendoza. Ring me up." The blind man felt for the card.

"That will be twenty boxes at two hundred fifty dollars each, Mr. Knox."

"*Muy bueno*," said Knox in bad Spanish with an equally bad accent. He leaned toward Willie and whispered conspiratorially. "I smoke real Cubans myself, but I give these away for business. A cigar box with your name on it isn't a bad business card, now is it?"

"No, it isn't," Willie agreed. The girls each rewarded Willie with a smile for the correct answer, the exact same smile.

Cesar processed the credit card, his fingers reading the lettering to get it right side up. Knox looked around through his amber shades.

"Have you decided to sell me this place, Mendoza?"

Cesar smiled at his own fingers. "Oh no, Mr. Knox. What would I do?"

"You'd run it for me." Knox turned again to Willie. "I've offered him a lot more than the place is worth. I also proposed a limited partnership and he said no. The only option I have is an unfriendly takeover. Organize his customers and make him sell. Then I'd start a chain across the country. 'Blind Mendoza's Stogies,' with his face on the door."

He laughed and Cesar was chuckling, although only halfheartedly. "You won't do that to me, Mr. Knox."

Cesar laid the credit card receipt on the counter, and Knox signed it with a flourish and retrieved his card. Then he waved to his chauffeur, who marched in, picked up the two large boxes and lugged them back to the luxury liner.

"Always a pleasure doing business with you, Mendoza."

"*Igualmente*, Mr. Knox."

Knox turned on a sandaled heel and headed for the limo. The girls turned with him and twitched out. Willie watched the limo sail off.

"Just who is Mr. Knox?"

"He's an attorney and a businessman. Communications. Internet. That kind of thing. And he's a big cigar connoisseur."

"A connoisseur of females too."

"I didn't see them, but they smelled good. Like coconut oil."

"They look like panatellas, Cesar, long and lean."

Cesar, always the ladies' man, smiled. "Lately, Mr. Knox has also gone into the cigar business. He became partners with Don Ricardo Tirado, who makes Tirado Cigars. Mr. Knox put money into the company. It's good for Don Ricardo. And Mr. Knox has still remained loyal to me."

Willie looked down at the credit card receipt for five thousand dollars. "Yes, I'd say he's very loyal."

Cesar agreed. "I told you, Willie. There are days it rains money in this store. By the way, you shouldn't take any payment from Victoria Espada for your services. I'll pay you."

They negotiated terms and Willie gave Cesar a day rate lower than usual. He also got the name and address of Victoria Espada.

"She's there now," Cesar said.

"Call her and tell her I'm coming." Willie gazed up at the old poster of the woman. He wondered if she looked anything like that now. She was forty years older. He could only hope.

"We'll see each other soon, Cesar."

"So to speak, amigo. So to speak."

CHAPTER FOUR

Willie caught the South Dixie Highway, cruised past Coconut Grove, then headed east toward the bay. It took him into a neighborhood of junglish vegetation and rambling houses on the edge of the land, houses that had survived decades of hurricanes and tropical blows of every degree.

He found the address right on the water. The property sat behind a low stucco wall that was almost totally taken over by kudzu vine. He saw two buildings: one a large, two-story mansion and the other a smaller house that looked like a guest cottage or servants' quarters. They were both finished in pink stucco, although the paint had been allowed to fade and chip.

Kudzu had also covered those walls and seemed to be holding the structures together. Around the houses were planted a few wind-blown fruit trees, limes particularly and some sea grapes, all of them twisted by onshore breezes. The grass looked like it hadn't been cut in a couple of months. All in all, the place was grand, but a bit abandoned, a kind of tropical haunted house.

Willie drove through an open gate and took the gravel driveway. He reached a young, blonde woman with a ponytail, wearing a black halter top and camouflage-colored shorts. She was washing a black jeep next to the big house. A German shepherd lay nearby.

"I'm looking for the Espada property," Willie said to her out the window.

"This is it."

"How about Mrs. Victoria Espada?"

"Oh, they don't live here in the big house. We rent this place." She pointed to the smaller house, which sat closer to the water. "They live over there."

Willie glanced that way. The structure was cut off from the rest of the property by an untamed ficus hedge. The house faced the water, with its back to the main residence. It had its own driveway and a large black Cadillac, at least fifteen years old, was parked there.

"Are they home?"

"The mother and daughter are almost always home, as far as I can tell," the young woman said. "They don't leave this property too often. It's like they're afraid if they leave, they won't know how to get back." She flicked her blonde eyebrows.

She was informative, if just a bit callous. Willie thanked her and took the gravel fork that led him to the smaller house. He parked next to the ficus hedge and walked to the door. The house was one story but had a rotting balustrade around the roof and what was either a deck or a kind of widow's watch up top. Crimson curtains hung in the windows and were matched in color by an arbor of bougainvillea growing on the leeward side of the house.

Next to the arbor, facing the bay, stood an easel and on it a partially completed oil, a dramatic seascape made of raging waves. Flattened tubes of paint and several rags lay on a table next to it. It was a barely contained storm of a painting. Willie looked out over the bay. It wasn't stormy at all, but if one of your family members had committed suicide out there then maybe you always saw the sea that way, in turmoil.

He used a brass knocker that was in the form of a lighthouse and discolored by verdigris. Moments later the door was opened by a small, dark young woman, obviously a cleaning lady—very likely Nicaraguan or Honduran. She wore a *Star Wars* T-shirt that depicted one of the Skywalkers wielding a laser sword. She herself held a feather duster with some of the same flourish. Willie smiled and asked the intergalactic Central American girl for the lady of the house. The girl didn't smile back. From somewhere inside he heard a CD or tape, a piano rendition of the passionate old Cuban standard, "Siboney."

The girl led him into the living room, where he was asked to wait. The room was painted a faded sea-blue color and crammed with tasteful old furniture, to the point where you could barely move. Crowded into that living room were a couple of couches covered in wine-colored fabric, an antique sideboard, an old sea chest, two stuffed chairs, which were gold in color, various small tables and, near the French doors' that looked out on the bay, a baby grand piano. A very large Persian rug lay under it all, almost filling the room. It looked as if there had been a shipwreck nearby and the Espadas had been able to salvage a large amount of good stuff. But it was more likely that moving out of the big house into this smaller one they had kept as much furniture as they could.

The walls were as busy as the floor plan, with paintings and photographs everywhere, many of them of famous Cuban landmarks. The largest was a painting of Morro Castle, the colonial fortress overlooking Havana Bay. But the one that really drew Willie's attention was the original oil of the poster that Cesar had hanging in his shop. In this version, Victoria Espada's skin was even whiter, her hair blacker, the fire in her eyes more intense. Willie felt what he had experienced as a boy looking at those women pictured on the cigar boxes—that cigars were tied to all sorts of adventures and manly pleasures beyond description.

Beneath the painting, on the piano, sat family photographs. Some were in color and included graduation and birthday photos of a young man and a young woman who Willie assumed were Victoria Espada's twins, Carlos and his sister.

Other photos were in black and white and quite old. One was of a young man dressed in a dark zoot suit and a black fedora. He was handsome but pale and his smile was tentative. Willie wondered if it was the late Ernesto Espada, who had taken the long swim. Finally, there was a photo that depicted a large, rambling farmhouse, surrounded by tobacco fields, with a majestic tropical mountain rising behind it. Willie couldn't guess when it had been taken, but it was certainly Cuba and looked idyllic, something out of a dream. The room Willie stood in looked as if it might be a reproduction of a room inside that same farmhouse, a dream inside a dream, a memory inside a memory.

He was still studying the photos when two women walked into the room. For a moment Willie froze, looking from one to the other, then to the painting on the wall, and then back to them again. What he saw challenged his sense of reality.

He was staring at a lady in a black dress, with a black mantilla draped over her shoulders in the traditional fashion, who he figured had to be Victoria Espada. Probably in her late fifties now, she was still striking, although you could see the effect of her rough fortune. The skin was drawn over the high cheekbones, streaks of white coursed through her hair. The dark eyes, however, had lost none of their intensity. Under them were dark rings, probably from loss of sleep in recent days due to the disappearance of her son. All in all, she seemed a bit feverish.

The younger woman was in her thirties and dressed in a gauzy white cotton low-cut blouse that resembled the one in the painting. She was, in fact, almost a double of the lady in the painting. The raven hair, snow-white skin and smoldering eyes were all in evidence. It was as if he were seeing the same woman at two different periods in her life, but at the same moment and in the same room. It was a bit freaky.

The older woman spoke to him.

"I'm Victoria Espada and this is my daughter, Esther. Thank you for coming." Her voice was grave and regal.

Neither offered her hand and Willie nodded to each of them. He still held the photo of the ranch house. "Is this where you lived in Cuba?"

Victoria looked at it. "Yes, that was our small kingdom in the province of Pinar del Río. There my family grew fine tobacco and my husband's family made very fine cigars from it. Kings and presidents smoked our cigars, Mr. Cuesta. Of course, that was very long ago, before the gods turned against us."

Willie nodded in commiseration and then pointed to the photo of the man in the fedora. "I assume that is your late husband."

"Yes, and may those same gods bless his soul. He died young."

"That's what I've been told."

She met his gaze now with dramatic intensity and delivered a soliloquy. "My husband died of a broken heart, Mr. Cuesta. He never wanted to leave his homeland or that farm you see there. But we were forced to because of the communist revolution. The next few years were very difficult, searching the world for a livelihood. He went from Spain to the Canary Islands to Central America to the Caribbean, trying to find a way to keep alive the family business, which had lasted for more than a century. It was a struggle and that struggle killed him before his time."

She spoke with exaggerated gravity, a sadness that Willie wasn't accustomed to hearing, except maybe on a stage. It was a performance, one she had probably given many times, one that seemed to say: "You have heard about my husband's drinking and suicide, but I will tell you the true story." She was protector of her husband's memory. There were worse things to be.

Willie had no idea what to say after that. He could see out the window, past the big house and out to the bay.

"This is beautiful property you have."

She looked out at it as well. "My husband and I had some money in this country when we first came here, and we purchased it. After my husband died, my children and I continued to live in the big house for many years, until we could no longer afford to maintain it. Several years ago, we had to move in here." Her tone made it clear what a tragedy that was, a queen relegated to servants' quarters.

Willie glanced at Esther Espada, who had drifted to the opposite side of the room and was shuffling through papers on an old rolltop desk. He admired her broad white shoulders and slim waist. He didn't mention that to her mother.

"Surely your children have been able to help you," he said.

Victoria Espada's gaze moved to her daughter. "Esther is an artist. I have insisted that she follow her muse. I didn't want exile to rob her of that. She has done what she could over the years. She's a good daughter."

Then she reached for the photo of a young man in a prom tuxedo, who also looked very much like her, with large dark eyes. "And my son, Carlos, has tried very hard to make a success in the business world, but just like our family in general, he has always had bad fortune." She shook her head. "I think you'll find, Mr. Cuesta, that we are cursed."

Willie didn't know from curses, but he was sympathetic to her problem. Victoria Espada was only a few years younger than his own mother and in the deep-set dark eyes, he saw a resemblance.

"Cesar tells me your son is missing."

The old woman looked desolately at the photo in her hand. "Yes, and I'm very worried."

"I'm told he's been gone about two weeks."

She nodded. "One morning he left with his suitcase. He told me he was going on a business trip to the Dominican Republic. We haven't seen or heard from him since."

"Have you gotten in touch with the authorities down there?"

She continued to stare at the photo. "They told my daughter they had no record of him ever arriving in that country. The airlines had no record of him. After he left here, he disappeared from the face of the earth."

"How about his boss, Mr. Cooler, at Great American Tobacco?"

She shook her head. "Mr. Cooler knows nothing. He told us that Carlos was not scheduled or authorized to take any business trip to the Dominican Republic or anywhere else. My son has never done anything like this in the past. Something must have happened to him."

Willie looked down at the prom photo of Carlos Espada. Could the smiling, tuxedoed fellow have gone off to rob a bank, as Cesar feared? Who could tell? But he understood now why Cesar had been worried about his asking Victoria Espada about that possibility. This was a woman into whose life you did not want to introduce that kind of worry.

"Do you have any idea where your son might have gone, Mrs. Espada?"

She didn't have a chance to answer. Esther returned holding a manila envelope.

"We found this under his mattress just a couple of days ago. We hadn't looked there before."

Willie opened the envelope and found two eight-by-ten black-and-white photos. The first pictured Carlos Espada dressed in a suit and tie, apparently attending a reception. Surrounded by many other people, he was speaking with an extremely voluptuous blonde woman, maybe thirty, in a small, tight dress.

The second photo depicted the same two people, but this time they were sitting by themselves on a beach. Carlos wore bathing trunks and the woman a dark bikini. They were talking and this time they looked very serious. The photo was grainier than the first, appeared to have been taken at a distance and very likely without their knowledge.

Attached to the second photo was a small white slip of paper. On it was written one word in Spanish: "*¡Cuidado!*" It meant "Careful!" or "Beware!"

Willie flipped the photos over. He found no dates when they had been processed. But on the back of the first one someone had printed "Atlanta" and on the second was printed "D.R."—the Dominican Republic. He turned them back over and studied them.

If he was looking for a reason for Carlos Espada's disappearance, this blonde looked much more likely a reason than a life of crime.

"Do you have any idea of the circumstances of these photos?"

Esther Espada pointed at the first photo. "This one was probably taken at one of the cigar distributors' conventions that Carlos often attends. I know one was held in Atlanta about a month ago. The other photo, we have no idea. As my mother told you, Carlos was not in the Dominican Republic on business."

The bathing suit shot certainly didn't look like business.

"Do you know who this woman is?"

Esther Espada's response was an icy stare and a curt shake of the head. It was the sort of reaction Willie would have expected from a wife, not a sister.

"But I will tell you this," she said. "Carlos would not have simply run off with a woman and abandoned us. He would never do that."

Given the looks of the blonde woman, Willie wasn't so sure. But it was clear that neither his mother nor sister would accept that. Carlos was the prince in this royal court in exile and he was noble.

"So, you think maybe something happened to him and that this woman was involved."

The women nodded solemnly in unison and Victoria answered. "Over the years there have been people who believed we still had money. Maybe this woman is that type. Maybe she thinks we can pay some kind of ransom."

"Who can I ask about this woman? Who knows your son well, beside you?"

Esther Espada answered. "My brother has never had a lot of friends. He has always stayed close to the family. I think you'll have to ask people he knows in the cigar business."

"Like his boss, Mr. Cooler."

"Yes."

"Is there anyone else?"

Esther Espada pointed at the first photo again. "The man stand-ing on the other side of that blonde woman is Don Ricardo Tirado, owner of the Tirado Cigar Company and formerly a competitor of ours. He probably knows that woman. She seems like his type."

Willie looked at the photo and saw a tall, thin, rakish old man with a cane in one hand and a cigar in the other. He was clearly ogling the woman, although he didn't appear to be with her and Car-los. Given Esther's tone, that was just as well. She obviously didn't approve of him.

"Can I see Carlos' room?"

Esther led him down a short hallway, past a couple of closed doors to a small room at the back of the house. Carlos Espada's bed-room was a bit like a monk's cell, furnished with a single bed, a bureau and two photos on the walls, both of his late father. The clos-et contained a couple of suits and other clothes. The only unusual find was under some old bank statements in the drawer of the night table: it was a small clipping from a Spanish-language newspaper about a double murder, two men found dead in an apartment late at night in North Miami. It wasn't dated, but wasn't discolored and appeared fairly recent. The article was very brief, saying only that the men had been dead for days and they had not been identified. There were no other details. He held it up so Esther could read it.

"Any idea what this is about?"

Esther read it warily and shook her head. "No."

Willie wondered if the article had anything to do with the warn-ing attached to the photos of Carlos and the blond woman, but he didn't say so to Carlos' sister.

He put the clipping in his pocket, and they returned to the living room. Willie took the photos and also copied down numbers for Nathan Cooler. Then the two women saw him out. Victoria Espada held his hand an extra moment. Willie looked at hers, which was gnarled like one of the trees outside. The look in her eyes was somber.

"If you find Carlos, please tell him to come back. We will ask no questions. None at all. Tell him to please not lose faith in the family. We only want to know he's safe."

Then she said something to him that Willie would recall more than once in subsequent days.

"You should take care as well. For several decades now the forces around us have not been friendly ones, Mr. Cuesta. I want you to know I'll pray for you."

CHAPTER FIVE

Willie climbed back in the car, called Great American Tobacco, and was advised that Nathan Cooler wasn't in. He was expected back in two hours. So, Willie took a chance and headed for the Tirado Cigar Company.

It was located on Calle Ocho, about fifteen blocks toward the bay from Willie's place, in an area known as East Little Havana. This stretch of the barrio had always been rougher than Willie's neighborhood farther west. Once called Riverside and inhabited by Jews, in the early sixties the neighborhood had been taken over by Cuban exiles.

Out went the smell of gefilte fish and the sound of Yiddish; in came the aroma of *arroz con pollo* and the crooning of *boleros.* Unfortunately, some fifteen years later, Cuban and Colombian drug smugglers also moved in. They shot it out in the streets in the early eighties, sometimes from car to car, creating a Latin version of gangland Chicago.

Those troubles eventually passed, but not before many of the Cubans had moved on. They were replaced by the latest desperate wave of refugees, this time from Central America, who traveled with their own tales of civil war and their own nightmares. The area was still labeled Little Havana, but it was now populated with the ghosts of various nationalities.

In the midst of all that, the Tirado Cigars workshop hadn't moved. Willie remembered the sign being there when he was a kid. On occasion he had stopped, stared through the front window and watched the cigar makers rolling each cigar by hand, the way they always had in Cuba. Maybe the shop had survived in that notorious neighborhood because nobody considered cigars worth stealing.

That had been true in the old days. But after the boom, with some cigars going for a lot of money, maybe that wasn't true anymore.

He pulled up now and walked into the one-room workshop. A small sales counter sat just inside the door, but the attendant was busy with a customer. Willie saw that the factory hadn't changed. About twenty old, scarred, wooden work desks crowded the room. The space was high-ceilinged, but long banks of fluorescent lights hung down to illuminate the desktops. Between those fixtures hung revolving ceiling fans that seemed so low they might slice a person's head off. Under those fans, hunched at the desks, sat the cigar rollers, at least half of them women. Piles of dried and cured tobacco leaves lay on the desks on either side of the roller, like sheaths of aged, cured human skin.

From a boombox perched in the middle of the room a popular song sounded in Spanish. It was about a man who sends his *querida* smoke signals of love, which get lost in shifting winds. As Willie listened and waited, he watched the cigar roller nearest him as she worked.

Middle-aged, heavyset, but attractive, she wore her red hair tied in a bright yellow bandana. The principal tool she employed was a crescent-shaped knife blade, which fit into the palm of her hand and with which she sliced and shaped the tobacco leaf. Her hands moved extremely quickly, bunching the tobacco, pressing the bunches into cigar molds, wielding her blade in long crescent-shaped flourishes to create the wrapper, wrapping and then rolling the cigar with the flat palm of her hand, and finally slipping the cigar into a species of paper cutter and chopping off the end with a whack of her hand in a way that would make any man wince. With an unlit cigar clenched in her teeth, she glanced at Willie mischievously. He noticed that taped to her desk she kept a color photo of a husband or boyfriend and decided he definitely wouldn't want to be that guy.

The customer departed and the attendant, a young brown-haired woman in big glasses, asked if she could assist him.

"I'd like to see Don Ricardo Tirado." Willie handed her a business card, she read it, then disappeared into a back room. The singer was still sending his smoke signals.

The attendant returned and walked Willie through the workshop to the office in the back. On the way he passed more workers slipping bands on cigars, while others counted and arranged them in cigar boxes embossed with gold.

Just outside the door to the office, the woman stopped and whispered to him. "You shouldn't speak to him too long. He had a stroke last year and he is not as strong as he was."

Willie said he understood. She opened the wooden door, ushered him in and closed it behind him. The small office was crowded with several bales of cured tobacco and a three-legged cigar maker's table, which leaned in one corner, apparently awaiting repair. Along one wall, a trestle table was stacked with cigar boxes of different brands, maybe gifts, maybe the wares of his competitors, which Tirado purchased in order to compare them with his own product.

The walls were hung with sepia-colored photographs of the cigar workshops of old Cuba. Men and women worked at tables just like those outside, but dozens and dozens of them in a warehouse-sized space. All the rollers were dressed in the styles of the fifties and stared into the camera with innocent, deer-in-the-headlight expressions that people didn't seem to be capable of anymore. Behind the desk hung a bigger photograph, that of a large Spanish Colonial building with the name of the company emblazoned above the door: Tabacos Tirado. It had to be the old headquarters in Havana. It was an elaborate but still graceful building out of what had been an elaborate but graceful past, now long gone.

The man positioned behind the mahogany desk in the middle of the room was much like that building, past his prime, but still graceful to the eye. Some people, no matter what befalls them, never lose their style. Ricardo Tirado's suit was a gray, double-breasted number, with pearl-white buttons, cut sleekly to his slim figure. His white shirt and sky-blue tie were both silk. In the lapel of his suit jacket he sported a pin in the form of the Cuban flag. His hair was gray and cobweb thin, and his face long and drawn, beneath age-spotted skin. You could see he had once, many moons ago, answered to the title of "dashing young man." Even now his gray eyes, the same color as the suit, were full of verve.

He held a cigar maker's knife and was cutting open his own cigars, apparently to inspect their workmanship. Scattered on the desk before him were pins with red heads on them. It was a custom in some cigar factories that a worker who delivered a bad batch was given a red pin. Three red pins and you were fired. Willie remembered a sad old Cuban song about "*el tercer alfiler.*"

Tirado laid down the knife, lifted an old, knotted cane, gripped it in his right hand and pointed it at the door.

"Don't tell me. I bet she said for you not to talk for very long. That just the breath from your mouth would knock me over because I'm so weak."

Willie smiled. "I won't lie to you. Yes, that's what she said."

The old man shook his head in fake frustration. "I'm decayed, but not moribund. The women out there, they pray for me, but I tell them it will do no good. I was too much of a sinner in my youth. Too much rum, too much dancing and too many women. No, God won't listen to their prayers."

He smiled wryly, then picked up the cigar he had been smoking and puffed on it, a sign of his incorrigibility. Willie could just picture the dashing young Tirado in randy old Havana, which in the forties and fifties had the reputation of the carousing capital of the world. The best rum, nightclubs that resounded with rumba until dawn. Casinos and women renowned the earth over. If you were one of the leading cigar makers, you probably had entree everywhere. Willie would like to have sampled the pleasures of old Havana with a guy like Ricardo Tirado, although they had clearly taken their toll.

"You can't be so bad off," Willie said. "Your business has grown, and I see you're still running it."

The old man shook his head. "Don't be ridiculous. Managers out there in the workshop run everything. They allow me to come here every day and make believe I'm still important. It's just as well I don't run it, because this business is getting more and more difficult."

"Because it has grown?"

"Because the competition has become distasteful, criminal, now that people smell more money. Your competitors try to buy your tobacco crops from your growers and to steal your workers. A farmer in Nicaragua promises to sell you his tobacco and then he turns around and sells it to someone who offered him a nickel more. The same with cigar rollers. They are always being hired away from you. Stolen! If I pay seventy-five cents a cigar, the competitors offer eighty, and their cigars are still bad. There are plagues that affect tobacco, and apparently there are also plagues that affect the people in the trade. We are in the middle of one. The business has become filled with pirates."

He puffed at his cigar furiously. The old man had his own agenda, as was often the way with old men. He hadn't even asked Willie why he was there, but it was time to get down to business. The "*neety greety*," as Cesar Mendoza might say.

"I understand that you still attend the cigar conventions."

Tirado flicked his sparse eyebrows. "Of course. I wouldn't miss any of those. It's the only chance I'm given to indulge my old vices. We have one coming up here in Miami in a few days and I'll be going there as well."

Willie removed a photo of Carlos Espada and the unknown young woman from its manila envelope and handed it to the old man.

"Do you remember being at this reception in Atlanta?"

Tirado took glasses off the desk, wire-rim bifocals, examined the photo and nodded. "Yes, of course I remember. I'm not senile, *hombre*. That was only about a month ago. It was the first convention they let me attend since I had the stroke. You can see here that I've escaped my keepers and I'm on my way to the bar for a mojito."

"Do you recognize the two people standing next to you?"

The old man squinted through the cloud of cigar smoke he had generated. He jabbed the photo with a gnarled finger. "The man looks like Carlos Espada. His father was Ernesto Espada, who was a cigar maker, but he died many years ago."

"Carlos has been missing for more than two weeks. That's why I'm here. I wonder if you might know the young woman with him?"

Tirado shook his head. "No, I don't know her. She resembles an American girlfriend I had in Havana many years ago. But these days they don't allow me to know anyone who looks like that. They are afraid it will give me another stroke." He glanced at the photo again. "But young Espada here seems friendly with her. That surprises me. He isn't the type. He has always been serious like his father." There was the hint of disdain in his voice. The Espadas didn't like Tirado, the libertine, and he apparently didn't care for them either.

"You knew Ernesto Espada?"

"Of course, I knew him. His family was prominent in the business. They were one of the old dynasties."

"Was he a drinking buddy of yours?"

Tirado shook his head. "Back in Cuba he hardly drank at all, as I remember. And when he began to drink here, he was a solitary drinker. The next thing I knew he had killed himself and left his wife with two children."

"Do you know Victoria Espada?"

Tirado rolled his eyes. "Yes, of course, hombre. For fifty years. We were all raised together in Pinar del Río. I was a few years older, but we still went to the same dances. When I was twenty my father sent me off to Havana to learn our company's operations there and she was eventually sent to Havana to study. I knew her there too." He squinted into the past and shook his head.

"*Dios mío*, she was beautiful. A work of nature. Men would follow her around like street dogs in heat. I wasn't any better. I followed her to the country clubs and searched for her in the great nightclubs—the Sans Souci, the Riviera, the Montmartre. I danced with her any chance she allowed me. Several times I begged her to marry me, but she wasn't interested."

He shrugged. "Of course, my reputation was already rather colorful. With a girl as conservative as Victoria, I wasn't going to get very far. Instead, she returned to Pinar del Río and married Ernesto Espada, the son of her father's business associate."

He shook his head ruefully.

"I take it you didn't approve," Willie said.

"It was a tragic mistake. He was never the man for her. He left her a widow before she was twenty-five, two small children on her hands and not much money. After he died, I showed up at her door, but again she wouldn't have me. She never remarried, a terrible waste of beauty. Me, I went on my way to the devil."

Ricardo Tirado might have danced with the devil, with or without Victoria Espada. He was the eternal rake, Cuban style. Then again, maybe he was being serious. Maybe love would have slowed him down. Maybe he did see it as a tragedy, although he played it for laughs.

Tirado was watching him as if he could read Willie's thoughts. Then he started to say something but stopped. Willie raised his eyebrows. "Yes?"

Tirado shook his head. "It's not important. I have my secrets, but they wouldn't be important to you. We were speaking of the Espadas and their misfortunes."

"They lost their business, and your operation has prospered," Willie said.

"I went through the same difficult years that they did. I lost everything. For a time, thirty years ago, anyone leaving Cuba was allowed to bring two boxes of cigars. I would wait outside the gate at the airport, buy those cigars from people and then resell them for a small profit. I eventually managed to start this factory, but my operation has grown only lately, since the great boom started. I took on an American partner who has money."

"Richard Knox."

The old man looked surprised. "Do you know him?"

"I met him briefly just a while ago."

"Between the American and me we had the capital to take advantage. But the Espada brand, a great cigar in its time, had been dormant too long and they had no means to revive it. I understand that young Espada is working over at Great American."

"He was, until he disappeared."

Just then the young woman with the glasses knocked and stuck her head in.

"A call from the Dominican Republic," she said.

Tirado frowned, started to reach for the phone, glanced at Willie and then turned back to the woman. "Tell him I'll call him back. Right now. I'm busy." The attendant withdrew.

"You have business down in the D.R.?" Willie asked.

"We have a plant there. We make most of our cigars there . . . Where were we?"

"I was telling you that Carlos Espada was working for Nathan Cooler over at Great American Tobacco, but then Carlos dropped from sight."

The old man grimaced. He didn't seem to care for Nathan Cooler either. Moments later, Willie found out why. The old man's attention was suddenly distracted by something happening out on the street. He lifted his cane and pointed it out the window.

"Those sons of bitches are back, trying to steal my workers." He hauled himself out of the chair and headed out through the workshop as fast as the cane allowed. Willie stayed on his heels.

On the sidewalk they found a short, dark man with a shaved head and wraparound mirrored sunglasses. He wore a green shirt open down his chest and a thick gold chain dangling into his black chest hairs. He held a roll of money in his hand.

Ricardo Tirado tottered to within about six feet of him and shook his cane. "I've told you to stay away from my workers, you son of a bitch."

The man smiled, exposing several gold-capped teeth. "I am standing on public property, *viejo*. There is nothing you can do. If you won't pay your workers top dollar, then we will."

"Yes, and when your latest contract is filled, you fire them again. But you won't tell them that. Get away from here."

The shorter man continued to smile. Willie now understood why Tirado referred to his competitors as pirates. The man definitely had the look.

"I don't have to go anywhere, but I will because I don't want you to have another stroke, old man. Your workers already know where to come."

He gave Tirado a mock salute, crossed the street, climbed into what looked to be a very new gold Lincoln and drove off.

"Who is he?" Willie asked.

Tirado was still breathing hard with rage. "His name is Calderón. Mario Calderón. He used to work for me. Now he works for Nathan Cooler at Great American Tobacco. He comes here and tries to lure my cigar rollers away. He's a traitor. I'll kill him before he kills me. When you go to see Cooler, you can tell him that."

The lady in the glasses had rushed out and was holding onto the old man's arm, trying to lead him back inside and scolding him in Spanish. Willie thanked Tirado for his time and left him a card.

As he pulled away, the old man was staggering tiredly back into his workshop, which he had just defended from pirates.

CHAPTER SIX

Willie knew the Great American Tobacco Company was located out Flagler Street, on the western edge of Little Havana. He had passed the building all his life.

Miami is a relatively new city, only a century in existence, and no structure in it can be called very old. But the factory seemed to defy that chronology. Its soiled, blood-red brick and clouded windows brought to mind the nineteenth-century mill towns in New England. It was rundown and desolate. At least that was how Willie remembered it.

But as he arrived at the address it became clear that the big boom had also benefited Great American. The building was being refurbished in great style—if not good taste. Masons had covered up the dingy old brick and given the rectangular, two-story building a brown stucco finish, vaguely cigar-colored.

Painted between the first story and the second, much like a cigar band, was a stripe of red paint with gold trim above and below. Calligraphed in gold script on that band were the words GREAT AMERICAN. Between the two words was the company's symbol, a rearing white stallion. The place looked like something you might smoke.

Willie parked across the street, entered through the front door, and found equally tasteful renovations in progress inside as well. The walls and carpet both matched the exterior decor, the same brown with red-and-gold trim. A reception desk sat against the back wall and behind it hung a large oil painting of the rearing horse. Painters continued to work in a corner of that lobby, and he saw drop cloths spreading down a hallway.

Behind the desk sat a petite young receptionist in a flowered dress and mauve lipstick. She was watching the painters warily, as if she were afraid they would try to paint her too—brown with a red band around her waist. Maybe a horse on the belt buckle. She looked as if she would put up a fight.

Willie approached her. "I'd like to see Mr. Nathan Cooler, please."

He handed the girl his card and she looked at it as suspiciously as she'd been looking at the painters.

"Do you have an appointment?"

"No, but if you could please tell Mr. Cooler that I'm here at the request of Mrs. Victoria Espada, I think he'll see me."

The girl picked up the phone and passed on Willie's request. A minute later an older secretary, a bit more robust, came down the spiral staircase from the second floor and led Willie back up the stairs.

Cubicles were being constructed, offices partitioned. The institutional art consisted of large depictions of the company's different cigars, all photographed against black backgrounds so that they resembled strangely designed space stations floating in a void.

A side door opened, and Willie caught a glimpse of a lower level and of machines used to make mass-produced cigars—chopping, shaping, wrapping, packing. Beyond them he saw a separate section where cigars were being hand-rolled, the way they were at the Tirado factory. Willie wondered how many of those rollers had been lured away from Don Ricardo.

The secretary pointed toward a pair of double wooden doors at the very end of the corridor and told him to go in. Willie did as he was told, knocking once, stepping inside and closing the door behind him.

He had expected to enter a fairly conventional corporate office, albeit one with a brown-and-red cigar color scheme. Instead, he found about ten pairs of eyes fixed on him. It made him stop and stare around in amazement. These weren't corporate types looking at him. They were Indians, native Americans, in full regalia—feather war bonnets, war paint, etc. Willie had somehow walked in on a nineteenth-century meeting of the tribes.

It took him a moment to comprehend that Nathan Cooler had decorated his office with man-sized, antique cigar-store Indians, the kind that cigar sellers had once stationed on the sidewalks outside their shops to attract customers. They were all carved out of wood. A few featured tomahawks or held bows with arrows pointed at Willie. On closer inspection, he realized that a couple of them weren't Indians at all, but sultans wrapped in turbans, probably used to advertise Turkish tobacco. One of them, lurking very near Willie, gripped a menacing scimitar.

Suddenly a figure moved. It wasn't one of the Indians or sultans, but Nathan Cooler, and he came from behind one of the warriors. He was laughing. A real jokester this Nathan Cooler.

Fair-skinned, broad-shouldered, he was about sixty years old, at least six feet four, burly and handsome. He was as wide as Richard Tirado was thin and was dressed casually in gray slacks and a navy guayabera. The shirt accentuated his eyes, which were a startling shade of blue. His complexion was florid. The ensemble was topped off by a white Panama hat with a blue band.

Cooler was the only figure in the room without a weapon, although he kept a colonnade of cigars in his shirt pocket, like arrows in a quiver.

"This is my board of directors," he said with the hint of a Southern accent.

Willie nodded. "I hope they get along, given the way they're armed."

Cooler smiled and motioned Willie to a chair. Willie threaded his way through the Apaches, Comanches and sheiks and sat down across a desk from Cooler.

The big man looked at Willie's business card. "I assume you've been retained by Victoria Espada to find Carlos?"

"That's right."

Cooler rocked back in his executive easy chair. "If you ask me, and I've been in this business quite a long time, he's just off on a bender somewhere. Salesmen tend to do that sort of thing. He'll be back."

"That's good because I'm starting to think the same thing."

Cooler seemed pleased to have someone agree with him. Maybe Victoria Espada had been expressing her worries to him.

"Salesmen have pressures," he said. "Sometimes they need a little R and R."

Willie removed the photos from the folder. "Well, I don't know how much rest and relaxation he's getting with this girl. But I imagine he's working off some tension."

Cooler took the photos from him. It was clear he hadn't seen them before. He studied both and looked back at Willie. "This is who he's with?"

Willie shrugged. "It certainly looks like it."

Cooler handed them back. "Well, that solves that."

"I take it the lady isn't a business contact."

Cooler shook his head. "Not that I know of. If she were, she'd be my business contact." Cooler rocked back and smiled.

Willie squinted at him. "For a boss whose salesman just disappeared for two weeks, without giving you notice so he could frolic with a blonde in the Dominican Republic, you certainly are understanding, Mr. Cooler."

The big man in the Panama swiveled from side to side.

"I was young once. These things happen." On the wall behind him were various photos taken over the years of Cooler with friends. He had been blond and ruggedly handsome back then and Willie imagined that Mr. Cooler had enjoyed the company of women. There were no family photos on the wall or the desk, leading Willie to assume that Cooler was a bachelor.

"It sounds like you run an unusually understanding and democratic company here," Willie said. "When can I come work for you?"

"If you can sell stogies, you can start tomorrow."

They were two laughing and joking good-old-boys, Willie and Mr. Cooler. Of course, Cooler's personnel policies made no sense for a successful company and Willie made another little joke about it.

"With your vacation policies I'd say it would be good to work for you, but not too good to own your stock."

Cooler didn't like that. It offended the corporate titan in him. Willie could see it behind the blue eyes, but all Cooler did was shrug.

"I've known Carlos Espada since he was in diapers. Maybe he feels he can take a bit of advantage because the boss is an old friend of the family and because I know he'll get his work done."

"That's funny. From what I've heard. he's had a lot of trouble getting that work done. In fact, I've been told that he isn't a very good salesman and that you keep him on just as a favor to his mother."

Cooler looked disappointed in Willie, in his lack of charity or possibly in his lack of insight into the business.

"Maybe he isn't the best agent I have out there, but the family name is worth a lot, especially here in South Florida. The Espadas were great cigar makers. It works out for the company and he's a good kid."

Willie nodded. Cooler's generosity of spirit was impressive.

"You'll see, he'll be back," Cooler said. "In fact, there's a cigar convention this week here in Miami at the Hamilton Hotel, and I bet you he'll be there. I'll leave you a couple of tickets. You can be my guest." Cooler wrote Willie's name on a list.

Willie thanked him and said he would surely be there. Cooler got up, signaling that the interview was over. It was only then that Willie remembered the scene at Tirado Cigar. He told Cooler about it and about Don Ricardo Tirado's threat. The big man was irked, but not at Tirado.

"I've told Calderón various times not to bother the other companies, especially not firms like Tirado. It only creates bad blood and bad word of mouth in the public."

"He's trying to hire away their workers."

Cooler grimaced. "I've told him not to do that. I'll talk to him again."

They walked to the door. Willie encouraged him to call if he heard anything about Carlos Espada. Cooler said he would, and they shook hands. On the one hand, Cooler seemed a perfectly capable man; on the other, employees like Carlos Espada and Mario Calderón appeared to do as they pleased. It didn't make a lot of sense and Willie wondered why it worked that way. He glanced at all the Indians, the board of directors. If they knew, they weren't telling.

Willie said good-bye and headed back down the long hallway as Cooler closed the door behind him. About halfway down he passed a young woman carrying flies.

"Can you tell me where Carlos Espada's office is?"

The woman pointed to the last door on the left. "It's right there, but Mr. Espada hasn't been in."

Willie held up the folder with photos in it. "I know. I just need to drop this on his desk for Mr. Cooler."

Willie waited for the woman to disappear, then opened Espada's office and slipped inside, easing the door shut behind him. What he saw knocked him back a step. Someone had trashed the place. In fact, it looked as if a tornado had hit it. The drawers of a file cabinet and wooden desk were open, and papers were strewn everywhere. Cigar boxes had been emptied and stogies lay all around.

But the damage wasn't just the result of a search. The furniture had been knocked over, pictures had been ripped off the wall and stomped, and holes had been staved in the plaster-board walls. It appeared as if there had been a fight, or rather a gang rumble.

Willie searched for signs of blood, but didn't see any, which was a miracle. He did find a briefcase with some sales slips, Carlos Espada's business cards and more cigars inside. If Espada had gone on a business trip, he had done it without his cowhide.

Willie was still picking through the case when the door to the office opened. Cooler stood staring at him.

"You don't belong in here, Mr. Cuesta." The big man wasn't happy. He was no longer the easygoing supreme leader he had been in his office. His face was red beneath the white Panama.

"What happened to Carlos Espada?"

"I told you, he took off."

Willie looked around him. "I might take off too if somebody was this angry at me."

"This was an act of vandalism. Some kids got in here. That's all."

"And the only office they vandalized was Carlos Espada's, who happens to be missing? That's quite a coincidence."

"Coincidences happen, Mr. Cuesta. Now I'll have to ask you to leave."

Cooler's tone, and size, didn't leave much room for argument. As Willie passed Carlos Espada's desk he picked up a cigar lying there. If you visited a cigar factory, you should get a free sample. Willie bid Cooler good afternoon.

CHAPTER SEVEN

Willie sat outside Great American for a while waiting to see if Cooler went anywhere. But he didn't. The only thing that moved was the sun, until it was slanting right through the windshield and making the air conditioner strain. Then Willie put the car in gear and headed to Cesar's shop.

The old man was still behind his counter when Willie walked in. "I'm back, *viejo*."

"Willie? What happened, *muchacho?*"

Cesar was smoking a cigar, as always, and was also sneaking a bit of rum from a flask he kept in his briefcase. It was that time of day. He poured a second shot glass for his guest and Willie told him to freshen his own. He might need it.

Then he told the old man about his conversations with the Espadas, Tirado and Cooler, and finally, reluctantly, about the scene in Carlos' wrecked office.

Cesar's face fell. "That doesn't sound good. It doesn't sound good at all. What do you think happened to him?"

"I don't know."

"What did Nathan Cooler say?"

Willie clipped the cigar that he'd picked up from Carlos Espada's desk. He stoked it up and waved the smoke away from his face.

"Nathan Cooler didn't want to talk about it. He walked me out of the building to make sure no one else talked about it either."

Cesar's grimace deepened. "But it makes no sense. Why wouldn't he, if someone destroyed one of his offices?"

"I can't say. I don't know Nathan Cooler."

"I'm familiar with him. To me, he has always seemed like a good man. He has known Carlos and his family for many years. He should be helping to find Carlos."

Willie sipped his rum. "Does Cooler have a nasty streak? Could he have been the one who wrecked that office? He's big enough."

"I've never heard he was violent."

"Maybe he's spared you because you're blind. Or maybe he doesn't want to talk because business is good, and he doesn't want to rock the boat."

"I've never thought of him as that kind of man."

"Did Carlos Espada have any enemies in the business who might have done this?"

The blind man shook his head. "He isn't like that, Willie."

The phone rang then, and Cesar picked it up. His face brightened momentarily.

"*Sí, mi amor*," Cesar said. "But right now, I can't talk. I have a situation."

Cesar listened. It sounded like he had one of his girlfriends on the other end.

"We'll see each other a bit later. I want to speak with you."

Willie was about to move away and give him some privacy, but the old man hung up. They stood in silence. Willie sipped his rum and smoked his cigar. Cesar stared into that inner darkness of his, maybe trying to picture Carlos, who he had in fact never seen. Or perhaps trying to intuit what had happened in that office. Then his nose twitched and he turned to Willie.

"What is that you're smoking?"

Willie took the cigar from his mouth. "It's a little number I picked up in Carlos Espada's office before I was asked to leave so abruptly. It's called *El Embajador*—The Ambassador."

Cesar frowned and shook his head. "That's no Ambassador, muchacho. The only place they make the Amabassador is in Cuba."

Willie shrugged. "Maybe Carlos bought some from a smuggler."

The old man grew stern. "What you're smoking is not a real Havana. Believe me." He tapped his nose with a finger. "What does the cigar band look like?"

"It's black with gold lettering."

Cesar nodded. 'That's the Ambassador band all right. Let me have it."

Willie handed him the stogie, mouthpiece first. The blind man pulled a watch chain from his pocket and used a clipper attached to it to expertly cut off the live ember. He ran the cigar under his nose, then cut it open, end to end, with a penknife, like a surgeon at work. He smelled the inside and then examined the tobaccos with his expert fingers, before he let it drop into the ashtray.

"That's no Ambassador. The tobaccos are Dominican, from the area around Santiago. The cigar is a counterfeit."

"Don't blame me, *viejo*. He had some of them in his office."

"It's illegal to have them, Willie. They're phony."

"Well, when we find Carlos, we'll have to turn him over to the police."

The old man had gone stock-still, absorbed in that inner darkness again. Willie frowned.

"What is it, *viejo*?"

"I told you that Carlos would always come and talk to me. Well, about a month ago he stopped by and what he asked me about was counterfeit cigars."

Willie shrugged. "What about them? I don't know anything about counterfeit smokes."

Cesar puffed his stogie. "It's big business, Willie. It started a few years back when the smugglers couldn't keep up with the demand for real Cuban cigars. Every day I have somebody walk in here and ask me where they can get genuine Havanas. I say that I don't know. It's illegal to sell them in the US because of the embargo against Cuba. That's all I tell them. But I'm sure most of them make contact with the underground market."

"You mean the smugglers."

"I mean the smugglers and now the counterfeiters, which is even a bigger business. These are guys who make cigars and then give them seals and boxes just like the genuine Havanas. They even know the codes for the different factories where the best cigars are made and they put those codes in each box, just like the Cuban government does." He reached down into the ashtray and fingered the tobacco there.

"The Ambassadors, the real ones, were created in the last few years by the tobacco industry in Cuba. They were made specifically for Castro and his diplomats to give as presents to political leaders around the world. That's why they are called Ambassadors. They use the very best Cuban tobacco and only a handful of the very best cigar rollers are allowed to touch them. Many people say they are the finest cigar ever made. The ultimate Havana, Willie. Every knowledgeable cigar smoker in the world wants to smoke one. Do you know how much a box of twenty-five will cost you in the underground market?"

"Tell me."

"At least five thousand dollars. I'm told some people have paid twice that."

Willie looked at the broken leaves in the ashtray and whistled. "That's a lot of change."

"Not for some people. High rollers in New York, Los Angeles, London, Paris buy them and hand them out to impress their business associates. Most people don't know the real Ambassador from the fake ones. The counterfeiters make them for a hundred dollars a box and sell them for thousands. They fake other top-quality Havanas, too, and sell them all over the world. It's a luxury racket that involves millions of dollars, Willie. And it's a dangerous racket, too. About a month ago they found two guys dead up in North Miami. Do you remember that?"

Willie squinted. Then he reached into his shirt pocket and brought out the brief article he had found in Carlos Espada's bedroom.

"There was something in the paper," he said.

The blind man nodded. "I didn't read it in the paper, but I heard about it later. Everybody in our business knew. They found those guys with all sorts of counterfeit boxes and seals. They also found them with their throats cut from here to here." The old man dragged his finger across his larynx.

"You think someone was trying to rob them?"

"Maybe. But it could also be for two other reasons. First, that some other people wanted to be in the counterfeiting business, and they didn't want to share the market."

"And the second."

"That they were killed by Castro's people."

Willie's eyebrows went up. "Castro?"

"I know that people blame Castro for every bad thing that goes on here, but in this case his government has very large interests at stake. If the market is poisoned by bad counterfeits, people will stop buying Cuban cigars and that means his government will lose a lot of money. God knows, he certainly has the agents here to do the dirty work."

Cesar stopped, still fingering the tobacco in the ashtray, like a man reading tea leaves. Willie knew they were both thinking the same thing.

"Carlos wanted to make money fast," Willie said. "You think he got involved in this scam?"

"I told you he was asking me about it. Who made them? How much they charged? Things like that."

"And what did you tell him?"

"That I knew they made a lot of money, but I didn't know who they were."

Willie sipped his rum. "That doesn't mean he got involved with it, *viejo*. All he did was ask."

"Yes, but then he disappeared. Now you find his office destroyed and phony cigars."

Willie was wondering about the blonde woman in the photographs. She was still a more likely motive for disappearing as far as Willie was concerned. He told Cesar about her, but the old man just shook his head.

"For me or for you she would be a reason to take off. But his mother and sister are right. Carlos isn't that kind. I think it's something crazy he's done."

The blind man had turned to him, and Willie could see himself reflected in the black glasses. It was as if Willie were the only thought in Cesar's mind.

"I told you I have a bad feeling about all this, Willie."

"I understand. I'll find out what I can, *viejo*."

"I know you will. Just be careful, *muchacho*."

CHAPTER EIGHT

Willie rode the elevator to the third floor of the Miami Dade Police Department, found the glass door marked "Economic Crimes Unit," and entered.

Willie remembered the Econ Crimes Unit being plastered with wanted posters of small-time grifters, both guys and gals. They were check kiters, Ponzi scheme artists, phony lottery barons, ersatz salesmen of real estate and insurance. Because South Florida was home to so many senior citizens, who were seen as easy prey, it attracted more than its quota of chiselers.

Wanted posters still provided a major element of the decor, but what had changed was the number of computer terminals in the room. The worktable at which Sergeant Bernie Egan sat sported three of them and he was staring at the middle one. He called out a greeting to Willie but stayed glued to his screen. Willie approached behind him and saw that Bernie was studying a lottery website.

"This place looks like an Internet cafe," Willie said.

Bernie nodded. "Weasels have embraced the new technology, Willie. There are so many ways to swindle people via the web, it's a marvel. When people can make bets or transfer money by pressing a key in their home, then you know some of our sleazier citizens are going to be online."

He tapped the screen in front of him. "These gentlemen here are offering you a chance to play lotteries everywhere from Idaho to Indonesia. One of the winning lottery numbers is pegged to hog shares over in Java. All you have to do is give them the number of your credit card and they'll buy tickets for you. Then they go out and buy pigs in Pago Pago and fix the lottery so they win and you lose."

Bernie beamed at Willie, cackled with glee, signed off from his lottery site and swiveled his chair in Willie's direction.

"So, what can I do for you?"

Bernie Egan was himself a beady-eyed guy who had once said to Willie: "I know how weasels think because I would have made a good weasel myself."

Short, sallow, slim, late thirties, he had thinning sandy hair and tinted glasses over those small, mouse-brown, shifty eyes. A green visor protected his eyes against the glare of the fluorescent lights above. He wore a faded white shirt and a very narrow dark tie and dark dress pants. All in all, he was extremely plain, nondescript, which was the best look for a weasel, but also for a cop who hunted weasels. Willie sat down in a swivel chair next to him.

"I'm not here to discuss anything high-tech, Bernie. I'm working on a case that may involve cigar counterfeiting."

Bernie brightened. "Ah, good old-fashioned, low-tech consumer fraud. Low tech, but big money."

"That's what I hear, and fairly dangerous, too. I heard about those two guys who got killed up in North Miami."

Bernie suddenly pushed off with one foot and went wheeling across the room in his swivel chair, stopping at a gray filing cabinet. He opened a drawer, rifled some files and returned with one. Out of it he picked about a dozen crime scene photos, which he handed to Willie.

They showed the outside of an ordinary apartment building, then the interior of an ordinary apartment and, finally, a small back room in that apartment. What had happened in that room was not ordinary at all. The bodies of two men lay on the floor, twisted in fear and pain, riddled with bullets, their throats cut for good measure, their eyes lifeless. Scattered all around them were upended and crushed cigar boxes and loose cigars. Willie grimaced and Bernie nodded.

"Yes, I'd say it's getting dangerous indeed. These guys were turning out Havanas by the crate. Homicide hasn't closed that case yet. In fact, they haven't gotten far at all. The question is: Were they killed by competitors or by people they cheated?" Bernie brightened again and shifted into a Groucho Marx imitation. "Crack the case, win a fake cigar."

"Do we know who these two unlucky gentlemen were?"

Bernie shrugged. "Just two low-level guys who had worked in the tobacco business in Cuba. Back on the island they had rolled Havanas and they decided to do the same in North Miami—despite the fact they didn't have any Cuban tobacco. All they had was phony boxes and bands, but that was apparently enough.

"We traced their product to resorts in the Caribbean and to bankers in Switzerland. They were hobnobbing with the rich and famous and doing very well. The girlfriend of one of them told us they were being pressured by somebody to go out of business, but they didn't see why they should." Bernie pointed at the photos. "Now we know why they should have."

Willie glanced at the images again. "Yes, we certainly do." He handed the photos back. "Now it's my turn to show you some photos. But they aren't as hard to look at."

He handed Bernie the two shots of Carlos Espada and his blonde bombshell.

"I have a missing person I'm looking for who might have gotten involved with some of the guys in this racket. His name is Carlos Espada. I'm wondering if you've heard the name in your travels or seen that face."

Bernie scrutinized the photos and shook his head. "Negative. What makes you think he's into faking Cuban cigars?"

"I'm not sure he is. Also, he's not the kind of guy who would be capable of doing what was done to those guys in North Miami. At least I don't believe so. In fact, I think there's much more chance of his ending up like those two guys. I'm wondering if there's anyone else who has knowledge of that business and might have knowledge of Mr. Espada."

Bernie thought about it, had a sudden inspiration and swiveled back to his computer. He typed, clicked, typed some more and tapped the screen with a finger.

"Here we have a local expert on the current state of that business. So expert and so current that he was arrested by members of our unit only about a month ago."

He was pointing at an arrest record for a certain Rolando Falcón, age twenty-four, registered at an address in the city of Hialeah. The screen said he had been apprehended in possession of counterfeit cigars that he had rolled in his very own home.

"Is he in jail?"

Bernie shook his head. "No. He made bail and I understand the charges may be dropped. He claims he wasn't selling them himself, but delivering them to someone else, and that he didn't know that the cigars he made were being peddled as genuine Havanas. It's a first offense, so he'll probably get off. And the guy he was delivering to has disappeared. Maybe it was your boy, Espada. If it was, I'm sure you'll let us know."

Bernie smiled brightly at Willie. Willie smiled back. Cesar wasn't paying him to surrender Victoria Espada's son to the police, but Willie would help Bernie as much as possible.

Bernie printed out the arrest form and gave it to Willie.

"It's a blue apartment building a couple blocks from the fire station in Hialeah. You can't miss it."

Willie thanked Bernie and said he would be in touch if he stumbled onto anything that would be useful to the police department.

Bernie beamed. "Don' t take any exploding cigars, Willie."

* * *

Ten minutes later Willie was rolling down Okeechobee Road into Hialeah, a growing metropolis that was even more Cuban than Miami. In Hialeah you couldn't spit without hitting someone from Havana, Santiago, Santa Clara or some other town in Cuba. The spoken language of the neighborhoods was Cuban Spanish. The names on the stores and advertisements on billboards—from *Café Cubano* to *bodegas* and *bicicletas*—were in *español*. Signs in store windows announcing "We speak English here," were not unusual. Anglo culture was making a last stand but was losing. Just as surely as Custer had lost.

Willie turned north into the heart of the town, spotted the fire station, turned west and went two blocks. The blue building Bernie had mentioned came into view. Its color resembled skies painted by Van Gogh. You couldn't miss it.

It was a two-story garden complex, although the term "garden" had to be applied loosely. Parking out front, Willie walked through the front entrance into an open central courtyard. No grass grew there due to lack of sun. Rusting metal mailboxes were built into the wall on the right side. Inscribed on the wall above them were innumerable graffiti, about all sorts of people who had lived there and loved each other. "Marta loves Ramiro"; "Consuela loves Junior." The place didn't look real good, but it apparently had been a hotbed of romance.

Of the sixteen mailboxes, only about half bore name tags and none said Falcón. Willie looked around. Loud rock-and-roll leaked from one of the apartments on the second floor. As Willie gazed up, the door to that apartment opened, the music suddenly growing louder. A young woman walked out dressed totally in black, with bright purple hair and matching lipstick. She closed the door behind her.

Willie watched her as she descended the stairs, approached the mailboxes and unlocked one that was not labeled. She was about twenty years old, with cocoa-colored skin and dark brown eyes. The contrast of the purple hair and lip gloss against the tawny skin was very exotic. Willie figured that in some Amazonian jungle there might be a bird blessed with those colors, but only there. She also wore a nose stud and several small silver earrings in the one ear he could see. On her right hip, just visible beneath the lace edge of her short black blouse, there was a tattoo, a braided snake.

She glanced up at Willie and he smiled. She turned on the indifference, avoided his gaze and inspected the mail. Relatively few participants in Miami's punk or late punk scene were Hispanic. Most immigrant families were still in the stage of assimilating, to some degree. They no longer would surrender their language, music, dances and traditions, as other generations had, but they weren't into blatant acts of rebellion against mainstream US culture, i.e. violet hair. Not usually. Latin punks were rare birds.

She closed the mailbox and was about to fly the coop, but Willie cornered her.

"Excuse me. I'm looking for someone who lives here, and I wonder if you could help me. His name is Rolando Falcón."

Her eyes darted vaguely toward the second story and quickly back to Willie. When she spoke it was with an accent, a melodic voice and a ready falsehood. "I'm sorry. I can't."

Willie took out a card and gave it to her.

"I'm not a policeman. I'm not here to cause any trouble. I just need a word with Mr. Falcón."

Willie's shirt bore a pattern of white palm fronds against a dark blue background. He certainly didn't look like the establishment. But he didn't have purple hair either. He was a creature from another part of the forest and that was enough for her.

"I'm sorry," she said, and she stepped around Willie and left the building.

He glanced up at the apartment she had abandoned, climbed the stairs and knocked on the jalousie door. The music remained very loud, and he got no answer. Next to the door was a porthole window and he peered through it but saw nobody. He knocked again, this time waiting for a momentary dip in the decibel level. The volume declined and the door opened.

The young man standing before him was clearly from the same corner of the forest as the girl, although from a slightly different species. He was also Latino, in his twenties, short and wiry. His T-shirt and jeans were black, and he wore a large gold earring. But his plumage, his hair, was spiky and bright orange. A tattooed dragon had wound its tail around his right forearm.

He looked Willie up and down warily, as if it were Willie who was outrageously dressed and coiffed. "Can I help you with something?" His syntax was correct, but his accent was pronounced. The last word came out "son-sing." On the CD player a man was spouting in Spanish about how much lips can hurt.

"Mr. Falcón?"

"*Sí, hombre.*"

Willie handed him a business card. The kid read it and his eyes flared. For a moment Willie was sure Falcón would close the door and he positioned his foot to fend off that move. But the kid had second and even third thoughts. "An investigator, huh?" he said finally.

"That's right."

Falcón sized him up with a whimsical expression. "Just like in the movies. Dirty Harry. Make my day." He said it with deliberation, as if he had learned his English watching old Clint Eastwood movies, which was perfectly possible. Although if he had learned the language from Clint, he should have done a better job of staying out of trouble.

Willie shook his head. "No, not exactly. I think Dirty Harry was a policeman. I work for myself."

"Oh, yeah?"

"Yeah. Do you mind if I get out of the sun?"

Falcón considered the idea and then allowed Willie to step inside. The apartment was small and dark. It was Willie's understanding that the brightest birds lived in the darkest parts of the forest. Well, Falcón lived in the dark as well. The only decoration seemed to be posters papering the walls, mostly of musicians and musical groups, both Latin American rockers and US rappers, who Willie had heard of vaguely, but whose music he didn't know. More boys and girls in black, they turned their market-oriented alienation on Willie from all angles.

Falcón lowered the music further and came back. "What do you want?"

"I'm looking for someone you might know. His name is Carlos Espada."

The kid frowned. "I don't know nobody called that."

Willie had a feeling Falcón would have answered the same way no matter who he was asked about, including his own mama. Willie held up his empty hands.

"Like I said, I'm not a policeman and I'm not here to cause you trouble. But I know you got busted a few weeks ago, charged with being part of a scheme to crank out counterfeit cigars. I also know you were probably innocent and because of that maybe you can help me."

Falcón was a very cool customer for a kid his age. He took a good twenty seconds to size up Willie and decide how to handle him. He reminded Willie of himself at that age: a bit of a wiseass, a bit whimsical, a bit self-conscious, with lots of phony aplomb. When he spoke, his tone was measured, as if he were repeating an account for the tenth time to a team of investigators.

"I don't know nothing about that. My *abuelo*—my grandfather—and my father, they made cigars in Cuba, and I'm making cigars since I'm a boy. I come here five years ago from Cuba and I need work. I'm rolling cigars at a cigar club on Miami Beach and this guy he ask me if I want to make extra money. So, I roll cigars for him. I roll them right here."

He pointed to a formica table in the cramped kitchenette.

"I don't know that he's selling them and saying they are from Havana. He just comes here and picks them up. Then one day the detectives come and they tell me I'm a criminal." He shook his head as if in shock and raised his orange eyebrows. "Wow, *hombre!*"

That was pretty much what Bernie had said.

"Who was the guy?"

"He tells me his name is Fausto. That's all I know. He buys the cigars I make for one dollar and he sells them for twenty or thirty dollars. He reep me off."

Yes, he certainly had "reeped" Falcón off.

"What did he look like?" Falcón shrugged. "Like everybody else, *hermano*."

For a guy with bright orange hair, that was probably true. Willie took out the photo of Carlos Espada and the young blonde woman.

"Was this him?"

Falcón's eyes welled with recognition, at least Willie thought they did, but then glazed over. He shook his head like a zombie, so that his big gold earring swung back and forth. In the background another song had begun, this one a strange ballad about a torture cell.

"It don't look like him," he said.

"Are you sure? Look again."

Falcón was already shaking his head. Meanwhile, Willie's gaze fell on the table right next to the door. Lying on it was a small box of matches and written on that container was "Great American Tobacco." Willie had seen similar boxes in Carlos Espada's office and one on Nathan Cooler's desk. He picked it up.

"Been over at Great American looking for work or has somebody from the company been here?"

Falcón read the box and shook his head. "You get those anywhere, *hombre*."

Willie threw the matches down, squinted at Falcón, giving him his best Clint Eastwood look, trying to tap into Falcón's old English lessons. He even put a steely edge on his voice, just like Clint, so that the punker would comprehend the gravity of the situation.

"This man is missing and his family is worried about him. They're Cubans like you." Well, not exactly like him, Willie thought, but they were Cubans. "Tell me where I find this man. Make my *mañana*."

Falcón shook his head slowly, his intelligent eyes not leaving Willie's. "It isn't *mañana,* man. It's today. And I tell you again, I don't know him."

But again, Willie didn't believe him. Of course, if Falcón were lying about his involvement in the counterfeiting scam, playing the innocent victim, the last guy he would want anyone to interview was his contact. That contact could have been Carlos Espada, also known as Fausto. To Willie, Falcón looked too hip to have been "reeped" off so easily. He also looked too smart to tell Willie anything he shouldn't.

"What was the name of the cigar club where you met this Fausto?"

Falcón considered that a moment, and then conceded an answer. "The Humidor. It's in Miami Beach on Washington Avenue."

Willie knew where it was. He pointed to the business card clutched in Falcón's hand.

"If you remember anything else, just whistle."

Falcón frowned and Willie left, just as a ballad came on in the background about fires in the rainforests and the deaths of God's most beautiful creatures.

CHAPTER NINE

William pulled up at his own place about an hour before sunset. He found the house full of afternoon heat, opened the windows and flipped on the ceiling fans. He said hello to the gecko and poured himself a cold beer, a Negra Modelo, with a generous squeeze of lime. Then he put on a Willy Chirino-CD and heard a song about a lady in black stockings and a guy who "never had any religion except the body of a woman."

Willie sipped his beer. He would change and head out to The Humidor on Miami Beach, but first he dialed the Espada house and asked for Esther. He recognized her deep voice when she came on.

"I have something I need to ask you," he said.

"What is it?"

"It has to do with your brother's activities lately and something your mother shouldn't hear."

She was silent a few moments. "Where are you?"

"At my place."

"Where is that?"

"Little Havana. You have my address on my card."

She hesitated, but briefly. "I'll be there."

"I'll be around back."

Willie poured himself a fresh beer, strolled down the back stairs, and lay in the hammock under the mango tree. From there he could listen to the adventures of Chirino and the lady in the black stockings. She spent the night, nabbed his wallet, disappeared before dawn, but also stole his heart. He seemed to think she was worth it.

Esther Espada arrived a half hour later, appearing just outside the gate. In the twilight she was even more beautiful than she had been earlier. Now she wore a green blouse and a short, black skirt.

Her hair was tied back with a red bandana, and she looked like a gypsy. Willie wished she were a gypsy, that she had some kind of magical powers that would change what he was starting to believe about her brother.

He opened the gate for her and offered her a drink. She accepted a glass of red wine. He went upstairs to pour it and watched her from the window. Sitting there alone, she looked sadder than she had earlier. She stared into the garden, at the bougainvillea, and Willie wondered what she was thinking.

She was still lost in thought when he walked up next to her with the wine. "The flowers are beautiful, aren't they?"

She glanced up at him. "You didn't call me to talk about flowers."

Willie sat in the lawn chair next to her. "No. I called you to talk about how your brother has been paying the bills lately."

"We told you. He works for Great American Tobacco as a salesman."

"I talked to Nathan Cooler. He said Carlos wasn't doing much business lately. In fact, he's not doing any business now, at least not for Cooler."

She pulled her fine chin back and the gaze in her eyes grew suspicious. "You're speaking in riddles. Tell me what you have to say."

Willie glanced at the flowers and then back at her. "There is a chance that your brother has become involved in the business of counterfeit cigars. If he has, then he may have put himself in danger, and something could have happened to him."

He told her about his trip to Great American and his stop in Carlos' office.

Her black eyes were suffused not with worry, but with anger. "We've had ill fortune in our family, Mr. Cuesta, but we are not criminals."

"I'm telling you what I saw and what's been communicated to me. Maybe I'm wrong," Willie said, none too convincingly.

"I'm sure you're wrong. Carlos would never do that. As much as we hate Castro, his driving us out of Cuba, and as much as we want to see his cigar industry fail, we are not crooks, swindlers."

She stared off into the hibiscus as the sun set and the shadows stretched toward them. "We've already had enough chaos and calamity in our family, Mr. Cuesta. You heard my mother's story. We have had to make our lives out of nothing."

Her hands moved in front of her those of a magician pulling hidden objects out of silk scarves. "We have been desperate, but we have never cheated, or defied the law. My brother is a noble person."

"We both know your family needs money," Willie said. "Maybe your brother got involved in something he shouldn't, not for his own sake, but because he was desperate to help you and your mother. Cesar told me your brother was at the end of his rope."

She was shaking her head resolutely. "We were only babies when our father died. But from the time he was just a boy Carlos always defended the honor of our family. My mother was a widow, a beautiful widow, and many men took an interest in her. My brother would stand at her side, staring them down, just in case their intentions weren't pure. Our father was a wonderful man. He was handsome, charming. My brother wasn't going to let anyone come close to my mother unless she considered them comparable to our father. It was the honor of the family he was protecting."

"And your mother never has found someone comparable."

"No."

"Did your brother do the same for you?"

She regarded him warily. Willie felt he was asking a personal question of someone who had never heard such an inquiry before. He figured no one had ever delved much into the life of the Espadas. It felt a bit dangerous, like uncharted territory. She made a decision about him and finally nodded.

"When I came of age, he made sure that men weren't looking for anything easy."

"And no one came along who made the grade in your case either?" Even as he asked it, he was thinking that it would be very hard to reach that grade.

She gave him a penetrating look.

"I've never married. Some legitimate suitors showed up at my door. There were also men who wanted to use the Espada name in their business ventures with cigars and others who believed we still had money, which we didn't. But I decided I couldn't leave my mother. Until I knew she was taken care of, her life stabilized, I wouldn't commit to anyone else. My brother made the same decision."

Willie wondered if she had "decided" anything, or if that position had been forced on her by a mother who glorified the past.

Since the first meeting, Willie had wondered about Victoria Espada. Over the years Willie had known many exile families. Some had washed up on the shores of several countries before arriving in Miami. Many had lost family members along the way. They had rebuilt their lives and gone on.

Victoria Espada had lost her husband, which was hard, and she had not weathered that tragedy well. A legendary beauty when she was young, she had certainly counted on life being easier than the one she had been forced to live. Thoroughbreds were more delicate than lesser specimens. Whatever the reason, something had set her apart. While others had remade their lives, Victoria had tried to hold on to a life that was lost. She lived like an exile within the exile community and her children seemed to be following in her footsteps. Or, at least, they had been until Carlos had disappeared.

Willie sipped his beer. "Maybe that's what your brother is trying to do—stabilize the economic life of the family, take care of your mother and let you live your life. "

She shook her head. "He should know this is no way to take care of our mother. She's at the point of going out of her mind. Two days ago, I found her standing on the edge of the water behind the house, talking, as if she were speaking to my father who died out there. I'm afraid she'll swim out there to meet him. My brother knows how delicate she is. He wouldn't go away like this of his own will. Do you understand?"

Willie said he did. He also decided not to tell her about her brother's possible contact with the punk cigar roller, Rolando Falcón. It would do no good.

"Can you tell me where your brother might have traveled in the last two weeks before he disappeared?"

"I told you what he told us. He said he had to go on business trips. Maybe they weren't for Great American Tobacco. Maybe he had found another way to make money, a legal way."

"Would you have a recent telephone bill I could look at, both phones in the house and cell phones?"

At first, she didn't like this idea, as if it were ignoble to pry into someone's phone calls. But she finally nodded.

"I don't think the bills have come yet, but I'll let you know as soon as they do."

There was nothing else to say, but she didn't move.

"And the woman in the photos?" she asked.

Willie shook his head. "I haven't found her yet."

She gave him her penetrating gaze but said nothing. The audience was over. Willie walked her out and watched her drive away. When he went back upstairs, he found himself humming the old song about a gypsy woman and the hell she played in a poor boy's life.

CHAPTER TEN

It was eight thirty when Willie swung onto Washington Avenue in South Beach. The club district was busy every night of the week, but not at that early hour. Most of the stores were already shuttered for the day, and the doors to the clubs were still closed. The strip seemed abandoned, like a movie set between takes of a crowd scene. It would be midnight before the streets would come alive again with club-goers, but that was fine with Willie. He wasn't looking for crowds. He was searching for one guy.

He managed to park just a block off Washington and walked to The Humidor. If the street seemed desolate and uninviting, The Humidor was something else again. It was cozy. The walls were covered in mahogany and red organza and when the padded, sound-proofed door closed behind him he felt he was walking into a large cigar box.

It was dimly lighted and had the feel of a plush speakeasy. Glistening wine glasses hung upside down over a small bar and a red-coated barman polished another one. About a half dozen small tables were spaced around, each one flanked by two high-backed red leather chairs and a matching love seat. A few shadowy individuals sat at those tables, only the embers of their smokes clearly visible.

The back wall was lined with open boxes of cigars, the house selection. Beyond that, up a flight of three red-carpeted stairs, stood a large, walk-in humidor, visible through a glass wall. From floor to ceiling it was paneled with dozens of cedar drawers, each featuring a gold lock and a gold name plate.

Willie walked across the room and entered the humidor. The temperature was a few degrees lower. He drifted around to keep warm, observing the drawers. Each gold plate was stenciled with the name of the owner of the cigars stored therein. Some names he didn't recognize. Others were familiar Miami-area businessmen, professionals and politicians. The back wall was reserved for the sports stars and entertainment personalities who often passed through Miami, the names you read about in the celebrity columns.

On the right-hand wall, near the bottom, he found a drawer etched with the name Carlos Espada—Great American Tobacco. Willie tried the handle discreetly and found it was locked.

He still had his hand on the lever when a female attendant walked in. She was a tall, green-eyed, auburn-haired woman in a very short, black skirt and tight red jacket, just like the barman's but cut lower. She didn't appear to have much on underneath it, just her own generous self. Like the drawers, she wore a gold name plate. Her name was Dana and she stood right over him.

"Can I help you?"

Willie stood up. "Just browsing."

"Maybe I can interest you in a private drawer." Her voice was low and breathy, like a smoky exhale.

"I'm not sure at the moment. How much does one cost?"

"Five hundred dollars per year, but with that you get a discount on our best cigars. And you also get my personalized attention."

She batted her long lashes at him as if maybe there was smoke in the air and it hurt her eyes, except there wasn't any smoke in the air.

"Just what do you mean by personalized attention?"

She gave him a coy look. "Well, let's put it this way. It doesn't mean I delve into the members' drawers. You weren't going to ask me if I did that, were you?"

"No, I wasn't."

"Good, because you can't imagine how many times I've been asked that since I started working here. 'Will you reach into our drawers?'"

"I can imagine."

"No, you can't," and she flapped her lashes at him sardonically some more. She was a smart girl for a cigar attendant. She tapped the glass top of the display case with a long, red-nailed finger.

"What personalized attention means is that I assist you in selecting a drawer, help you fill it with fine cigars, clip them and light them for you when you come here, if you please. I also lean over provocatively in front of you when I do it. It makes guys puff harder and smoke more cigars. The management likes that."

She gave him another clever look and he smiled back.

"The truth is I'm not here to join the club," Willie said. "I'm only an occasional cigar smoker and I think I'm not in the same economic class as most of your members."

She looked around. "Yes, we have some tycoons in here and superstars and up-and-comers."

Willie took out a business card and handed it to her. "This is who I am and I'm working on a case involving one of your club members. He's missing and his family is looking for him."

She read the card and looked up at Willie.

"Which one are we talking about?"

Willie pointed to the drawer belonging to Carlos Espada. "This gentleman right here."

She read the name, thought about it for several moments, glanced toward the barman and then whispered to Willie. "I'm quitting soon anyway. Too many guys wanting me to delve into their drawers . . . I can tell you that guy Espada hasn't been here in a while."

"How long?"

"At least a month, maybe more."

"What else can you tell me about him?"

She shrugged. "Not much. I know he works for a cigar company and the firm pays for the box. He never says much to me when he comes in. He's pleasant, courteous. He fetches his own cigars and lights them himself. He doesn't need me to bend over in front of him. He can puff all right on his own. And he doesn't look like the kind of guy who would run off."

"Well, we don't know that for sure. Maybe something happened to him."

She clearly didn't like the sound of that but said nothing.

"How about drinking? Did you ever see him drunk?" Willie was thinking of what Cooler had said about Carlos probably being off on a bender.

She shook her head. "No, he never drinks much at all. Maybe one glass of wine. He just comes in, gets his cigars and talks a while with whoever is here. He's a salesman. They need to talk people up."

Willie glanced at the box. "Can members keep other stuff in those boxes?"

"They can keep anything they want in there, as long as it isn't a controlled substance, if you know what I mean."

"I wonder what he has in there now." Willie figured counterfeit cigars might be considered a controlled substance.

She knew what he was getting at and shook her head. "I can't tell you that. I have a master key, but I can only use it if a member loses his key."

"I understand."

Finally, Willie took out the photos of Carlos Espada. "Just to make sure. This is the man we're talking about, right?"

She eyed the photos and grimaced. "Yes, that's him all right. But what's he doing with her?" She jabbed at the image of the blonde woman.

Willie raised his eyebrows. "Do you know her?"

"Oh, yeah, I know her. Her name is Dinah. She hangs out in here sometimes."

"What's her last name?"

She shook that off. "I don't know. She isn't the kind that goes by two names. Like Madonna or Cher. She's just Dinah."

"What can you tell me about her?"

She gave him her best catty look. "I can tell you she likes men with money, and it doesn't matter how old they are. That's why she's always in here. It isn't because she likes to smoke."

"When was the last time you saw her?"

That made her think. "Now that you mention it, she hasn't been here in a couple of weeks."

Willie pointed at the photo. "Did you ever see her with Espada?"

She shook her head. "No, never. I don't think he has the kind of money that attracts her. That's why I was surprised to see them in that photo together. She seems to go for real high rollers."

"Is she a working girl?"

"You mean a hooker? I don't know exactly what business arrangements she makes with her smokers. I hear she's spent a lot of time on yachts and took some vacations in the islands with members. Maybe she just lights their cigars, but I don't think so."

Willie looked around at the cedar drawers with their gold name plates. "Can you think of any of the high rollers she spent time with?"

She roamed around the room a bit and then tapped a drawer. "Mr. Knox."

Willie's brows danced. "Not Richard Knox?"

"That's right."

"Blond, well-tanned, medium build."

"That's him—and rich."

Willie looked at the drawer. It belonged to the same man who had sidled into Cesar Mendoza's store that morning with two women, one on each arm, neither of whom were Dinah or even blonde. The same Richard Knox who was partners with Don Ricardo Tirado.

"So, Dinah and Mr. Knox smoke together."

"You might put it that way. He owns a yacht. It's called *Fortune's Child*. I know because he's invited me to go on what he calls sailing soirees. I've never taken him up on it, but I'm pretty sure Dinah has."

"Do you have an address for Mr. Knox?"

She hesitated and Willie smiled.

"I can go home and get it off my computer program that has all the property listings. But you could save me the time."

She opened a drawer under the display case, took out what appeared to be a list of members, and gave Willie a Miami Beach address on Pine Tree Drive, not far away.

Willie thanked her for the information and asked her to give him a call if Carlos Espada or Dinah showed up. She said she would.

She eyed him warily. "You're not going to let on to Mr. Knox who told you all this, I hope. I'll need another job when I leave here, and I don't want to get burned. On top of that, he has a temper, a quick fuse."

"Don't worry. My lips may wrap themselves around a cigar, but not around your name, ever."

She looked at him wistfully. "Well, you don't have to go that far."

Willie smiled at her. "I'll be in touch."

"Do that. I'll bring the cigars."

CHAPTER ELEVEN

Willie found the Knox estate tucked behind a tall, white, stucco wall, about a quarter of a mile from the sea. Large, black, wrought-iron gates were adorned with a gilt monogram—"RK." Very discreet. Knox wanted to be hidden away, but not too hidden away.

Willie parked on the wide swale, walked to the gate and looked through it up a long, curving driveway toward the house. The manse sat amid a grove of eucalyptus trees and was built in a style that might be called post-modern Moorish revival. It featured lots of ter-racotta-colored stucco, braided columns, a satellite dish on the roof, and looked large enough to house a sizable harem. It was also equipped with a couple of Rottweilers who ran up and tried to eat the gate.

Willie pressed the doorbell. A woman's voice came over the intercom, he identified himself and asked for Mr. Knox. He was asked to wait, did so for about five minutes, and then heard someone call the slavering dogs. They sprinted back to the house, a buzzer sounded and the gates swung open momentously, as if Willie were being admitted into the pearly kingdom.

He climbed back in the car, drove to the house and reached the front door just as it opened. A black maid led him around the outside of the building to the backyard, which was bordered on three sides by tall ficus hedges. Willie found Knox lying next to a large, lighted oval pool, even though the sun had already set. He was reclining on a very wide chaise lounge with two tanning lights trained on him. He wore opaque black swimming goggles to protect his eyes. The tanning lights cast a glare around the backyard, partially illuminating a lush garden of white roses that looked otherworldly in that light.

From inside the mansion, Willie heard New Age music, which he always found more eerie than soothing.

Knox was wet, as if he had just pulled himself out of the pool, or maybe the bubbling Jacuzzi, which was right next to it. He wore only a black towel draped over his private parts and was drinking what appeared to be a martini with an olive. On either side of him lay the two women he'd been with earlier that day. They also wore towels and apparently nothing else, along with the matching smiles they had simulated the last time Willie had seen them. The reflection of the tanning lights off their teeth threatened to blind Willie.

Knox flipped up his black goggles. "Hello, Mr. Cuesta. What a great pleasure it is to see you again."

Willie stood at the foot of the chaise lounge staring down at the three of them. One of the women was massaging Knox's legs. The other was feeding herself a cherry from some kind of pink slush concoction she was drinking. She fed another one to Knox, although Willie didn't think a cherry would go very well with a martini. Looking at the blond businessman squeezed between the two dark beauties Willie was reminded of a sandwich. Turkey on whole wheat, or maybe pumpernickel.

"Why is it such a pleasure to see me?" Willie asked.

Knox held up his martini in a toast. "Almost everything in my life is a great pleasure, Mr. Cuesta, so I assume you will be." He smiled broadly and sipped his drink.

Willie smiled back, although not as broadly. Who could? He brought out the photos.

"I'm working on a case that Cesar Mendoza asked me to take, and I need to talk with this woman. I understand her name is Dinah and she hangs around boats. I thought you might know her."

Knox appraised both pictures and then nodded. "Yes, I've seen her around. Quite something, isn't she?"

"Yes, she is."

Knox deliberated over the photos an unusually long time, as if he would say something profound about her.

"She's the kind of woman who looks like she tastes good," he said finally. "Some women are just beautiful to look at. Others sound beautiful. She looks like she tastes good." He beamed at Willie. Clearly, this passed as character analysis for Mr. Knox.

Willie glanced at the photos in Knox's hand. "Do you know her last name?"

Knox shook his head. "I never know their last names."

"I see. Well, do you have any idea where I can find her?"

Knox grinned again, his white teeth glistening under the bright light. "That depends on why you're looking for her. Like I said, my life is full of pleasure, and I wouldn't want to cause this girl any pain."

"I certainly wouldn't want to cause the lady any displeasure either," Willie said. "I just want to talk to her about a man I'm looking for."

Willie explained his case.

Knox looked surprised. "Carlos Espada. You don't say."

"You know him?"

"I've bumped into him at cigar conventions and, of course, I've heard of the family. Renowned for quality."

"Well, right now he's renowned for being hard to find and I thought the girl might help me."

Knox glanced at the photos again. "The last time I saw her was about two weeks ago. It was down in the DR at a private club on the north coast called Costa Brava, the Gold Coast. Ever hear of it?"

"Not that I remember."

"That's too bad. Costa is a paradise. Do you know what paradise is, Mr. Cuesta?"

"I haven't made it there yet. You'll have to tell me."

"It's a place that is not only beautiful, perfect climate and reserved for the right people, but also a place where everybody does exactly as he or she wants, and nobody asks them questions. That's the thing about paradise no one tells you in church, Mr. Cuesta. Nobody asks any questions."

Willie had always worried that he would feel out of place in paradise. Now he knew for sure. Willie was the kind who asked questions.

"I take it when you saw this woman down there you didn't ask her who she was or what she was up to?"

Knox got a mischievous glow. "Oh, I know what she was up to. She was having the best time she could, just like everybody else. But

I didn't ask her any boring details, like her last name or what else she was doing."

"Did you notice her with Carlos Espada?"

"No, I don't remember seeing Espada, but I was off pursuing my own enchantment and I don't know who she was with all the time."

"Was she your guest down there?"

"That's a negative as well. She came on a yacht, I know that much. But it wasn't mine."

"Have any idea where that yacht came from?"

Knox thought about it and decided the answer wouldn't cause any pain. "You could try over at Hunter Island. You didn't hear it from me, but I'm pretty sure she was sailing with someone from there."

Hunter Island, which sat just off the edge of South Point in Miami Beach, was one of the most exclusive addresses in the county. You had to ride a private ferry to get there, and it was patrolled by a private police force. Even the paupers there paid a million and a half for the smallest condo.

Willie thanked Knox for the information.

The blond man beamed at him. "You see, your visit has been a pleasure, for you and for me. But I'm gonna have even more fun once you're gone." He glanced at the women on either side of him as if he were planning to feed one or both of them to the Rottweilers.

"Well, then I better not keep you," Willie said.

"You could join us if you'd like."

Willie looked from one woman to the other. "Unfortunately, I have work to do."

Knox shrugged. "Maybe next time."

The blond man flipped his black tanning goggles back into place. Willie said good-bye, cutting through the strangely illuminated rose garden, and left paradise as fast as he could.

CHAPTER TWELVE

It was still early when Willie arrived at his brother's nightclub, Caliente. Only 10:30 p.m. Most of the regular clientele were either still at dinner or hadn't even left home yet. It would be midnight before the house band, Chico Ruiz y Los Siete Vientos—The Seven Winds—started playing and it would be 1 a.m. before the place started jumping. By then they would be turning people away.

He left his car with Esteban, the chief valet, and entered through the front door, where a few well-dressed early arrivals stood in line. There was a nip in the air late at night and ladies were wearing jackets or wraps over their lovely bare shoulders. Willie and his staff would have to watch for "pony express riders," as Tommy called them. These were thieves who waited for a couple to hit the dance floor, then cruised by the empty table without breaking stride, nabbed expensive outerwear and/or handbags and headed right for the exit. You had to keep your eyes peeled for guys with purses.

Willie cut across the dance floor where a handful of couples already danced to an Oscar d'Leon number, this one about a wind that carried a song and a night that invited two people to make love.

Around those dancers, white tablecloths glistened on all three levels of the stadium seating. Candles on each table waited to be lighted. White-coated waiters hustled and when Willie passed the bar he caught the strong aroma of lime, as the bar staff sliced their supplies for the long night ahead. He stopped, ordered a lime daiquiri, picked it up and kept going.

He found his brother at the owner's table right next to the stage. Tommy, as always, was dressed for business, fitted out in his Calvin Klein tuxedo, keeping a calculating eye on the door. Willie sat next to him.

"How's things, *hermano*?"

Tommy nodded. "All right so far, but the night is young. And you?"

Willie shrugged. "So-so."

"Why so-so? Did you go to see Cesar?"

Willie nodded. "I'm looking for a nice boy who may be mixed up in some bad business."

"You're not looking here I hope."

"No, at least I don't think so."

Willie explained the case. Then he took out the photos of Carlos Espada and Dinah and showed them to his brother.

"Ever see either of these people in here?"

Tommy examined the photos. "I don't recognize the woman and I would remember if I'd seen her."

"I'm sure you would." Tommy had a historic weakness for blondes.

"But the guy may have been in here. He looks familiar."

"Well, if he comes back, you let me know."

Tommy went to check on the sound system while Willie studied the floor. As he did, his cell phone rang.

"Hello."

"Willie?" It was Amy.

He got up and headed for a quieter corner of the club. "How are you?"

She hesitated before answering. "I'm all right, I guess." A beep sounded on the line. "Hold on, will you? I'm still at work."

So Willie held. She was a busy girl, Amy. A successful public relations executive with accounts all over Miami and Latin America. Smart and beautiful too.

They had met almost a year earlier in the very middle of the dance floor right there at the club. Making his security rounds one Saturday night, Willie had cut through the whirling bodies of the salsa-dancing crowd and had suddenly found himself standing before a woman who was mysteriously by herself.

She was extremely pale-skinned, with big, brown eyes, bare shoulders and attractive in a tight black dress. At the moment she had an astonished look on her face, as if she had suddenly materialized right where she stood—or gotten lost on the way back to her table. She looked vulnerable, a damsel in distress.

"Lose your partner?" Willie asked over the music.

She studied him for a moment, as if he too had appeared out of nowhere.

"I don't think I ever had a partner, kind sir."

Willie—who, after all, was one of the hosts—held out his arms. She came into them, and they fell into a basic salsa step. Nothing fancy, but for a girl with no Latin blood, her rhythm was excellent. Willie told her so. Their eyes met and held for a moment.

"Thank you," she said and then turned away demurely.

The attraction had been immediate and unescapable. Her friends had eventually gone home without her, while she and Willie danced until very late, talked in between stints on the dance floor and drank champagne.

Willie handled most of the conversation, while she watched him out of the corner of her eye, amused by him, attracted, but also a bit wary. It was the wariness of a woman who knows right off that the man she has just met might end up in her bed, wonders just who he is and what will happen in the end.

It was dawn when Willie dropped his damsel in distress at her condo. They kissed, nothing more.

"I've never kissed a Latin man before," she confessed.

"How is it?"

She ran her tongue over her lips and nodded. "Vaguely spicy."

By the end of the next weekend, it had become more than vague. It had become passionate. In bed, her skin seemed even paler when contrasted with his. And as a lover she carried that same wariness in her eyes and a tremor of desire, a fragile quality, that Willie found irresistible.

Out of bed she treated him with the same whimsy that marked their first meeting. That combination of wit and passion was too much for Willie.

She became part of his life. At the club, the staff treated her like part of the family. Everyone loved Amy. Tommy gave her a regular table and wore a big Cheshire cat smile.

"It looks like she's got you where she wants you, *hermano*."

Even his mother, who had always seen Willie settling down with a Cuban girl, had altered her idea for his future after Amy had visited her shop.

"Maybe this is the one, a beautiful American girl."

Amy dragged him to receptions and parties in other parts of town, business crowds where you didn't usually bump into a former cop turned private investigator. She was making Willie's world wider. He had even gotten a couple of clients out of those occasions. Willie was an attraction, and everyone talked about what a handsome couple they made. Willie and Amy went through life, dancing, talking, making love and then doing them all again.

But after a few months, when they had started to talk about making a life together, the geological plates that made up their individual lives had started to collide. Amy wasn't pushy, but she mused about living somewhere else, while Willie had never thought of leaving Cuban Miami. She also brought up the fact that Willie could make more money working in corporate security and that the hours would be better.

"If you're going to have a normal life, you don't want to work in a nightclub until five in the morning several nights a week," she said. "Given your experience, you deserve better than that, Willie."

Normal life—that was the issue. Willie had never lived what anyone would consider a normal life. Willie's old man had been a musician and had worked and partied at night, sleeping during the day. Both Willie and Tommy had developed lives that had put them on the same schedule. Their mother had noted it early on.

"You're both like your father—vampires," she often said. "It's your tropical blood."

And working for somebody else had never been Willie's forte.

At first, Willie had not confronted Amy's ideas for their future and life had gone on. But his reluctance to discuss a move and any change in career had become obvious, until she had insisted, and they suddenly found themselves in crisis mode.

"People don't just dance their lives away, Willie."

Willie shrugged. "Maybe they should, Amy. Maybe they should."

Amy had accused him of being "afraid to commit." Willie hadn't looked at another woman seriously in months, even though the temptations at the club were always present and sometimes aggressively so.

"It isn't a question of committing, Amy, but committing to what? The All-American dream? A nine-to-five job working for some Anglo outfit and a little house out where nobody speaks Spanish? If that's what you're looking for, maybe you shouldn't have taken a lover you found in a salsa joint at two in the morning?"

The moment he'd said it, he'd been sorry. He was happy she had found him on that dance floor. He told her that, but she had walked out on him anyway and not answered his calls, either at home or at work. That was ten days earlier. It had been a long time since Willie had felt lonely, but he had experienced it lately. Now she was calling him and came back on the line.

"How are you?" she asked.

"So-so. I would be better if you hadn't stopped talking to me."

"I had to travel for work, and I also needed to think. I still need to think."

"So, you still won't see me."

She hesitated. "Yes, I want to see you. Can we meet tomorrow for coffee?"

They agreed to meet at his place the next afternoon. She didn't say "love you" before she hung up the way she usually did—but then neither did he.

* * *

Willie stayed a bit longer listening to Chico Ruiz and his boys go through their standards. He allowed himself to be dragged out on the floor by Ofelia, the older but still sexy office manager, for one extremely suggestive salsa number. With that rhythm still in his step, he said good night to Tommy and danced out the door.

Willie drove straight home and parked around the corner from his place. He found himself humming an old Willy Chirino tune about a perfect night made of champagne, music and love. Well, Willie would have to settle for music, a daiquiri, one dance and sleep.

He opened the door on the ground floor and headed up the nar-row stairs. The old lock on his apartment door gave him a moment's trouble, as always, but he got in. Even before he reached for the floor lamp, he realized something was wrong. In the living room, both closet doors were wide open. So were all the drawers of his desk. He hadn't left them that way. Whoever had rifled the desk had dumped papers on the floor.

He reached into his back holster and removed his .38 as he turned on the light. He saw in a moment how the intruder or intruders had entered. A small pane of glass in his back door was broken. It had been that way for several months and Willie had put off fixing it. He had made it easy for them. The door was still open. They hadn't bothered to close it on the way out.

Willie swore under his breath, crossed to the gaping door and looked down the exterior steps that led to the backyard. He saw no one.

He closed the door, glanced into the bedroom and saw that the bureau drawers had been ransacked as well. Willie inspected both rooms. He never left cash lying around and his other valuables—suits, stereo, VCR, computer—were all in place.

Nothing was missing, but something was there that hadn't been before. An aroma hung in the air. In fact, a very thin veil of smoke was visible.

Willie walked back into the bedroom and turned toward the bathroom door. He gripped his handgun tightly and reached for the knob, but he didn't do it quickly enough. He was standing flat-footed when the door came flying open, hit him squarely on the right shoulder, knocked the gun from his hand and sent him flying so that he rammed the bed rail with the small of his back and then fell to the floor.

The blow stunned him and before he could react, they had him. A very large man grabbed him from behind, dragged him to his feet and applied a full Nelson. A second intruder ripped down the mosquito netting from the bed and wrapped it around Willie's head so that Willie was looking through multiple layers of gauze. He could see a red cap over a dark face with a moustache and a burning cigar clenched in the mouth. But it was all out of focus.

"We're not going to tell you this twice," Fuzzy Face said with an accent. "Don't stick your face in our business, or you'll get burned."

He removed the cigar from his teeth. Then he brought it toward the gauze that covered Willie's face. He touched it to the material. The first layer of gauze disintegrated right in front of Willie's eye, the filaments turning a bright orange and then flaming out. Willie struggled, but the big man had him good.

The bright orange ember of the cigar came toward Willie's face again until he felt his lashes being singed. Another half inch and no eye, only excruciating pain. Willie clenched his eyes and gritted his teeth.

But the pain didn't follow. He felt the ember pull away, opened his eyes, and saw that Fuzzy Face had put the stogie back in his mouth. The mouth was moving.

"Don't be a fool," he said. "Mind your own business."

He didn't say anything else. He just nodded once at the giant. The giant dropped Willie, swung his foot and caught him on the side of the head, as if he were dropkicking a football. Willie's vision, already blurred by the netting, became that much more distorted.

By the time it cleared and he struggled to his feet, they were gone.

He unwrapped the mosquito netting from around his neck as he stumbled to the mirror in the bathroom. The lashes of his left eye had turned white at the ends from the heat of the cigar, so that one eye looked older than the other. He appeared to be a person unevenly aged.

He went back into the living room, picked up everything on the floor, including his .38, and confirmed that nothing was missing. He figured they had come to threaten him, but as long as they were on the premises, they had searched for something to steal. Why not?

He closed the back door and wedged a chair under the knob. He rehung the mosquito netting, which was now distinguished by a small, round, charred hole right above him. He turned off the light and eventually fell asleep, staring up at that spot as if it were a bullet hole in the night sky.

CHAPTER THIRTEEN

Willie woke the next morning with a thin shaft of sunlight falling through the bullet hole and hitting him in the face like a laser. Behind his eyes his head pained him from the kick he'd received. He hoped the laser would cut that pain out of him, but it didn't. He cursed Fuzzy Face and the other goon and dragged himself out of bed.

He fetched ibuprofen from the medicine cabinet and then heated milk for *café con leche*. It was just ready, and the headache was starting to subside when the downstairs bell rang. He had no appointments for the morning. He rarely did, because of his late nights at the club. He was still naked, so he slipped into his ratty, black, silk bathrobe. Given his visitors of the night before, he also grabbed his handgun.

He eased his way down the stairs and peeked around the curtain that covered the door. Standing on the front steps he found a short, pale, extremely dapper, white-haired man dressed in what appeared to be a very expensive dark blue Italian suit. Beyond him, parked at the curb, stood a black Lincoln limousine with a driver. It wasn't as long as Richard Knox's limo, but Willie's block didn't get a lot of limousines. He figured either the guy was very lost and needed directions or he was an extremely upscale assassin. Willie took a chance and opened the door.

"Can I help you?"

The man looked Willie up and down and grimaced. Willie couldn't be sure if he was unhappy about the gun, which Willie had neglected to drop into the pocket of the robe, or the robe itself which obviously didn't meet the man's sartorial standards.

"I'm looking for Mr. Cuesta," the small man said with an accent that wasn't Hispanic, but vaguely French. "I was given this address, but I may be mistaken."

"You're not mistaken. I'm Willie Cuesta. What can I do for you?"

The man produced a leather sheath from inside the pocket of his suit and passed Willie a business card. It identified him as Jean-Philippe Montand, president of Montand Tobacco, AG, Geneva, Switzerland.

He glanced at the robe and gun again. "I know it is very early, but I would appreciate a few minutes of your time."

"You're not early, I'm late," Willie said, opening the door and pocketing the gun.

Willie led the dapper man upstairs and deposited him in a chair in the living room. Montand moved carefully, avoiding contact with any obstacles as if he were avoiding contamination. He declined coffee, so Willie sat down across from him with his large *café con leche* and two *empanadas* he'd bought at the bakery across the street two days earlier. In his ratty robe, he was the picture of business formality.

His visitor had snowy white hair that came down on his forehead in a sharp widow's peak and his eyes were slate gray. His nose was pronounced and his chin sharp. He wore cologne and was the only man in the cigar business who Willie had spoken to who didn't smell of cigar. Very continental, very contained. The only thing that broke the glacier-like composure was a swollen blue vein that veered across his left temple and disappeared into his hairline. If you looked at it closely, you could see it pulsing slightly. It indicated, possibly, some hidden tension. Willie glanced at the card once more.

"I hope you haven't come all the way from Switzerland just to see me," he said. "You could have called."

Montand shook his head. "No. I spend considerable amounts of my time in the Caribbean and in Miami."

He didn't seem very happy about it. He gazed around at Willie's rattan furniture and potted palms and didn't appear impressed by the decor either.

"I see," Willie said.

"I'm in the tobacco business. But you can see that, can't you?" he said, pointing at the card in Willie's hand.

"Yes, I can. I'm not sure, but I think I've even heard of your cigars."

The other man shrugged. "You may have, but we don't market in the United States. We sell mostly in Europe."

"I see."

"You may not know this, but Geneva has long been a center for the tobacco trade in Europe. We have had dealings with the tobacco producing islands for many decades, and with Miami."

"I didn't know that."

The other man nodded curtly but said nothing. The gaze in his eyes was chilly, as if he were still back in the Alps.

Willie sipped his coffee and patted his lips with his napkin. "I still don't know why that has brought you to my door." Willie was starting to wonder if the guy wasn't an assassin after all and just liked to take his time.

"I'm sure you don't. I'm here because I'm told you're looking for Carlos Espada."

"Yes, that's true, but I didn't know it was public knowledge. How did you know?"

He shrugged. "I don't want to be indiscreet, Mr. Cuesta. So let's just say I heard it—how do you Americans say—through the grapevine."

"I see," Willie said, although he didn't understand why his source should be a secret. "Well, do you know where he is?"

The Swiss man shook his head. "No, I don't."

"That's too bad."

Montand met that with silence. Willie, who had just woken up, was getting a little irritated. Maybe the other man sensed that.

"But Carlos Espada did speak to me by phone not long ago," Montand said.

"How long ago?"

"About one week."

"You don't say. Where was he?"

"I don't know that."

"What did he say to you?"

"He didn't say much, but he did ask me some things."

"Like what?"

"He asked me about some illegal practices that he had heard were going on in the cigar business."

"We aren't speaking about counterfeiting Havanas, are we?"

Montand wasn't surprised that Willie knew this. "Yes, we are speaking about counterfeiting."

"And what did you tell him?"

"I didn't tell him anything because I don't know anything about counterfeiting."

"I see. Then, why did he call you?"

"I don't know really. Maybe because I have been in the business a long time and he has known me a long time."

"What did you talk about?"

"Nothing. I asked after his mother and sister and that was all. He hung up."

Willie nodded but said nothing. What could he say? This man had arrived in the morning, practically dragging him out of bed, to tell him that he didn't know anything that could help him. And to tell him this several different times. All of this after Willie had been assaulted just the night before.

The Swiss man uncrossed his legs, hitched the other pant leg and crossed them in the other direction.

"I got that phone call from him and now I hear that he's disappeared. It left me very concerned. I'm just wondering what else you can tell me about what might have happened to him."

Willie sipped his coffee. It was clear Mr. Montand hadn't come to tell him anything—except that he, Montand, was not a counterfeiter. That might be true and it might not. What he really wanted was to pick Willie's brain about Carlos Espada.

"Well, I can't tell you any more than you already know."

That disturbed Montand. His aristocratic nostrils flared. "You can't? You haven't found any sign of him?"

Willie shook his head. "No."

"You didn't find anyone who had seen him or heard from him or anyone who might know where he is?"

"No, I haven't. What's your interest in this, if you don't mind my asking?"

"Only a concern for Carlos Espada. I knew his father and have known his mother many years. I don't want you to misunderstand. I came to you because I didn't want to tell his mother about the conversation Carlos and I had. I'm afraid Carlos may have become involved in something unseemly."

Willie thought of the photos and of the golden girl, Dinah, but he wasn't going to tell Montand about that. In fact, he wasn't going to tell him anything. Willie didn't like this tailor's dummy sitting before him, even if he looked like he belonged to a very expensive tailor.

First of all, Willie had a headache. On top of that, Montand hadn't done much but violate a private conversation with Carlos Espada and—maybe deliberately—smeared Espada. If Carlos had merely asked him what he knew about counterfeiting, why had Montand assumed that Carlos "had gotten involved" in it. Despite his savoir faire, Montand's ill will was apparent. No, the little Swiss man had not come to help, and what he was really up to, Willie didn't know, but it made him that much more concerned for Carlos Espada.

Montand had apparently found Willie not to his liking either. He got up now, once again being careful not to touch anything that might contaminate his couture.

"I won't take any more of your time," he said.

Willie didn't argue. They went down the stairs together. Before Montand went out he turned to Willie.

"In the course of talking to people in the cigar business you may hear certain rumors about me."

Willie's brows arched with interest. "I haven't heard any so far, but what rumors will those be?"

Montand shook his head. "It's not for me to tell you. But I'm advising you not to believe everything you hear."

Willie shook his head. "I never do."

He watched as the Swiss man strode out to his waiting town car, got in and took off.

CHAPTER FOURTEEN

Willie shaved, showered and dressed. He slipped into a white guayabera, gray linen slacks and loafers and sat down at his desk.

First, he checked his phone messages, which he hadn't managed to listen to the night before, due to the rude behavior of Fuzzy Face and his friend.

He found only one message, but it was from Cesar Mendoza.

"Willie, call me. I heard from Carlos Espada. There's something wrong with him. He sounded crazy. He asked me to tell him about his father's death, about those last days. I told him I couldn't help him, that I hadn't seen Ernesto Espada in several weeks before he committed suicide. But Carlos wouldn't listen. He told me I was lying. He asked me other strange questions and grew very angry on the phone. I'm worried, Willie. Come see me right away."

Willie tried Cesar, first at the shop and then at home. In both places all he reached was answering machines. In both places, Willie told Cesar to call him, gave him the number of his cell phone and rang off.

Next, Willie called Sergeant Bernie Egan at Economic Crimes.

"Hey, Willie. *¿Qué pasa?* How's the case going?"

"I need a favor, *compadre*. Can you do a quick criminal records check for me?"

"Fire away."

"The name is Richard Knox." Willie gave him the current address on Pine Tree Drive. "I'd say he's in his 'late thirties.'"

Willie could hear Bernie's fingers clicking on his computer keyboard. About thirty seconds later he'd gotten a hit.

"I think I have him. Age thirty-nine. Blond hair. Five foot ten."

"That's him. What does it say?"

There was a silence of a half minute while Bernie read the record. "It says he's never been convicted of anything. Besides a couple of traffic hassles, he's only been arrested once, but he beat the rap."

"What were the charges?"

"Criminal conspiracy, racketeering, tax evasion. There's a long list of co-defendants here, all of them Latin—Campos, Murillo, Martinez, et cetera. The charges were brought in the early nineties. It looks narcotics-related."

"Gotcha."

"Does this have to do with the cigar case?"

"I'm not sure, but I'll let you know, Bernie. *Gracias.*" He hung up.

The last call he made was to Don Ricardo Tirado. The old man answered the phone himself.

"Don Ricardo, it's Willie Cuesta, the private investigator."

In the background Willie could hear the music of the cigar rollers. The old man grunted into the phone.

"More questions?"

"Just one. Do you know a man named Jean-Philippe Montand?" Willie read the name from the business card.

Tirado made another sound into the phone, not a happy one.

"Yes, of course I know him. Everyone in the business does."

"What should I know about him."

"That he does business with Castro. Because he's based in Europe and not the United States, he can still deal in Cuban tobacco. He can't market it here, but he does everywhere else. And some people think he comes here to Miami to spy on us for Castro. I'm one of those who believe it. He's a scoundrel. Is that enough?"

"I guess so."

"Then, *buenos días.*" The old man hung up and so did Willie. He sat staring at the phone, remembering what Cesar had told him about the deaths of the two cigar counterfeiters up in North Miami and how some cigar insiders suspected it had been done by Castro agents. Willie didn't believe that and Montand didn't look much like a man who would slit anyone's throat. It might get his cuffs bloody. On the other hand, he could easily gather information for his business partners in Havana. That was what he had probably been doing during his baffling visit.

Willie was still staring at the phone when the doorbell rang again. Willie went down to answer it, this time concealing the gun in his back holster. He found Amy, which was much better than finding Montand.

She wore a dark suit and a red silk blouse and looked like she might have lost a pound or two in the past ten days. She looked good, but she always looked good. They exchanged a peck on the cheeks, which was not their usual way of doing things.

"Shall we drink our coffee here?" Willie asked.

She glanced up the stairs and then shook her head. "No, we better not."

They both knew what she meant: after ten days, one look at the bed and that would be that. Instead, Willie closed the door, and they went into the Cuban coffee joint next door. She ordered an American coffee, Willie a *cortadito* and they sat in the corner. From a radio came a bolero, a man singing to his love, who was the dawn of his days and made him see stars at night.

She took a few moments to taste her coffee and Willie gave her time. "I'm sorry I haven't returned your calls," she said finally.

"I'm sorry about what I said. I didn't mean it that way."

She nodded. "I know you didn't. That's not why I didn't call you. The issues here don't have to do with one angry exchange. They go deeper and I needed time to think."

"And what did you come up with?"

She shrugged. "Nothing too profound. For one thing, what really attracted me to you at first was that you were exotic. The whole Latin lover thing."

Willie winced and she nodded.

"Yes, it sounds shallow, but how deep can it be when you first meet someone? I liked the atmosphere of it, the music, the dancing, the club and, at the middle of it, this smart, good-looking guy. I was bored and I was looking for something a little different, a little dangerous and you were it."

Willie cocked an eyebrow. "That's me all right, dangerous . . . I'm not a thug, Amy."

"I don't mean it that way. I mean you're something that a nice white girl from Middle America, like me, isn't supposed to want. In fact our mothers warned us about guys like you who spend their nights in clubs until dawn, surrounded by women dressed to kill—men who want to hold onto you even after the music is over and even after you drive home."

"The club is my job. I get paid for it and the only one I've gone home with when the music ended—at least since I met you—is you."

She nodded. "I know that. But in the back of my head I have ideas stored about what my married life will be like. It doesn't seem to include *merengue* until dawn five times per week, no matter how much I've enjoyed that at times. I thought you were just an adventure, Willie, but I've reached the point in my life where the only adventure is who I'll end up with, have children with, and all of a sudden I'm getting visions of a husband who comes through the door at six in the evening everyday, or at least not at six in the morning after the club or after a surveillance on some investigative business."

Willie shrugged. "I don't keep farmer's hours. What can I say?"

She nodded and went on. "You also share all this history with your family and these other people around you, which I don't share and never will. It's like a secret society."

"That's history. We're talking present and future and we're not in Cuba or anywhere else in Latin America. We're here."

She shook her head. "When you're in a relationship, your history always matters, it always comes to the surface. All these things make me wonder, Willie. And then at other times none of this matters at all. I think of all the good things we have."

She was talking about affection, the absurd sense of humor that had marked their meeting and which they still shared, as well as the unusually strong physical desire they felt for each other. At least that was what occurred to Willie. She apparently was thinking the same things. Their eyes met and she looked away demurely, the same way she had during their first dance. Then she looked back at him.

"The question is, can you take what happens on a dance floor and in a bed and make it work in the rest of life."

Willie shrugged. "Cubans have been doing that for centuries." He smiled. It was a joke, although not far from the truth.

Amy didn't laugh. "I think I love you, Willie, but I'm wondering if we can ever make it work together, if down deep we can come to terms. If I can introduce you into those Middle-American dreams of mine and make it work out. I'm still figuring it out."

Willie didn't know what to say. To tell her that he might change his way of life to any significant degree would probably be a lie. His work at the club he did for his brother, Tommy. She was right, he and Tommy were close. And, as his mother had pointed out, his lifestyle was in his blood. Then again, he had gone several years since his divorce and not found anyone with whom he wanted to spend a lot of time, until he'd bumped into Amy by mistake on that dance floor.

They were still looking at each other and she shrugged again. "Let's not think about it anymore for the moment. I'm tired of thinking about it. What's new with your work?"

He filled her in on the Espada case but left out the visit by Fuzzy Face.

She thought about that. "People in my office buy smuggled Cuban cigars and give them to our clients."

Willie's brows danced. "Is that right?"

"Well, we're in P.R. in Miami. We schmooze, buy drinks and we hand out cigars. I wonder if the guys I work with are getting real Havanas, or if they're getting ripped off."

"Who do they buy them from?"

"I don't know, but sometimes they buy quite a few boxes. They spend a lot of money. I'll have to ask where they go for them."

"I'd appreciate it."

She drained her coffee. "I better be going now."

"When will I see you again?"

"I can't tell you, but you will. For the moment, let's just say we're friends and see what happens."

She gave him another peck on the lips and walked out. He drained his *cortadito*, which tasted more bitter than usual.

CHAPTER FIFTEEN

Willie drove a few blocks west on Calle Ocho to his mother's *botánica*. He parked out front, walked past the two life-sized Santeria deities who guarded the front entrance against evil intruders. He passed through the portion of the store where natural medicines and potions were displayed and found his mother working in the back room. She was shoving a root-like material into a hand-operated grinder. Despite her sixty-five years, she turned the crank like a young butcher making sausage. You didn't want to mess with Mama.

She looked up as he walked in. "There you are. I was expecting you."

His mother offered spiritual consultations and was said to have powers of divination. She could tell when he was about to arrive, at least she claimed she could.

Willie planted a kiss on her forehead. "Here, let me do that."

He took over the grinder. "What do you have here?"

"That is a root called bull's horn," his mother said. "I'm receiving many requests for natural medicines that will increase the virility of old men, men who have trouble answering the call to love."

Willie stopped in mid-grind and looked at the roots lying in the pile. What he saw didn't really resemble bull's horn very much. It was more phallic than that. When he was a little kid, he would sneak his friends into his mother's shop so they could see the weird medicines. Bull penis, that's what they had called it back then, had always been a major attraction. His mother handed him another one.

"Usually, I just sell the whole thing, but this woman told me she didn't think either she or her husband had the strength to grind it. If he's that debilitated, I don't know that anything will help him, but we'll see."

Willie turned the crank some more. "Why don't they just use Viagra?"

His mother shook her head. "Viagra is expensive for people like these. That's why I'm getting so many requests. Couples with more money are using Viagra and the women are coming back with tremendous stories. So, my customers come to me and it's my job to find natural remedies they can afford. This particular medicine has worked very well for some men, including one of your older male relatives, but I won't tell you which one."

Willie was glad of that. He didn't want to know which of his uncles was ingesting this stuff in hopes of romantic transport. He finished grinding the specimen and his mother poured the resultant powder into a vial.

"This he'll mix with some *guarapo*, maybe in the blender." *Guarapo* was sugar cane juice; combined with bull horn it would make quite a Cuban cocktail.

The backroom of his mother's store was also the kitchen of her house. The living room, dining room and bedrooms were located on the two floors above. Willie had grown up there.

Right now, his mother was heating him some *picadillo* for lunch. Willie sat at the table to wait. There was no place in the world as familiar as that kitchen. No scene was as grounding as that of his mother standing next to the stove, a dish towel tossed over her shoulder, like a cut man in a fighter's corner. For forty years, they had lived these silent moments, but Willie felt they connected to something even further back than that, to people who had lived by firelight in caverns and caves. It was a place of refuge from anything and everything else.

Finally, his mother broke the silence and asked him if he'd had work lately. Since he'd left the Miami PD, she worried constantly about his making a living. So, Willie confided in her about the call from Cesar Mendoza, who she knew, the Espada family, the fact that Carlos had gone missing and the conversations with Espada's mother and sister.

She served him his *picadillo* and rice and sat across from him.

"I remember the name of that family on cigar boxes," she said. "A very respected family. I think the mother is right that the gods turned against them for some reason. I wonder why?"

Willie also told her of the possibility that Carlos Espada was mixed up in cigar counterfeiting, how big a business it apparently was, and, lastly, about the photos of Espada and the blonde woman found under Carlos' mattress.

She raised her eyebrows the way Willie always did. Of course, it was a tic that he had picked up from her and no one else.

"When you have that much money involved then you are probably going to have trouble and you're also going to get women like that."

His mother already disapproved of Dinah. Mama was always on the lookout for a wife for Willie, but she had apparently already dismissed this woman, who hung out at cigar conventions.

"How is Amy?" she asked in an offhand manner, although he knew it was of vital importance to her.

"Amy is fine. I just had coffee with her."

His mother nodded and asked nothing else. Willie had not mentioned to her his problems with Amy, but he was sure Tommy had.

He cleaned his plate with a piece of Cuban bread, drained his coffee, got up and gave her a kiss on the cheek.

She held on to his sleeve. "Be careful, Willie."

"I'm always careful, Mama. You know that."

"I know you're not always careful. I know more than you think. I spend much of my time in contact with the spirits, but that doesn't mean that I don't know what you are up to, *hijo*."

Willie knew this was true. His mother was the original magical realist, except she never mixed the two. She saw mysticism as a way to hedge against the harsh realities of life, especially Cuban exile life. But she never lost sight of those realities.

Willie stood up, kissed her and told her not to worry. She got up as well and went back to her grinder. She would take care of the ones who wanted to make love and Willie would see to the citizens with less romantic pursuits.

* * *

He got back in the LeBaron and drove another few blocks west toward Cesar Mendoza's store. Maybe the old man was there by now.

But when Willie arrived he found a red CLOSED sign propped in the window. It was right side up and Willie wondered if that was luck, or if the blind man had a system for getting it right.

The store hours stenciled on the door said the shop was open from 10 a.m. to 8 p.m., but the inside was dark, and the doorknob wouldn't turn. Willie cupped his hands against the glass and gazed in. Lights were on and a half-smoked cigar sat in an ashtray on the sales counter. The dolly Cesar had used to deliver Knox his stogies was leaning against the wall next to the cold-storage compartment.

Willie knocked, just in case Cesar was working in the back room, but he got no response. He craned his head so he could see behind the sales counter and spotted something lying on the floor behind it. He saw just the tip of Cesar's brown leather briefcase. Worry creased Willie's brow. The blind man never went anywhere without that case.

Willie went to the bridal store next door. Only one saleswoman was working, a pale, thirtyish woman with a nice smile and hands clenched at her waist like a bridesmaid. Willie didn't smile back.

"Are you getting married?" she asked.

"Not today. I was trying to find Mr. Mendoza who runs the shop next door."

"Isn't he there? He's always there at this hour."

"The shop is closed. You didn't notice if he came and left?"

She shook her head. "We don't really have much contact. His customers and mine are really different folks, if you know what I mean. Very few of my ladies smoke cigars."

"I understand. I'm afraid something's happened to him."

Willie went back out and the saleswoman followed him. She watched as he removed his gun from his back holster and grabbed it by the barrel.

"Stand back," he told her. He smacked the glass door panel and it shattered into pieces. No alarm sounded. Willie reached through the gaping glass and opened the door from the inside.

He ground glass under his heels as he stepped in and ducked behind the sales counter.

The register was gaping and empty, and Cesar's briefcase lay open, face down on the floor, with its contents strewn. They included several cigars, a retractable white cane with a red tip, a personal telephone directory with the numbers inscribed in braille, an extra *guayabera,* and a bottle of cologne for those assignations Cesar bragged about. But Willie had a feeling Cesar wasn't making love at the moment.

He walked into the back room and found it empty, except for crates in which cigars had been shipped and some cleaning supplies. The back door was bolted.

He went back into the front room and turned toward the cold-storage locker. He crossed to it, reached for the handle, stopped, brought out his handkerchief, wrapped it around his hand and then pulled it open.

Cesar Mendoza sat on a stack of cigar boxes in the far corner of the compartment. He looked as if he had just plopped down to take a breather in the midst of storing cigars. The problem was Cesar wasn't breathing. The front of his white guayabera was soaked with blood. Willie crouched down and saw that Cesar's throat had been neatly slit, almost ear to ear. Right next to the dead man's foot lay a chavette, one of the hand-sized, semicircular blades used to make cigars. Its cutting edge was discolored by what had to be Cesar's blood. The blind man's dark glasses lay in his lap. His eyes were open and appeared to be looking right at the bloody blade. Of course, Cesar, the blind man, had probably never seen it coming.

Willie heard a gasp behind him and found the saleswoman from next door.

"You better call the police," Willie told her. "Tell them we have a homicide here."

* * *

Patrol cars pulled up in two minutes and it took no more than half an hour for homicide to arrive, in the person of Sergeant Lester Grand. Grand was a wide-bodied black guy, about six-four, two hundred and sixty pounds, who had once played offensive tackle up at Gainesville, but had blown out a knee before he could turn pro. Instead, he had come home to Miami and turned cop. He had also married a diminutive but tough Dominican woman, with whom he'd had no less than six kids, all boys, who were brown and huge and looked a bit like the Samoans who play in the NFL. The family appeared to be on the genetic cutting edge of millennial Miami.

Grand strolled into the cold storage for a minute and then got out of the way of the crime scene techs. He spoke briefly to the saleswoman, who obviously couldn't tell him much, and then he moved on to Willie.

"Long time no see, Willie."

"Not long enough, given the circumstances."

"No doubt. What's your connection to this, if you don't mind my asking?"

"Cesar was a friend of the family." Willie hesitated. "And I'm working a case he was interested in."

Grand didn't conceal his own interest. "What case was that?"

"I'm looking for a missing person, a friend of Mr. Mendoza's."

"Who's that."

"A guy named Carlos Espada, also in the cigar business. He dropped out of sight a couple of weeks ago."

"Do you think the guy could have done this?"

Willie shook his head. "Cesar was looking for Espada because he was afraid something might have happened to him, not because he was afraid of him. Espada has no violence in his past. The truth is I think Espada just took off with a girlfriend."

Willie didn't tell him that the missing man might be involved in anything illegal. Nor did he tell him that Espada had been in touch with Cesar just the night before. He wouldn't tell him that until he had a chance to talk to Victoria and Esther Espada, and maybe he wouldn't tell him at all. What he did tell Grand was that he had not talked to Mendoza since the day before and had no idea what might have happened to him.

Grand drifted away and stared at the open register, which was being dusted for prints.

"So, this could be nothing more than a robbery. But why the hell kill an old blind man to take his money? He probably wouldn't put up much of a fight and he probably wouldn't be able to identify you."

Willie shook his head. "Makes no sense, but bad shit often makes no sense."

"Ain't that the truth."

Willie asked Grand if there was anything more he could do and Grand said no, not at the moment. Willie left him his card, took a last look at Cesar and left.

* * *

He drove back to his place and fell into the chair that overlooked the garden. He sat there stock-still, wracking his brain, gathering his senses, trying to control his frustration and his anger.

He was still there when the phone rang. It was Amy.

"Willie?"

"Uh-huh."

"Listen, I spoke with the guys at work and they don't want to discuss where they get those Havana cigars."

Willie's chin came up. "They don't, huh?"

"No. They don't want to expose the firm to any bad publicity, and they especially don't want to discuss anything that might come back to haunt our clients who have bought those cigars."

Willie tried to contain his anger. "I see. They have some business concerns, do they?"

"We *are* a P.R. company, Willie. It's our job to look out for the image of a client and his or her business concerns."

Willie's knuckles were white on the phone. "Yeah, well you tell your friends that a man was found dead today, his throat slit. He was an old friend of mine. And the executives at your office can tell me what they know, or they'll be under subpoena telling the police. Because I don't give a fuck about their business concerns and their fucking P.R. Okay, Amy?"

On the other end there was a gasp and then silence. "I'm sorry about your friend, Willie," Amy said finally, her voice shaking. Then Willie heard the line go dead.

He hung up as well. Seconds later he wanted to pick up the phone and call her back and apologize, but he didn't. It was too late. He'd fucked up again. The next day, he'd send flowers. Maybe she'd understand. Maybe.

CHAPTER SIXTEEN

A n hour later Willie pulled off the Seventy-ninth Street Causeway and into the parking lot of Pelican Harbor Marina. It sat on the western shore of Biscayne Bay. Gorgeous dark blue waters stretched about five miles to the east, all the way to the hazy high-rise condos on Miami Beach.

The marina shared the site with a seabird hospital. Injured pelicans sat on pilings like patients in a ward. Cats hung out on the pier beneath them, but didn't bother the birds, maybe because any fish scraps the pelicans dropped, the cats took care of. And maybe because the pelicans were bigger than the cats.

Willie passed them and ducked into the dockmaster's office and asked for Clarence Ross, his old mentor in the Miami PD Intelligence Unit, now retired.

"Oh yeah, he's here, working on his boat, supposedly," said the dockmaster, who had a waist as wide around as a life preserver and a hook nose. "But I haven't seen him do much more than drink beer and shoot the shit with the other boaters."

"That sounds like him."

It didn't take Willie long to locate Ross. He was on his seventeen-foot sea craft, *The Fugitive*. Ross sat slouched in a deck chair with his feet up on a gunwale, guzzling beer with an attractive, well-tanned, gray-haired lady. He was wearing his blue captain's cap with the gold anchor embroidered over the brim, an old *guayabera* and bleached jeans. He spotted Willie walking down the pier.

"Oh no, here comes the *compadre*," he said in his broad cracker accent. "Something must be wrong in paradise."

Willie was introduced to the lady, Amelia, who had warm brown eyes and didn't look a day over sixty, a few years younger than Ross.

She excused herself and ambled down the pier a few berths to a lovely sailboat that was about forty feet long.

Ross sipped his beer, watching her. "I know what you're thinking, amigo. That she's not in my class."

"The boat or the woman."

"Both. But you're wrong. We're talking about taking a little sail
over to the Bahamas, Amelia and I. She'd be captain and I'd be first
mate, a much higher rank than I ever reached in the Navy."

"You never got that far up in the police department either."

"That's true, too."

But they both knew that the only reason Ross had never been
commander of the Intelligence Unit was because he had no desire to
be. Bureaucracy didn't appeal to him. Catching criminals did appeal
to him, and before he'd retired he had caught almost as many bad
guys as he had caught fish over the years.

He kicked the styrofoam cooler at his feet.

"Grab a beer and sit."

Willie stepped down into the boat and did as ordered.

Ross swigged from his bottle and fixed his incisive gaze on his
visitor. "You look like you have something on your mind, other than
my love life."

"A friend of mine was murdered."

Willie gave him the details and Ross scowled.

"I'm real sorry. Sounds like he was quite a gentleman."

They drank their beers in silence.

"I need to pick your brain a bit," Willie said finally. "Does the
name Richard Knox mean anything to you? A guy about forty,
apparently a local. He has lots of money although I don't know if he
had it back when you might have known him."

"Do you think this customer killed your friend?"

"I don't know about that, but he may have a connection."

The old man squinted into the distance and massaged the loose
skin under his chin.

"The name sounds vaguely familiar, which means he probably
did something he shouldn't have."

"I think so, too, but I didn't find any criminal record on him. All
I know is he was once charged with criminal conspiracy and tax evasion but beat those raps. I also know that he sails around the

Caribbean a lot and has a lot of money from unknown sources, at least unknown to me. He claims he's made it in Internet technology, the World Wide Web, but maybe it was some other kind of web."

"So, I take it you think he might be in the narcotics business."

"Or he used to be."

Ross squinted some more, searching through that long memory which contained a boyhood on a dirt farm near the Georgia-Florida border, some exciting years in the Navy during World War II, then lots of fishing and forty years of police work at the heart of Miami's roguish luster.

"Yeah, I think I do remember a fellow by that name. He was an attorney."

"Bingo."

"If I recall, he was mixed up with drug dealers, defended them possibly, enjoyed large fees, but was also suspected of being part of the business. Nobody could catch him inside the henhouse though. The guys he was mixed up with were moving cocaine from various islands in the Caribbean."

"That sounds about right."

"How is he connected to your friend who was killed?"

So, Willie told Ross about the Espada case, all the conversations of the past two days.

Ross brightened. "I use to smoke an Espada stogie every once in a while and they were as smooth as the best moonshine. Of course, that was back before Castro, in the days when normal folk could get Havanas. It's too bad the family has run into so much trouble."

"Yes, it is. Do you know anything about cigar counterfeiters?"

Ross shook his head. "It's a relatively new criminal enterprise, so I never had to fight it myself when I was on the force. I only know what I read in the papers and what I hear from old friends downtown. Sounds like that little sideline has gotten rough."

"You mean the two guys murdered in North Miami."

"Yes, sir. That's as rough as it gets."

"Well, investigating it also has its pleasures. A large cigar convention opens here tomorrow at the Hamilton Hotel. Dozens of cigar companies are going to be giving away free cigars. I've been invited and I can bring a guest. I think they expect me to escort somebody better looking than you, but that's their problem."

"So I'll get a lot of free stogies."

"Exactly and I'll get free advice on my case."

Ross gave him a wry look. "Two of my greatest vices: cigars and sounding like an expert. You certainly know how to tempt a man."

"You'll have to tell your friend, Amelia, to wait for you a couple of days."

"We weren't planning to leave right away, and the cigars will be nice to smoke on deck at night gazing at the stars."

Willie stood up. "I'll call you with details. Don't spend too much energy working on the boat."

"I'll do my best," Ross said. "And I'm sorry about your friend."

Willie left him and headed for another marina, this one down at Hunter Island.

CHAPTER SEVENTEEN

On the way, Willie called information and asked for the number of the security director's office on Hunter Island. He dialed, gave his name and asked for Tom Moore, the boss.

Moore had once been a major in the Miami PD, in charge of the Patrol Division. He had called it quits in his early fifties after receiving a very attractive offer from Hunter Island. He assumed command of the guards on the island, including those who secured the private ferry. He said at the time that he felt like an admiral with his own small Navy. In total, he directed about twenty-five troops.

In exchange, he was housed in his own two-bedroom condo on the most exclusive island in South Florida, with use of tennis courts, golf course, skeet-shooting range, etc. Moore didn't own the condo, but he lived among multimillionaires, banked most of his salary and invested his pension check based on the expert advice of the high rollers around him. This was the sweet deal of all sweet deals, especially for a guy who had spent most of his career cruising around crummy neighborhoods.

Yes, he had to keep an eye out for potential kidnappers, but the private ferry and the two patrol boats circling the island made a snatch very difficult indeed. Apart from that, the most serious incidents he had to deal with was one Ferrari denting the fender of another on the ferry, or a trust-fund baby having a few too many and barfing on the croquet lawn.

Moore's deep voice came on the other end of the line.

"Is that you, Willie? Where are you?"

"Over here on the mainland with the rest of the commoners, Tom."

"What's up?"

94

Willie quickly explained the Carlos Espada missing persons case, and the death of Cesar Mendoza.

"I'll show you the photo of this woman and if you've seen her, maybe you can help me find her to talk to her."

"I'm not sure I can do that, Willie. This is a private island, with the accent on private. And you're not a policeman anymore."

"Gotcha, but the guy who's missing was seen with this lady. Now he's gone. And then another man shows up dead. I would think you'd want to at least look at her photo, to see if it's the same sister, before something unpleasant happens to one of your crown princes over there. You know what they say, 'An ounce of prevention,' Tom. I figured I'd do you the favor."

Moore gave it a few moments thought, just long enough to rationalize.

"So maybe it's in the interest of our community to confirm that this woman was not involved with either of those men. I mean, you're worried about the well-being of the residents here and not just your case."

"Always, Tom."

"And you won't unnecessarily molest my benefactors, the good burghers of this island."

"I wouldn't think of doing that, Tom. I have only the greatest respect for the filthy rich."

"Okay, I'll call over to the ferry and put your name on the visitors' list. Come straight to my office when you get off. And try not to dent any of the BMWs before you get here."

* * *

Willie drove south to the MacArthur Causeway, where he caught the ferry to the island. One of Moore's security cops, a big guy who looked like a Florida state trooper in his wide-brimmed hat, found Willie's name and gave him a pass. Willie rolled onto the ferry without mangling the Mercedes that was on one side of him or smacking his junker into the Jaguar in front of him.

The ride to the island took about five minutes. The palm trees and the coral-colored condos appeared against a beautiful horizon, the best horizon money could buy. If Carlos Espada and his girlfriend were looking for a place to peddle their expensive stogies—their phony Havanas—this would be it.

Willie drove off the ferry and was honored with a special escort—a cop in a golf cart—who ushered him to the security office. Along the way he passed the golf course, health club, squash and tennis courts, etc. Life looked pretty rigorous on the island.

Moore was waiting. Dressed in the same crisp khaki uniform as his troops, he was a heavyset guy with a round, pink face, a few fronds of hair on top and an easygoing disposition. Of course, if you lived and worked on the island, being easygoing was easy.

"Long time no see, Willie. You look like you're doing well."

"So-so, but I still don't get invited over here very often."

Moore shrugged. "I don't think you'd like it. They don't dance a lot of salsa over here."

Willie brought out the photos of Carlos Espada and the elusive Dinah. Moore scrutinized them and then winced.

"Yeah, I have spotted this fair girl here on our fair island, unfortunately. I'm pretty sure of it. I recognize the golden tan and the gold on her fingers."

"Do you remember exactly where you saw all that gold?"

"Yes. I believe it was at the marina."

They rode Moore's executive golf cart over to the docks. It was a small installation, but the array of vessels was impressive—sailboats fifty and sixty feet long; cabin cruisers just as big, and a few full-fledged luxury yachts half a block in length. Some of them, according to Moore, came equipped with screening rooms and discos.

"Onassis had nothing on some of these neighbors," Moore said.

They parked the golf cart in front of the dockmaster's office. This facility was spiffier than the office over at Pelican Harbor. It looked like a cabana at a ritzy hotel. Inside, they found a neat little man, extremely tanned, with a bristly gray crewcut and a gap-toothed smile, whose name was Mullins. He was on the phone and while they waited Willie checked out some of the supplies Mullins had for sale.

They were unusual maritime wares, kept in stock for an unusual clientele. They included not only the traditional life vests, fishing supplies, lines, fuses, etc., but sets of martini glasses, a food section that featured both beluga and osetra caviar, satellite radios that could be equipped with stock tickers and a bulletin board where massage professionals of both sexes offered their services for extended cruises. Willie saw that "Roberta" was known for "deep tissue, Swedish and shiatsu massage for your pleasure, as far south as the tenth latitude."

Mullins hung up the phone and Moore introduced Willie, who produced the photo of Espada with the mystery woman. Mullins eyed it and tapped the image.

"Yes, sir, she's been around here. In fact, she may still be on one of the yachts."

Willie's brows danced. "Which yacht is that?"

"It's called *The Oracle*. It's the biggest boat we have right now, about one hundred twenty feet."

Willie had seen it as they drove in. Moore had pointed to it and told him it was equipped with a Jacuzzi on the top deck.

"It's owned by a corporation headquartered up in the Northeast and they use it to entertain their big clients," Mullins said "I've seen her on deck schmoozing with the guests, kind of like a hostess."

"Kind of," Willie said.

Mullins frowned. "Do you think she's up to no good? I haven't heard any complaints."

Willie shook his head. "No, I don't think the corporate guests will complain about her, not the way she looks."

Willie explained his search for Espada and that he just wanted a word with the lady. He and Moore thanked Mullins and then drove the golf cart to *The Oracle*.

One crew member was on deck burnishing the brass. He was a young bare-chested, muscular kid who was so bronzed he looked as if he'd used the brass polish on himself. Moore asked him if a woman by the name of Dinah was on board. The kid turned, looked up toward the top deck where the Jacuzzi was installed and called her name.

A moment later, a blonde head appeared above the edge of the tub. It was attached to bare, golden shoulders. In fact, for a brief moment, a fraction of a second, Willie and Moore were treated to a glimpse of extremely golden and gorgeous breasts. Then she turned away, slipped into a silver bikini, stood up and disappeared into the yacht. A minute later she sauntered down the gangway toward them.

She looked much as she had in the photos, except she glistened with Jacuzzi water and she toted a tiny cell phone. If she was a kidnapper, or an accomplice to murder, she was very relaxed about it all.

"What can I do for you gentlemen?" She put a little twist on the word "gentlemen" and her eyes pulsed with pleasure. She apparently liked men in uniform—Moore—and men out of uniform too: Willie.

Moore introduced himself and Willie. "Mr. Cuesta here is an old acquaintance of mine from the Miami Police Department and he's working on a missing person case."

Moore didn't bring up the murder of Cesar Mendoza, which was the smart way to go about it. He also didn't mention that Willie was no longer a policeman, and Willie didn't correct him. He would let her assume what she wanted.

"He won't take much of your time, just a question or two."

Willie showed her the two photographs. "I'm looking for the gentleman with you in both these photos."

She studied them. "That's me, isn't it? In all my glory."

Willie nodded. "Yes, it is."

She focused on the photos some more, shook her golden ringlets and offered Willie a vacant expression.

"But I couldn't tell you on a bet who the guy is."

Willie's face clouded over. "You couldn't, huh?"

"No. You have to understand, I go to lots of parties, and I meet lots of guys." She shrugged. "If I had a dollar for every guy I've talked to in the last year, I could go to Vegas and stay quite a while, honey."

Willie held up the photo of the reception.

"This man's name is Carlos Espada. He's employed in the tobacco business. This photo was apparently taken at a cigar convention in Atlanta about a month ago. Does that make the nickel drop?"

She shrugged. "I was there all right. I go to lots of smokers, and I drink a lot of champagne at them. Champagne is good for my mood, but it doesn't do a lot for my memory."

Willie held up the other photo. "Here you're not drinking champagne. It was taken in the Dominican Republic. You're looking into his eyes and no one else is around. That magic moment. You're telling me you don't remember this either?"

She cocked a hip and put a hand on it. "Amigo, in the Dominican Republic I'm even more popular than I am here. Those boys down there would sell the family farm just to talk to me. He was just one guy I talked to." She flashed her eyes lasciviously.

"He's not Dominican. He's from here. He may have been involved in counterfeiting cigars."

She shrugged again. "Not with me."

Her cell phone rang, and she answered. Her eyes lit up. "Hello, big spender. Yes, it was me who beeped you." She listened. "I'm like a million dollars, but right now I have a man here searching for someone I supposedly knew in the Dominican Republic. He has photos and I just can't remember the guy." She giggled, cocked her hip and listened, running a hand through her ringlets.

"You do that," she said finally. "I'll be waiting."

She hung up and beamed at Willie. "See what I mean. And you expect me to remember one poor boy I met on a beach for a minute."

Willie wanted to see what he might extract from that bankrupt memory with another question, especially if she'd known Cesar Mendoza, but she excused herself, "to tinkle." She ducked below decks and Moore turned to Willie.

"I'm not sure I believe her, but we can't do much more, Willie. We don't want to upset the captains of enterprise who own this boat by leaning on their hostess."

"I just want to ask her one more question, Tom, and then I'll be out of here."

They waited a few minutes for her—a long tinkle—and then they were both distracted by the sound of an approaching speedboat. It was a low-slung, black cigarette boat. Its nose was up, and a large rooster-tail of spray rose behind, as it ran fast and noisy, parallel with the island. Whoever was at the controls was feeling gaudy. Moore frowned because the noise would certainly bother the residents.

As he and Willie watched, the rooster swerved, coming even closer to the docks of the Hunter Island marina. That was when Willie saw Dinah. She had sneaked off the other side of the yacht, still wearing her silver bikini, but now she also wore a large straw hat and carried a small suitcase. She was running along the dock toward the swerving cigarette boat.

Willie went sprinting after her as the speedboat veered toward the pier, gearing down so that it almost stopped. Willie was gaining on her, but then he saw a man in the boat raise his hand. It had a gun in it. That sent Willie diving for the dock. The gun let off a loud "pop" and a whistling noise. It took Willie moments to realize it was a flare gun and he watched the smoking missile arc and then explode.

The cigarette boat slid perfectly toward the dock, just as Dinah arrived at the end, and a hand came out to her. She reached for it and was plucked neatly off the planks onto the boat. A split second later, the driver slammed the throttle back. The boat reared up and turned away sharply, heading back out into the bay. Willie reached the end of the pier just in time for the spray to hit him from head to toe. The salt water stung his eyes. But the face of the man who had pulled Dinah off the pier was perfectly clear to him. It was Carlos Espada.

* * *

Tom Moore loaned Willie a towel, tucked him back in the golf cart and drove him to his car with only one request:

"Please don't come back."

Willie returned to the ferry. His thoughts ran in crosscurrents. Carlos Espada was alive and apparently in good health. His mother and sister would be glad to hear that much.

On the other hand, he was involved with Dinah—who was certainly in good health—and whatever they were mixed up in, they didn't want to discuss it. At least not with Willie. That would be very worrisome news for Espada's loved ones, especially now that Cesar was dead.

Willie drove back to his place and before he changed his wet clothes or even sat down he called the Espada house. When Esther answered, he told her that Cesar Mendoza was dead. He also told her how and where he had seen her brother and, finally, relayed to her the message Cesar had received from Carlos.

"Do you know why your brother would say those things? Why is he asking questions about how your father died?"

She was silent for a time. When she did speak, she rambled.

"My brother isn't well. He has said things before because my father's suicide is so very difficult for him. He would prefer that my father had been killed and not that he chose to kill himself and abandon us. Carlos himself has had suicidal tendencies because of the pain it has caused him and maybe that is why he is taking these chances now. Maybe it's a death wish. You need to find him and bring him home as soon as you can."

Willie started to speak, but she cut him off.

"I have to go now and tell my mother about Mr. Mendoza before she hears it from someone else. Please find Carlos, Mr. Cuesta, before something happens to him as well." Then she hung up.

Willie poured himself a rum to warm his wet flesh. Then he poured another one and drank it to the memory of Cesar Mendoza, a nice man who, almost certainly, hadn't deserved to die. He sat and thought about Cesar a long time—and then he poured himself another rum.

CHAPTER EIGHTEEN

Clarence Ross wore his white silk dress guayabera with the baby blue embroidery and his only pair of dress pants; he'd even shaved for the occasion, which made him almost unrecognizable.

"I owe you for this, amigo," he said to Willie.

"Don't I know it, old man. Just don't puff yourself to death."

It was early the next evening and they approached the rambling Hamilton Hotel, which hosted the South Florida Cigar Convention and Smoker. The Hamilton was an old, Mediterranean-revival structure, about ten stories tall, with a bell tower on top. Painted a rose color, in the sunset light it was incandescent. The royal palms out front had grown to full height over the decades and formed a magisterial processional lane leading up to the door. A long line of luxury cars snaked down the driveway from the valet post. Willie figured most of the limousines in town had to be there.

Willie and Ross skipped the valet line, found a space in the parking lot and headed for the entrance. Just inside the door stood a young lady in a very short gold shift. She flashed a dazzling smile and handed them each a complementary cigar clipper, courtesy of the hotel.

"Be careful you don't cut yourself," she cautioned Willie. Willie assured her he wouldn't.

The convention had imposed its "cigar boom" style on what was normally a classical decor. The lobby of the hotel featured a white marble floor, white marble columns with jade-green cornices, sober tapestries on the walls and a vaulted ceiling. All in all, it recreated the atmosphere of a cathedral. But now, suspended from the ceiling, hung three huge facsimiles of cigars, each about three yards long and a foot in diameter. They compromised the grandeur of the place just a bit.

Over the entrance to the main ballroom hung a large red banner, which also announced the convention, depicting a satyr-like creature smoking a stogie. Paying customers were queued up waiting to go in; several hundred had shown up, almost all of them men, with only a handful of women in the line. Willie looked carefully but didn't see Dinah. She had apparently decided to skip this particular party. He didn't see Carlos Espada either.

What he did see were television camera crews working the crowd. The death of Cesar Mendoza, a folkloric figure in the community, was big local news, both on the stations and in the paper. Now the reporters were pumping the cigar makers and smokers about the legendary tobacconist. Willie didn't want to be interviewed. His name hadn't come out in the news, but maybe Sergeant Lester Grand had mentioned it to a stray journalist who might be lying in wait.

Willie and Ross avoided the cameras and went to the convention booth to pick up the guest passes. Nathan Cooler had left Willie's name on his list, despite the run-in at Carlos Espada's office. Willie also stopped at the hotel registration desk and inquired if a Mr. Carlos Espada had checked in. The young black woman with the Caribbean accent who worked behind the counter told him that no one by that name was registered.

Willie thanked her. He and Ross strolled by the smokers waiting in line and entered the ballroom. That cavernous space also had been taken over by the cigar vendors. Its decor was much like that of the lobby, but all along its walls and in an island in the middle of the room companies had constructed booths, hung banners bearing their logos and were distributing samples of their stogies. It had the look of an indoor bazaar. As they entered, both Ross and Willie were handed canvas carry-all bags in which they could collect their free cigar samples. It was trick-or-treat for big boys.

They stopped at a free bar in the middle of the ballroom and then drifted around along with the other smokers. The representatives of the cigar companies dressed in varying styles. Some wore suits, but a few dressed in guayaberas and straw *guajiro* hats or Panamas. One of them was done up in a black silk smoking jacket and sipped a martini. The booths were crowded with eager customers who plucked the free samples from the cigar reps in the same way jumping dolphins pluck fish from the teeth of the attendants at the Seaquarium. It was a feeding frenzy.

Most of those customers kept a lighted cigar clenched between their own teeth and the smoke suffused the room, drifting up into the large chandeliers.

"It's like Chernobyl in here," Willie said to Ross, after about a half hour of going booth to booth.

"It's like Christmas in here, bub." By now Ross was carrying both bags in one hand and collecting two samples at each booth. He had a big stogie in his mouth and a vintage bourbon in his free hand. He was like a boll weevil attacking a big old cotton field.

After a while, Willie let Ross go hunt for the cigars while he roamed around on his own. Sprinkled around the room were other entrepreneurs exploiting the high life that had become associated with expensive tobacco. Yacht brokers and manufacturers of private jets were on hand, as were dealers of Rolls, Bentley, Lamborghini and other luxury automobiles. You could join a polo club up in Palm Beach County or sign up for a roving backgammon tournament that traveled to London, Ibiza, Monte Carlo and Saint Martin.

One international real estate broker offered European chateaus for sale, while another traded exclusively in private islands. He was hawking one, just off the coast of Scotland, which he insisted was a steal at three million dollars. Even in the photo the place appeared chilly. Willie told the broker he was thinking more along the lines of something with palm trees, but he would let him know.

All in all, the convention was a kind of fantasy land, a theme park for hedonism. Lost in the smoke, possibly, was the person who had killed Cesar. The blind man had died at the height of "the boom" and Willie wondered if he had died because of it. Maybe Cesar had known something about someone who now had too much to lose.

Willie kept moving, looking out for the cigar makers he had met on the Espada case. Some of the companies had enlisted rollers who were constructing cigars for the customers right on the spot. At one display, Willie saw the orange-haired Rolando Falcón, apparently hired for the night to do his thing. He was wearing a T-shirt with the name of the cigar company stenciled on it, but otherwise he looked the same as he had the day before. He wielded the crescent-shaped cigar knife with great style, like a young street fighter with a switchblade.

Willie caught sight of Nathan Cooler at the Great American Tobacco booth. He wore his trademark white Panama hat with the blue band. Next to him stood Calderón, his henchman. Calderón's head looked freshly shaved, but he wore a dark suit and white turtleneck, not a shirt opened down to his navel. His big gold chain was apparently tucked away under his clothes. So was his nastiness. He wore a big smile for his customers.

On the other side of the room Willie spied Don Ricardo Tirado, wearing a finely embroidered guayabera, greeting fans of his cigars. Tirado was positioned so that he didn't have to see his nemesis, Calderón. Next to him stood Richard Knox, his partner, basking in the old man's glory.

Then Jean-Philippe Montand came into view. The Geneva-based cigar distributor had just entered the ballroom. He was short, but given his mane of white hair, Willie couldn't miss him as he crossed the floor and approached the Tirado booth. Willie remembered what old Don Ricardo had said about Montand, that he was a scoundrel and a spy. He figured he would see some kind of confrontation.

The moment Tirado spotted Montand his chin came up. Willie could see the warmth disappear from the old man's countenance and disdain fill his eyes. But Montand advanced anyway, leaned toward the glaring Tirado and began to speak to him privately, in the midst of all the commotion.

The Swiss man spoke rapidly, his eyes fixed on the old Cuban. And whatever it was he had to say, Tirado was interested. He didn't unclench his jaw, but Willie could see he was listening. He asked Montand a couple of short questions and at least one of the answers seemed to surprise him.

At the end of the conversation Tirado nodded curtly. Then both men glanced at their watches, as if they were agreeing on a time to speak again. A moment later, Montand turned away and Willie watched him hurry out of the ballroom. For two men who were supposedly blood enemies, it appeared they had managed to agree on something.

Tirado was too busy for Willie to ask him about it right then. But Willie and Ross had invitations to attend the dinner afterward and Tirado would presumably be there. Willie could ask him then about the "spy."

Meanwhile, Willie turned his attention to the half dozen women in the room. Several of those seemed to be genuine cigar enthusiasts, or at least they represented real smokers because they were hustling from booth to booth collecting samples. But Willie noticed a few others who seemed to pass their time grazing. In particular, he spotted a tall redhead with big hair, maybe forty, done up in a silver dress and a gaudy rhinestone choker. She hung out around the champagne stalls.

Willie strolled over, accepted a glass of Veuve Cliquot from an attendant and found himself standing next to her. She sipped her champagne and glanced at him, her eyes bubbling with interest.

"I haven't seen you before at a convention. You're new."

"You come to a lot of these little soirees, do you?"

Her eyes flared with amusement. "All the time. I like men who smoke cigars."

They introduced themselves. Her name was Rochelle. She claimed to work in "human relations."

"You having a good time tonight?" she asked.

"Not so far, but you never know."

"No, you never know. Things could improve any minute," she said, still bubbling.

"My evening would improve immediately if I could find this woman I know. Her name is Dinah, a blonde. She usually turns out for these get-togethers. Ever meet her?"

The mention of Dinah didn't make Red happy. She lost her bubbly interest, and her gaze went flat.

"Oh yeah I've seen her. She's cheap if you ask me. As cheap as a machine-made cigar."

"Is that right?"

"Yes, it is. She started hanging around the cigar bars and the conventions a couple of months ago. Moving very fast."

"In which direction?"

"In the direction of anybody who looked like he had a lot of money, that's what direction."

Red had become momentarily distracted, exchanging a smile with a passing smoker. A moment later she turned back to Willie, extinguishing the smile.

Willie sipped his own bubbly. Of course, here was a woman about forty, dealing with a rival who looked to be in her early thirties. And she herself wasn't exactly standing there waiting for the 8:05 to Orlando. If Willie wasn't mistaken, she was there looking for someone who might fill her later years not only with cigar smoke, but with creature comforts. A younger woman, like Dinah, could only get in her way.

"Did Dinah ever mention to you where she worked?"

She shook her head. "She never mentioned anything to me at all, but I don't think she did much of what you would call work. What she was doing was always looking to make deals."

"What kind of deals?"

"She wanted to get her hands on some Havanas. She said she knew people who would pay a fortune any time for anything they thought came from Havana."

Willie's eyes flared. "So, the cigars didn't really have to be Havanas. They could have been counterfeit."

She scrunched up her nose and her voice dropped. "You never say that word around here. People don't like it. But that was the idea."

That afternoon Willie had Xeroxed the photos of Espada and Dinah and he produced them.

"Ever see her with this gentleman here?"

She glanced at the photos. "I remember seeing him at conventions. Maybe I saw her with him once, but I'm not sure. They weren't an item, that much I know."

She eyed Willie up and down appreciatively. "I don't think he's anybody you need to be jealous about, honey. I also think you could do better than Dinah any day. The longer you age tobacco, the better it is usually. That can be true of women too."

Red's despair was showing now, but Willie nodded. "I agree. But you know how it is. When somebody gets under your skin."

"Yeah, well I'd be careful if I were you. That girl comes in contact with your skin she'll burn you. She's dangerous. I can tell."

"Do you think she could be dangerous enough to kill some-body?"

She shrugged. "I know she carries a gun. I saw it in her purse one night in the powder room at a cigar smoker. Like I said, be care-ful."

"Thanks for the tip."

"If you don't mind, time's a wastin'."

She practiced her bubbly smile on him once more and then sashayed into the crowd.

Willie sipped another glass of champagne, waiting for the throng to thin out. After a while Ross walked up. His two carry-all bags brimmed with cigars. He carried one in each hand like a dairy farmer lugging pails of milk from the barn, careful not to spill any.

"I've got enough good 'ceegars' here to change the pollution level in the city of Miami, bub."

"The pollution index has already been affected," Willie said, waving away the hazy air around them. "I think it's time to make for the buffet."

"I think it's past time. I'm right behind ya."

CHAPTER NINETEEN

illie and Ross flashed their special guest passes and were
admitted to the elevator for the mezzanine level. When the
doors slid open, they found themselves standing before a bank of
tables laden with hors d'oeuvres. On the very center table stood an
ice sculpture of the same satyr pictured on the banner in the lobby.
He was smoking a cigar made of ice, although the heat was getting
to it and large drops of water fell from the tip.

A young woman with platinum-blonde hair and almost unprece-
dented decolletage served them caviar.

"This was in Russia yesterday," she said.

"I was in Orlando just last week, darlin'" Ross said, chomping
down on a cracker covered with the small black eggs.

She wasn't impressed and they moved on to the bar, where they
collected more champagne. A girl came by dressed in a leotard covered with dark green layers of cloth cut in spade shapes, so that she
looked as if her bare shoulders and lovely neck were emerging from
a tobacco plant. Willie had never seen anything quite like it and
probably no one else had either. She carried a tray with more caviar
and crackers and allowed Willie and Ross to snatch a couple.

A Latin orchestra was playing a salty old song about a rough
barrio in Havana where everyone smoked cigars. Willie was listening, when he found Don Ricardo Tirado standing next to him. The
old patriarch gripped his gnarled cane in one hand and what
appeared to be a rather large whiskey on the rocks in the other. As
he'd told Willie, cigar conventions were his only respite from the life
of moderation that had been forced on him by his doctors. Right
now, he was living dangerously.

Willie greeted him. It took the old man a moment to place him. "Mr. Cuesta, no?"

"That's right." Willie introduced Ross. "Are you enjoying the evening?"

The old man nodded. "So far, yes. And as long as I can avoid my caretakers, I plan to continue to enjoy it." He looked around furtively and sipped his whiskey. He turned back to Willie. "I'm told you were the one who found Cesar Mendoza yesterday."

"A very bad day, indeed."

Tirado nodded and lifted his whiskey. "I think we should drink a toast to his memory." They touched glasses and the old man took a gulp of his drink. It was a large gulp. Tirado and Cesar were contemporaries, and it was always worrisome to see a contemporary die, no matter the circumstances.

"Did you know Cesar Mendoza well?" Willie asked.

Tirado rolled his eyes. "Did I know him well? I knew him too well." His eyes twinkled, the way Willie had seen them do during their first meeting. He tapped Willie's lapel. "Cesar was a devil. He loved the nightclubs. He loved to dance. He adored women. In Havana we used to carouse together and it didn't matter a bit that he was blind. In fact, he attracted women the way sugar attracts flies. He's dead, but let me assure you he rung every bit of pleasure out of life before he died."

He took another hit from his drink and looked back at Willie. "Remembering our wayward youth. That's the only way I can keep from thinking of him as dead."

"Who do you think murdered him?"

"I have no idea. I assume it was a robbery. His business was going very well and he must have had money around. His good fortune probably killed him."

"It's strange that it would come only weeks after those two cigar rollers were murdered in North Miami. They had their throats slit as well. People say they were involved in counterfeiting."

Tirado grimaced. "It's as I told you the other day, the boom has attracted criminals. Some of the individuals involved are as bad as some of the tobacco being used to make cigars. Before, no one killed anyone in the cigar trade. There was no reason. There wasn't enough money in it. Now they're finding people in the business dead all over the city."

"Let's say Cesar wasn't killed by thieves. Was there anybody in the cigar trade who had anything against him?"

Tirado shook his head. "No one that I know. As you saw when you visited my factory, we are not all as friendly as we seem here. But Cesar sold everyone's product. He didn't favor anyone." Tirado shrugged. "Maybe one of his girlfriends killed him. That's more likely."

"Is it?"

Tirado thought about that. "Not being able to see was Cesar's greatest gift as a seducer," he said finally, "and he also thought it was his greatest protection. Women found him endlessly appealing as a lover and since the boom started and he had more money, he took even more lovers. Cesar played the role to the maximum. He told me he could discourse on the texture of a woman's skin for half an hour without using the same word twice. He said he was better at describing a woman he had never seen than he was at talking about tobacco. Their smell, their texture, their body—no matter what they looked like. Of course to Cesar, that didn't matter, because he couldn't see. If a homely woman had a melodious voice, a tender touch and a good heart, it didn't matter how she had aged, she could still be the object of his passions. He treated them all as if they were great beauties, whether they were hotel maids or business executives."

Tirado shook his head. "But the problem was Cesar sometimes liked to blend his mistresses the way we blend tobaccos in a cigar. He liked more than one at a time. He said if a woman found him with another, he would tell her, 'I thought it was you, *mi amor*. I'm only a poor blind man.' It was amusing, but that could get a man killed. Don't you think?"

Willie agreed with a lift of the eyebrows. "Do you know who he was seeing lately?" Tirado's wry expression remained in place. "He wasn't *seeing* anybody. You mean who was he screwing?"

"Exactly."

"Cesar was always discreet. He never revealed names." He hesitated a moment. "But I did run into him at a restaurant about a week ago and he was with a woman that night."

"Do you know who she was?"

Tirado met Willie's gaze. "He was eating with Victoria Espada."
Willie's eyebrows danced. "Is that so?"

Tirado shook his head. "There was never any romance between
Cesar and Victoria, only friendship. In fact, Victoria, as far as anyone
knows, has not had a romance since her husband committed suicide
many years ago. I told you that the other day. But maybe she can
help you in some other way."

Of course, Tirado himself had been unable to win Victoria Espada. Maybe he was underestimating Cesar, who remained very close
to the family. But Willie didn't offer that.

"You said earlier that Cesar had no enemies. How about Jean-
Philippe Montand?"

Tirado's gaze iced over. "What about him?"

"A spy and a scoundrel, you called him yesterday. Did Cesar feel
the same?"

Tirado shrugged. "I doubt it. Cesar had a different attitude
toward people. How do the Americans say—live and let live."

"I saw *you* speaking to Montand a little while ago, downstairs."

That irritated the old man. "I wasn't speaking to him, he was
speaking to me."

"Cigar business?"

Tirado shook his head brusquely. "I don't do business with Montand."

"Then I guess it was just a little friendly chat."

"It was nothing of importance."

Another girl in a tobacco plant outfit cruised by. Tirado was
momentarily distracted by her. In her wake came the blond figure of
Richard Knox. The "pumpernickel ladies" were at his side. They
also wore Tobacco Girl outfits, but with red belts that said "Tirado
Cigars."

Knox greeted Willie and Don Ricardo. He was wearing a white
suit and the same amber shades he'd worn the first time Willie had
met him. He greeted Willie with his perpetual smile.

"Isn't this wonderful?"

Willie nodded politely. Tirado excused himself and said he was
going for another drink.

"Before the nursemaids find me."

Knox put his arm around the old man's shoulder. "Have one more, but go easy, *compadre*. We don't want to lose you now that business is booming. The girls here will take care of you."

Knox's ever-present bookends took Tirado, one by each arm, and eased him toward the bar. The old man looked them over, beamed at Willie, and didn't argue. Ross also excused himself and headed off looking for their dinner table. Knox watched them go and turned back to Willie.

"I can't afford to lose Tirado right now. He's the figurehead for the business, the symbol of quality."

Willie sipped his champagne. "Yes, it would be bad for business right now if he died."

Knox grimaced. "I didn't mean it to sound that way. Did you locate the woman you were looking for yesterday?"

Willie nodded. "Oh yeah, I found her, and then I lost her again."

Knox smiled. "Well, she did look fast, not exactly the female you settle down with. Did she tell you where to find Espada?"

Willie thought about that a moment and then answered truthfully.

"No, she said she didn't remember ever meeting him. And she didn't have time to tell me anything else."

Willie tasted his champagne. "I suppose you've heard what happened to Cesar Mendoza."

Knox nodded. "Of course. I heard last night." He shook his head ruefully. "You do business with a man one day, and the next day he's dead."

A thought occurred to Knox, and he wagged a finger near Willie's face. "If you find these counterfeiters, you should ask them where they were when Cesar was killed?"

Willie frowned. "Why's that?"

"Because counterfeiters didn't like Cesar. He told me once that people would bring him cigars they'd bought, supposedly Cubans. Cesar would just take a whiff and know they were fake. Some of those customers returned those cigars. Cesar was a kind of consumer protection agency for smokers. Who knows, maybe the counterfeiters got pissed off with him."

They both thought about Cesar for a few moments. It was Willie who broke the silence.

"Well, it looks like you'll be able to take over his business after all."

Knox didn't like that.

"It hadn't crossed my mind." But now it did. Willie could see Knox checking the imaginary profit statements in his head. He got to the bottom line and beamed at Willie. A smile as wide as a spreadsheet blossomed on his face.

"That's exactly what I should do. Start that chain I talked about, Blind Mendoza's Stogies. Put his photo in the window of every store. Work the story in the press. Nobody will ever forget Mendoza and we'll make money too."

Knox was already shifting into the development stage.

"Well, tell me when you're ready to sell stock," Willie said.

Knox said he'd do that. The loss of Cesar Mendoza had caused only a temporary dip in his spirits. He was rebounding quickly.

The blond man leaned toward him. "I'm having a little get-together up in my suite after dinner. Number 690. It should be spicy. Drop by."

"I'll do that."

Willie watched him head off into the crowd and then kept an eye on him as Knox retreated to a spot at the end of the bar where someone was waiting to speak to him. Mario Calderón greeted Knox. This was the same Calderón who had been taunting Ricardo Tirado, Knox's business partner, just two days before. Willie watched as the two men fell into an intense conversation. First, he'd seen Ricardo Tirado speaking with Jean-Philippe Montand. Now Knox and Calderón. Cigar conventions, he was starting to see, created surprising bedfellows.

Willie drained his wine and went looking for his own bedfellows at his table.

CHAPTER TWENTY

A minute later Willie was seated with Ross at one of the large, round tables covered in glistening, white linen. Joining them were seven other conventioneers, all of whom were having a high time and doing business of one kind or another all at once.

They included a couple of heavyset cigar store owners, one from Tampa and another from Orlando; two smaller tobacco growers from Honduras; a girl dressed as a mermaid, who had buoys for breasts and had worked in a booth representing a fancy resort in the Virgin Islands; the gentleman who sold private islands; and, finally, the same red-haired woman who had trashed Dinah. Her name was Rochelle, but Willie thought of her as Red.

Red had insinuated herself next to the island salesman. Maybe she thought that if he liked her, he might lay a small bauble on her— let's say an atoll or a sandbar some place. The mermaid sat next to one of the Hondurans, who was already running his hands over her scales. Ross was beguiling the two cigar store owners with old tales of law enforcement.

Willie sat down with the mermaid on one side and the only empty chair on the other. The girl moved her tail out of the way before Willie sat on it, then she turned back to the Honduran. He was telling her about the hacienda he had in Honduran tobacco country and the beach house he kept in the Bay Islands off the north coast. Wonderful diving, he said, and sharks were no problem.

"I'll dive anytime," the mermaid cooed.

Red, meanwhile, had turned her attention from the island broker to the other Honduran, who was recounting for her the history of the boom. How the US economy had mushroomed and big cigars had become the symbol of the decade. By the mid-nineties money was being made in cigar tobacco hand over fist.

"Did that include you?" she asked sweetly.

"Well, yes it did, señorita," said the Honduran. He was leaning very close to her and staring at her cleavage, like a man yodeling into a canyon. Willie was afraid he would fall in.

"That must have been very exciting," said Red.

He said it was, but eventually business had slowed for many companies, and some had crashed. Red frowned at that.

"Did your business crash?"

"No, our business never crashed. We continue strong."

Red's smile returned. "That's wonderful."

"Yes, it was," he said, "but competition was very strong." He lifted his head from above her breasts for just a moment and looked around the room. "A few years ago, everybody in this room was very happy and very friendly. Now, some of the people are not so friendly." He shrugged and went back to surveying her landscape.

A waiter arrived to serve the wine. Willie chose a Louis Jadot 1989 Chassagne Montrachet, not because he'd ever had it before or heard of it, but because it was red. Then came the appetizer, a little ditty called Scallops with Pekey Toe Crab and Pickled Ginger in Blood Orange Dressing.

Willie had just dug in—if one can be said to dig into a Pekey Toe Crab—when the occupant of the tenth chair showed up. It turned out to be Jean-Philippe Montand. He apologized profusely to his tablemates. It was only after he'd sat that he noticed Willie next to him. He didn't seem happy about it.

The waiter served the newcomer some wine, and Montand took a large swig from it, larger than a gentleman of his cut usually consumed in one gulp. He put the glass down and turned to Willie. "I've been at the police station for several hours today."

"Is that so? What was the occasion?"

"They were questioning me about the murder of Cesar Mendoza. I understand you were the one who found him."

He seemed to blame Willie for causing him trouble with the police by reporting the dead body.

"That's right, but why would they question you?"

"Because I may have been the last one to see him alive—apart from whoever killed him"

That impressed Willie. "When was that?"

"Two days ago. We had dinner together. Cesar had called me. I hadn't spoken to him in some time and suddenly I found a message on my machine asking me to dine. I called him back and left a message, accepting. The police found that message on Cesar's answering machine, got my name and number, showed up at my condo here this afternoon and eventually requested that I accompany them, as you Americans say so quaintly, downtown. I told them I was a foreign businessman visiting their city in good faith, but it didn't matter."

"And what did you tell them?"

"That we ate at a restaurant in Coral Gables. That we drank Spanish wine. That Cesar ate baby scallops and that, to begin, we talked about the old days."

"Which old days are these?"

He assumed an urbane expression. "The very old days. I met Cesar in Spain back in the early sixties after he left Cuba. We used to spend long nights in the cafes there, smoking cigars, drinking. He talked about that a bit and he also talked about what Cesar always talked about back then—his latest affairs. The man never changed."

"Did he talk about any affair in particular?" Willie was thinking of what Tirado had said, that Cesar might have been killed by a lover.

Montand looked irritated. "What importance can that have?"

"Did he?"

The other man shrugged. "He told me a long story about a lover he had here for a time. One night this woman simply showed up at his house. He said at first he had no idea how she knew him, where she had seen or heard of him. In fact, he didn't know who she was."

"Really."

"Yes, really. She used the name Maria but admitted to him that it was a false name. She came to see him at least three nights per week. She always talked to him in a whisper, so if he encountered her somewhere else, he wouldn't recognize her voice. She never used perfume when she came to see him, for the same reason. So that he wouldn't pick up her scent somewhere. He said she made love with a tremendous appetite, like a woman who had been years without a lover. Their sessions lasted all night. She would leave just before dawn. Cesar said it was a good thing he wore opaque glasses because his eyes must have been swollen for months. He said he knew just from her manner that she was very beautiful and an aristocrat."

"How old was this woman? Young, old, what?"

Montand shook his head curtly. "I didn't ask for the salacious details, Mr. Cuesta."

"What happened between them?"

"One night she arrived unannounced and he was with another woman. He said she immediately left and never showed up again."

"And he never knew who she was?"

Montand met his gaze. "He said he knew from the very first month who she was, but never let her know that."

"Who was she?"

The Swiss man shook his head. "He didn't tell me. Cesar never told you that."

Willie sipped his wine and thought. "Did he mention that he had seen Victoria Espada lately?"

The other man was surprised by the question. "No, he never mentioned that. Do you think he was mixed up somehow with Mrs. Espada? She has always been a very beautiful woman, but extremely circumspect."

Willie shook his head. "I don't think anything. How about her son, Carlos Espada? Did he talk to you at all about Carlos and what he has been up to lately?"

Montand retreated even farther, to a higher point in his own personal Alps. He studied Willie with those glacial gray eyes of his and finally nodded.

"Yes, he did."

"What did he say?"

He hesitated. "That was why he asked me to dinner."

"To ask you about the counterfeiting business?"

Montand bristled. "Why would I know about that?"

Willie shrugged. "People say you have extremely close relations with the Cuban government. I'm sure the cigar industry types on the island try to keep track of who is trying to copy their cigars. It hurts their business."

Montand scowled. "Some old stories never die. I am not and never have been an agent of any kind for the Cuban government. I told you the first time I met you not to believe everything you hear. And you should not be repeating a story like that at this moment. Matters are dangerous enough right now in this city for a person in my business. It's as if the harvest is on and we are the plants. Someone is cutting people down."

Willie nodded. For a guy like Montand, who already had enemies in the business before the boom, recent events had to be especially uncomfortable. But Willie didn't have much sympathy for him. The Swiss man seemed like the type who would play all sides against the middle.

"Did Cesar ask you about counterfeiting or didn't he?"

"Yes, he asked, and I told him the same thing I told you. I know nothing about it. But it wasn't the principal topic he wanted to discuss with me."

That surprised Willie. "What was?"

"For some reason he wanted to talk about the death of Ernesto Espada. He wanted to know about his last days."

"What did you tell him? Were you here at the time?"

The other man nodded. "Yes, even then I kept a place here and I happened to be visiting at the time. As for the reasons for Ernesto Espada's suicide I knew what Ernesto had told me himself. That a business deal had fallen through. That he felt betrayed by life."

"Who was the business deal with?"

Montand shook his head. "That I don't know. He didn't say. There had been rumors that he would go into a partnership that would be based in Europe. The rumor was that Tirado was involved as well, but later Tirado denied it. I knew matters were extremely difficult for Espada. I had seen him in the Canary Islands and Mexico, and he was struggling, but now his situation had deteriorated even further. One day he told me about that deal falling through and days later I heard he was dead."

"And that was what you told Cesar?"

"Of course."

"And how did he respond?"

"He said that was his recollection as well."

Willie squinted. "He asked you about counterfeiting and the death of Ernesto Espada. What could one possibly have to do with the other? The first happened over thirty years ago and the other is happening now."

"I have no idea, but I have no desire to discuss either one of them any further."

That was just as well because the main course arrived then. It consisted of Roasted Loin of Bradley Ranch Venison with Spring Vegetables. Willie assumed the Bradley Ranch was where all the best deer hung out. That was followed by dessert, Valbona Dark Chocolate Mousse with Carmelized Cuban Bananas. It was served with thin wafers, although it should have come with the business card of a cardiologist.

Conversation died down during these last two courses, except for the mermaid, who would tell any man willing to listen about how much she loved to dive and the fact that she didn't need a tank. Then she'd giggle.

Coffee was just being served and cigars fired up when Willie saw Nathan Cooler get to his feet at a nearby table. Cooler tapped on a glass with a knife until the talking died down and he took off his Panama hat.

"We're gathered here in Miami this evening to celebrate a good year for most of us and to talk about how to increase profits next year," he began. "But something happened to all of us yesterday that can only be considered a loss, a great loss. Cesar Mendoza was killed."

Murmurs of agreement and commiseration were heard all around the room.

"As of this afternoon, the police were saying it was a robbery. I remember worrying about Cesar working by himself in that shop, worrying about who might come in off the street. But he did it for so many years that after a while I stopped worrying. Cesar was an institution. His shop was a landmark. And now he's gone."

He let that sink in a moment. "We all hope the police find who committed this crime, that the people responsible are not allowed to crawl back into some hole in this city and get away. Right now all we can do is drink to his memory."

Everybody toasted the blind man. Moments later the house lights were dimmed. Then spotlights illuminated a stage area just in front of the orchestra. The musicians began a medley of old cigar tunes, like the ones Cesar Mendoza had always played at his store.

In the midst of the first song, the Tobacco Girls marched onstage, formed a chorus line and began strutting their stuff and shaking their leaves. A handful of male dancers, dressed in the homespun white cotton and straw hats of tobacco cutters, came on next and tried to "harvest" the girls with long curved wooden knives. They cut underneath the girls leaping feet and over their swirling heads. A series of struggles were choreographed in which the lively and seductive plants eluded their would-be harvesters. It occurred to Willie that a Cuban ballet about seduction was a fitting tribute to Cesar.

The lights came down all the way and the orchestra segued into another tune, this one about tobacco fields that "get lost in the blue mist of desire." One Tobacco Girl and a male dancer fell into a sensuous dance. The singer sang about the woman "in flower" and the land aflame with desire.

In the end the cutters were able to harvest the field. The men carried the Tobacco Girls into the shadows to make love as the singer crooned about "a thousand sweet spirals of smoke" rising into the night sky over Pinar del Río.

When it ended, the audience applauded long and loud. The orchestra broke into a salsa tune and many of the people got up to dance. That was when Willie noticed two people at a back table near the door: Victoria and Esther Espada. The older woman was dressed much as she had been the first time they had met, all in black. Esther was in white, set off by a bright flower print wrap. Her black hair cascaded down over it. Willie excused himself to his tablemates and headed right for them.

CHAPTER TWENTY-ONE

Victoria and Esther weren't alone when Willie walked up. Several people were waiting to greet them. The Espada ladies were, after all, cigar aristocracy. Willie watched as they solemnly accepted one visitor after another. Finally, Willie's turn arrived and be stood before them, a humble retainer.

"I didn't know you ladies were coming tonight."

It was Victoria Espada who answered. "We didn't plan to be here either, until an hour before it started. Mr. Cooler convinced us to join him. He said many of Cesar Mendoza's friends would be here to pay him tribute and we wanted to be here as well. He was very loyal to us." The implication was that others had not been.

The circles under Victoria Espada's eyes were darker than they had been. She looked like she'd spent a rough night after hearing of Cesar's death.

"I tried to reach you today."

She shook her bead. "Cesar had a very old aunt who we have known all our lives. We have been with her all day planning the funeral and consoling her. We know what it is to have the fates turn against you, to lose someone suddenly."

"Had you spoken to Cesar since I saw you?"

She shook her head. "Neither of us had heard from him. If I had, I would have told him to be careful."

Willie studied her. "Why would that be? What did Cesar have to fear?"

"When people begin to disappear who have never disappeared, Mr. Cuesta. When strange women you have never seen or heard of before and who cannot possibly have anything to do with your family suddenly appear in your life, then the world is following different laws than it did before. One has to worry." The strange woman to whom she referred had to be Dinah.

"I understand."

Both the women were distracted momentarily as another Tobacco Girl walked by, this one dressed only in a thong and two discreetly placed cigar bands. Victoria Espada's eyes followed her with a look of high censure. What Willie was witnessing was the clash of two different female icons of cigar history. *Very* different.

They watched until the woman disappeared into the crowd and Victoria turned back to Willie. "Have you had any more word of my son?"

"No, señora. Nothing yet."

She shook her head. "I thought, after what happened to Cesar, that he would come here out of respect for an old friend. But possibly he has no respect for anyone anymore."

The pain she had expressed at their first meeting had turned into bitterness. Perhaps she heard that in her own voice and didn't like it. She looked up at Willie.

"Why don't you dance with my daughter? Maybe it will raise her spirits."

"My pleasure, señora."

He held a hand out to Esther Espada. She considered it a moment before she took it and allowed him to lead her to the dance floor.

The orchestra played an old *bolero* about a woman "who had in her heartbeat the rhythms of a song." Esther Espada came into Willie's arms and together they fell into that heartbeat. She gazed over his shoulder at the crowd around them.

"What do you think of the gathering?" he asked her.

Her dark eyes narrowed. "My father must be turning over in his grave."

"What do you mean?"

"I mean, if he were to see what some people have done to his business."

More than anyone else, Esther and Victoria Espada seemed out of place in this crowd. The traditions they came from, and held onto, didn't have much to do with girls dressed as mermaids, backgammon tournaments, stretch limos and Greek-revival *groseros* like Richard Knox.

"You don't think he would like the Tobacco Girls?"

She glared over his shoulder. "The business used to be run by families that had a certain history and certain standards. Some of the companies are still run that way, but other people have come in who are opportunists and farceurs as far as I can tell."

Contempt had filled her eyes. Willie had to wonder how much of it was her natural aristocratic disdain for bad taste and how much stemmed from frustration at her family's misfortune. It was probably a bit of both. She met his gaze.

"My brother has my father's blood in his veins. He is an innocent compared to most of these people. I've always known that. It didn't worry me until now, until Cesar Mendoza was killed."

Willie's eyebrows went up. "We don't know that Cesar was killed by someone in the business. It could have been a simple robbery."

"Do you believe that?"

Willie shrugged. "No, but I'm not sure yet."

"That newspaper article you found in Carlos' drawer, it had to do with two cigar rollers, didn't it? People here are talking about that."

"Yes, it did."

"And now Cesar is killed. It wasn't a simple robbery. It was something else. And I'm worried my brother may also be hurt by whoever hurt Cesar."

The music continued, but they had almost stopped moving. She stared at nothing, and Willie stared at her.

"On the other hand, he may simply have run off with a blonde," Willie said.

She gave him a cutting glance and then shook her head. "I'm going to tell you a story about my brother, Mr. Cuesta. When he was twenty-two years old he fell very much in love with a young Cuban girl here. She and her family had come over in the boatlift of 1980. She told him they were from Pinar del Río, and she had worked in the tobacco fields that had once belonged to my father. She said people who worked there still revered the memory of my father. The girl was very beautiful, and my brother idealized her. She was a connection to the past, to our father, to the life we lost.

"He introduced her to my mother and me. He told us that he planned to marry her. We weren't opposed in any way. But then my mother began to speak with her, began to ask her questions about the *vega*, about the house. The girl couldn't remember essential details, matters she should have known, certain landmarks on the property. It became clear that she wasn't who she said. She tried to argue with my mother, but it was no use. She had apparently heard of our family, thought we were still wealthy and decided to share in that wealth. She was a fake. My mother told Carlos as much and the girl was dismissed. Since then my brother is very wary of women who appear out of nowhere, Mr. Cuesta. In fact, he's wary of women in general. He would never be with a woman like that of his own will."

Willie shrugged. "Before the boom a lot of men in the cigar business had never been involved with women like that, but some of them are now."

He was recalling stories Cesar had told him about private parties in the VIP rooms of nightclubs or cigar salons.

"Some of these guys are burning up their profits as fast as their customers burn the cigars," Cesar had said. "Those stretch limousines are full of smoke, champagne and some very bare flesh, Willie."

She was shaking her head. "You don't understand our family, Mr. Cuesta. You don't understand what holds us together."

Willie squinted. He thought he did understand. It seemed to him that it wasn't only Carlos Espada who had tailored his life to his mother's protectionist family policy. He was holding in his arms a woman who was surpassingly beautiful and who also had never married, who had no life outside that little house on the edge of the bay. He put a soft spin on it.

"In your case, living at home must make it easier to live the life of an artist," he said. "To make ends meet."

She shrugged. "The truth is I would have preferred to be an actress, but that wasn't possible. I needed to stay closer to my mother." She looked up into his face and the corner of her mouth curled in a smile. "In a way I am an actress, except that all my life, every day, I play the same role."

Willie frowned. "What do you mean?"

She shrugged, wearing that same Mona Lisa smile, but didn't answer. He watched her out of the corner of his eye, as she stared over his shoulder with that same solemn, welling gaze, just like the old image on the cigar box. Willie thought he caught her meaning. Her family had left Cuba before she was born, but Esther Espada had been raised as if she were still back on that farm, still a member of the aristocracy of tobacco. The identity she had inherited, that role she spoke of, was based on a life she herself had never lived. It was a reality inherited from ancestors and recreated by her mother, for both Esther and her brother. But their lives couldn't help but eventually collide with reality. Her brother couldn't avoid running into business problems in real life and he couldn't help but meet a woman who played him like a fiddle. And his mother and sister would be dragged into reality with him.

As he held her in his arms, felt her breast against his, looked down on those bare white shoulders, her reality became more insistent. Because her body was no figment of the imagination, it was very real and very beautiful. Willie took a deep breath and figured he better stick to business.

"Another question is what your brother was doing in the Dominican Republic? Have you gotten the phone bill?"

Slowly, she came back to the present. She looked at him as if she was surprised to find herself in his arms. Then she nodded.

"Yes, I got it yesterday."

"Did you look at it yet?"

She shook her head. "But I'll bring it to you as soon as I can."

"Do that."

When the music ended, he escorted her back to her table. Her mother was waiting for her in order to leave. Willie bid them good night. He watched her bare shoulders disappear through the crowd.

He was still gazing in that direction when he noticed two other guests heading for the exit. Don Ricardo Tirado shuffled along, spiking the carpet with his cane. A couple of steps behind him walked Jean-Philippe Montand, who was checking his watch and saying something to Tirado.

Willie gave them time to get out the door and then he followed them, cutting through the writhing tobacco plants on the dance floor.

CHAPTER TWENTY-TWO

Willie reached the lobby just in time to see Montand and Tirado board an elevator by themselves. He watched the illuminated numbers and saw it rise to the seventh floor before it started back down.

As soon as it opened at the lobby level, Willie got in and rode it back up to seven. He got out and found a hallway wallpapered in coral brocade with matching carpeting. It was empty, except for a room service waiter, a gray-haired Latin man, who was just headed back down to the kitchen. Willie stopped him.

"A friend of mine just came up to this floor, but I can't remember the number of the room. An older man walking with a cane."

The waiter nodded and pointed back up the hall.

"The last suite on the left. He just went in there."

Willie thanked him and walked slowly up the hallway, giving the waiter plenty of time to make it to the service elevator. When he reached the door of Suite 717 he paused, checked to make sure no one else was coming out of the guest elevator and then put his ear to the door. He heard voices inside, several of them in conversation, but they weren't loud enough for Willie to make out what they were saying. Montand and Tirado certainly weren't arguing, or if they were, it was an extremely discreet fight.

Willie stepped away from the door before someone opened it and caught him eavesdropping. He backtracked to the elevator, not pressing the button, but trying to decide what to do. He wasn't sure whose room it was, Montand's, Tirado's or maybe someone else's. Knocking on the door would probably get him no further than he had gotten in his earlier questioning of both the Swiss man and Tirado. And it might get him hurt.

He was still standing there when the door to suite 717 opened and someone walked out. It was neither Montand nor Tirado. It was the young, orange-haired Rolando Falcón, of all people. Willie turned quickly so that Falcón would only see his back and he pressed the button for the elevator. Just what Falcón was doing in a room with the two men who had just walked in, Willie couldn't imagine. A man like Montand wouldn't be found dead in the same room with a character like Rolando. Not under normal circumstances. But these circumstances weren't normal at all.

Willie waited until Falcón was right behind him and then he turned. The kid was surprised and more than a little disturbed to see him there. Willie smiled.

"Rolando Falcón. The last person I expected to see. What brings you here?"

Willie had taken the words out of Falcón's mouth. The younger man frowned.

"I'm working for one of the companies and I was getting paid. What are you doing here?"

Willie pointed the opposite way down the hallway. "I was visiting a friend who is staying in the hotel."

Falcón believed Willie about as much as he trusted a fake Havana, but he said nothing. Willie wondered who else had been in that room, and what Falcón's real business was in that very busy suite.

The elevator arrived and they got in.

"As long as I bumped into you, I'll ask you the question of the day," Willie said. "Did you know Cesar Mendoza, the cigar dealer who was killed?"

Falcón shook his head. "I met him a couple of times at cigar shows, but I didn't know him too good."

"I'm told a man named Montand was a friend of his, a small, white-haired Swiss man. Ever hear of him?"

Falcón didn't take his eyes from Willie's.

"Never heard of him," he said, even though he had just been in the same room with Montand.

"I see," Willie said. "How about a cigar maker named Ricardo Tirado?"

The orange head shook again. "Don't know him."

The elevator door opened, and they stepped into the lobby. Falcón started to head for the door, but Willie took him by the elbow and turned him around.

"You didn't tell me the truth the last time I talked to you and you're not telling me any now. Mendoza was a friend of mine and I'm running out of patience. I can make things hard for you with the police."

Falcón tried to free his arm from Willie, but he couldn't. He looked around to see who might be watching. When he turned back, he looked scared.

"You better not do this, *hombre.* You don't understand what's going on here. Somebody is going to get hurt if you don't be careful."

"Somebody's already been hurt."

"Then it will be somebody else. You'll see."

He pulled his arm from Willie's grasp. The kid hurried off and Willie watched his bright orange hair disappear out the door.

Willie was still standing there when the elevator door slid open and Don Ricardo Tirado hobbled out. His meeting with Montand and whoever else was in that room had been short.

Willie intercepted him and was about to ask about this apparently secret meeting. But just then Cooler and Calderón approached the elevator.

The moment Tirado's gaze fell on Calderón his demeanor changed. The old man was no longer the gracious tobacco legend. Just as it had two days before, the sight of Calderón made Tirado lose it. He lifted his cane and shook it, this time coming even closer to the little man's bald head.

"You came to my workshop again this morning," Tirado yelled. "I'm telling you for the last time. If you ever come near my workers again, I'll kill you."

Calderón recoiled just far enough to avoid the cane. He put on the same slimy smile he had worn two days before. Tirado saw it and looked as if he would carry out his threat right then, or at least try to. But Cooler stepped between them.

"Ricardo, I'll take care of this. I promise it won't happen again."

Tirado turned on him. "I've heard that before, but you haven't taken care of it yet. I don't have that long to live anyway, and I won't let you or this viper you employ ruin my last days. I'm warning you."

Cooler appeared desolate. Calderón, partially concealed behind him, made things even worse.

"Old man, you can die when you want, but never will you do anything to me. Already once you tried to ruin me and it didn't work."

Tirado glared at him. Willie saw the old man's color change and not for the good. All those vices he had reminisced about so fondly had definitely taken their toll. A crowd was gathering around them as well, including the Tobacco Girls, who had drifted out of the ballroom and were heading for parties upstairs. Willie stepped between the two men and took Don Ricardo by the arm.

"Why don't we end this little tea party before somebody gets hurt."

Cooler looked relieved, but then turned angrily toward Calderón, who moved away from him and disappeared into the throng of Tobacco Girls, ducking for cover. Cooler went after him.

Willie led the old man away.

"I'm telling you the truth," Tirado, said struggling to catch his breath. "If I see that man outside my workshop or if I hear that he has contacted one of my workers, I'll shoot him."

"What did he mean when he said you tried to ruin him once?" Willie asked.

The old man sneered. "He means that when he worked for me I had to fire him."

"Why was that?"

"Because he was sneaking cigars and boxes out of the workshop and augmenting his income by selling them on the side."

"And then he went to work for Cooler?"

"Yes."

"Did Cooler know about the problems you had with Calderón?"

"Yes, he knew. He called me and I told him. But he was desperate for a foreman and hired him anyway. And that's when our two companies began to have trouble. I never had anything but courteous relations with Nathan Cooler before that. Now you see where we are."

Willie's eyes narrowed. Again, the relationship between Cooler and Calderón made no sense. It was like the old story of the elephant who was afraid of the mouse.

Tirado was gazing angrily after Cooler and Calderón and now turned back to Willie.

"Do you remember when we first met, I told you I had a secret, a secret not of importance to you. Well, I'll tell you now. The doctors have discovered a cancer in me. They say I have at the most six months to live. Do you understand that I have nothing to lose? Do you understand when I say I won't let that criminal poison my last days. Not him or anyone else."

Willie was speechless. Before he could respond, Tirado hobbled away from him. Willie had wanted to ask him about his meeting in suite 717, but he hadn't. He watched as the old man made his way across the lobby as fast as his cane could propel him and then out the door, as if it was the door to the next world.

Willie looked around him, but Calderón and Cooler were gone. He turned and went to the registration desk. The same attractive black woman with the island accent was still on duty.

"Me again," Willie said. "I'm looking for another friend. His name is Clarence Ross. I'm told he's in suite 717 but I want to make sure."

"Yes, sir," she said. And she began to tap away at her computer. Something popped up on her screen. She read it and began to shake her head.

"There is no Mr. Ross in suite 717 tonight."

Before she could stop him, Willie leaned over the counter and craned his neck so he could see the screen. She scowled and swiveled it away from him, but Willie had seen what he needed. Suite 717 was registered to a Mr. Hernández—Fausto Hernández.

Fausto. That was the name Falcón had mentioned the first time he had spoken to Willie. The name of the man who had contracted him to make counterfeit cigars.

Willie gave the desk clerk his sunniest Miami smile.

"Excuse me, *querida.*"

Once again, he rode the elevator to the seventh floor. This time he walked resolutely to suite 717, knocked on the door and prepared to confront either Carlos Espada or a stranger named Fausto with connections to the counterfeit scam.

He was about to knock again when it opened. The forbidding form of Sergeant Lester Grand filled almost the entire door frame. Grand didn't seem at all surprised to see Willie, which was a hell of a lot more than Willie could say about finding him there. You could have knocked Willie over with a small cigar.

Grand smiled. "Hello, Mr. Cuesta. Nice of you stop by. Come on in."

Willie did as he was asked, and the door was closed behind him. He found Grand in the company of two other plainclothes officers who didn't bother to stand up from their chairs. Grand didn't bother to introduce them. All three were smoking cigars. A large coffeepot sat on a room-service table along with lots of used cups and a couple of open notebooks and a tape recorder. The room had the look of a surveillance operation.

"We weren't expecting you," Grand said.

"Yeah, well, I was expecting a guy named Fausto Hernández."

Grand pointed to his own broad chest. "That's me. I'm Fausto Hernández."

"Really. I thought Fausto Hernández was a guy mixed up in the counterfeiting business."

Grand nodded. "We know. That's why we used it. Just to be cute and to see who might come to see us."

"I see," Willie said.

"Well, you've had lots of callers, Mr. Hernández."

"All of those were people we asked to come see us. We're questioning people who knew Cesar Mendoza, just like I questioned you."

"Find out anything interesting?"

Grand shook his head. "Not yet. How about you?"

"No, nothing. Do you still think it might have been a simple robbery?"

"We're not making any statements about who we think might have killed Cesar Mendoza."

"Have you found any connection between his death and those two rollers who got cut up in North Miami?"

"You mean apart from the wounds to the throat of each one?"

"Yes."

"That's something else I can't tell you. Do you have any other questions?"

"Yes. How's the family?"

"Just fine."

"Good. Then I think I'll be going."

"Good idea."

Willie nodded to the two plainclothes guys, who didn't nod back.

CHAPTER TWENTY-THREE

Willie returned to the main ballroom looking for Ross. He wanted to tell the old man about the Miami Police Department suite upstairs.

He was cutting across the dance floor when he spotted Nathan Cooler. The tall man stood near the bar with a drink in his hand, his Panama hat tilted back on his head, staring desolately into space. The dancing around him made Cooler seem that much more alone.

To Willie, it appeared as if Cooler had the weight of all the world on those big shoulders. Maybe it was the death of Cesar Mendoza. Maybe his curious relationship with Calderón was wearing him down. Maybe it was the fate of Carlos Espada. Or all three.

Willie was going to leave the big man to his thoughts, but Cooler spotted him and waved him down.

"Can I speak to you for a moment?"

"Certainly."

Cooler led him to a now-empty table at the rear of the ballroom, next to a potted elephant-ear plant. They sat across from each other.

"I understand you saw Carlos yesterday. His mother told me."

Willie gave him the details. Cooler thought them over and then leaned toward Willie, his big hands folded in front of him.

"I'm going to make you an offer, Mr. Cuesta. I'll pay you $25,000 if you find Carlos and bring him to me."

Willie's eyes widened about $25,000 worth.

"That's a lot of money."

"It's worth it to me."

"What exactly is worth that much to you?"

"Not having my company dragged through the mud."

"What kind of mud are we speaking of?"

134

Cooler didn't like having to spell it out. "I think you know. Carlos Espada may be mixed up in some business activities that aren't exactly legal."

"Yes, and I also know that the wreckage in his office wasn't caused by high school kids."

"No, it wasn't. I'm worried about who he's gotten himself involved with. People like that could wreck more than an office. They could destroy a whole business."

Willie was listening, but he was also wondering just how Cooler had arrived at the $25,000 figure. Was it keyed to the value of his company, or how much he thought it would take to buy Willie? It was an interesting issue.

"So, the first time we met you lied to protect your company."

Cooler shrugged his big shoulders. "Wouldn't you? It's all I've got."

The way he said it, it sounded like an admission of defeat, an assessment of a life that had produced only some sales figures and a refurbished factory. As always, Cooler was a bit of an enigma. He was apparently sensitive enough to see the poverty of what he was saying, but he hadn't been perceptive enough to create more of a life for himself in human terms.

Willie looked away into the dancing multitude and then back at Cooler. "So if I find Carlos I simply bring him to you and we just forget his sudden drift into crime."

"Exactly. He's a good kid. He won't do it again. I'll assure you of that. I'll break him in half if he does."

"And how about if the crimes he has committed are a bit more serious than falsifying cigars?"

Cooler grimaced. "What do you mean?"

"How about if he was involved in the death of Cesar Mendoza? Then what? Do we forget that, too, for $25,000?"

Cooler was stunned. "How can you think that? Carlos would never do anything like that."

"That's what you said about his peddling phony cigars."

"Why on earth would Carlos harm Cesar?"

Willie shrugged. "Cesar suspected Carlos was involved in that nasty little business. Maybe he was going to turn him in. If I know

Cesar, he might have done it just to keep the kid from getting killed. And Carlos is a desperate and unstable man."

Cooler was glaring at him but said nothing.

Willie shook his head. "I know you think you're trying to help, but that's not the way, not trying to cover up a murder."

"I'm not trying to cover up any killing. Carlos would never hurt Cesar."

"Given what Cesar said to me, we're not dealing with a sane human being here," Willie said. "I know Cesar had heard from Carlos and Cesar was scared by something Carlos said to him. Carlos was acting crazy on the phone. He was asking questions about Ernesto Espada's death. Do you know why he would do that?"

"I don't know any more than I've told you. But I'm sure Carlos Espada had nothing to do with Cesar Mendoza's death. Believe me, once you find him I'm sure we'll be able to prove that. And my offer still stands. You know where to contact me. Now, if you'll excuse me, I'm going home."

They both stood up and Willie watched the big man wade into the crowd. He suddenly didn't trust Nathan Cooler at all. All he knew for sure was that the big man wanted to get his hands on Carlos Espada before the police did and Willie wasn't sure why. Willie wasn't about to oblige him. Instead, he went searching for Ross.

CHAPTER TWENTY-FOUR

W illie finally found Ross at the caviar stall with another glass of champagne in his hand. The old man didn't seem at all tired of the good life.

First Willie told him about Sergeant Grand's grand accommodations upstairs.

"Sounds like the Miami Police are in full undercover mode," Ross said. "That's interestin'."

Willie also passed on Nathan Cooler's generous offer. That *really* impressed the old man.

"You could buy a lot of stogies with $25,000," he said.

Finally, Willie relayed Richard Knox's invitation to join his little "soiree."

"Sounds too good to pass up, bub. The night is young."

Willie gave in. Ross collected his two bags of free cigars, and they went back down to the lobby. They left the bags with the bell captain, then headed upstairs to Knox's lair. They could hear the party the moment they got off the elevator on the sixth floor, just one level below the police.

Just inside the door of suite 690 they bumped into the girl who had worked in the private-jets booth. She was wearing an extremely small stewardess uniform, which featured a kind of low-cut leotard with epaulettes on the shoulders, fish net stockings and two jet plane pins in the middle of her breasts. A silk sash hanging over one shoulder read "Fly Me." She handed Willie and Ross another glass of champagne each, which was the last thing they needed.

The room was already curtained in cigar smoke. Many of the men had shed their suit jackets and were in short sleeves, puffing away. Willie spotted the two Hondurans, who had sat at his table.

They were dancing to *merengue* music, one with the mermaid and the other with the big redhead. The mermaid danced *merengue* very well for a woman with scales and a tail. All the Tobacco Girls were crammed into the space as well, rubbing their leaves up against the other late-night male partiers. A few of the girls had seen their tobacco leaves wilt some, so that their breasts were in full flower. In the spirit of the floor show they all just had seen, a few of the gentlemen were actively trying to harvest them.

Willie and Ross stood just inside the door for a minute, taking it all in.

"I think what we have here, bub, is what they used to call an orgy," Ross murmured.

"I think they still call it that."

A Tobacco Girl sidled passed them and through a closed door into one of the two bedrooms. Over the next few minutes Willie and Ross watched partiers of both sexes go into and come out of those rooms. Then one of the doors opened and Richard Knox appeared. He spotted Willie and Ross and drifted over.

"Got here just in time, gentlemen. The proceedings are just getting good."

Willie rolled his eyes. "So we can see. Unfortunately, I think we'll have to be going. Lots of work to do in the morning."

"Oh, that's too bad."

"But there was something I wanted to ask you earlier. Are you the same Richard Knox, the attorney who used to defend drug dealers?"

Knox froze for a moment, his perpetual grin looking like a rictus. "What does that have to do with the current price of tobacco, Mr. Cuesta?"

"Nothing. I was just curious."

"I made my living in the courts at one time and I had all sorts of clients."

"I understand you were in the dock yourself at one time. Did they charge you with actually being on the mother ship unloading drugs, or did you do your work laundering money through the banks?"

Knox shook his head. "I've never been on such a cargo ship, Mr. Cuesta, and my dealings with banks have always been strictly above board."

"So you must have been hauled into federal court for accepting fees you knew were tainted, money with traces of cocaine on it."

Knox had lost his bonhomie. "Various attorneys got caught in the legal crosscurrents of the late eighties and early nineties, Mr. Cuesta. If you look it up in the court clerk's office, you'll see I successfully fought those charges and was never convicted of anything."

"I have looked it up."

"Good. Now go find a law library, or even just a civics classroom, and you'll read that everybody, including drug smugglers, are entitled to defense counsel. It's the American way."

"So, you did it on principle. I should have known that. You have the look of a man of principle." Behind his amber shades, the glee momentarily returned to Knox's gaze.

"I am a man of principle, Mr. Cuesta. The one thing I believe above all is that no one is allowed to ruin another person's good time. You are about to spoil mine. You wouldn't want to do that, would you?"

Knox brought the cigar up to his mouth and puffed on it. In doing so the hot ember came close to Willie's face. Behind it, Knox's eyes had gone cold. And for a moment Willie remembered his brush with Fuzzy Face and his large accomplice in his bedroom two nights before. He wondered if Knox was trying to make him remember. It certainly seemed like it. Willie waved the smoke away.

"I'm sure we'll meet again," Willie said.

Knox shook his head. "I'm not sure. I'm flying to the DR tomorrow. Sorry I can't invite you to come with me. Now, I better see to my other guests."

Willie drained his champagne. "Enjoy your evening."

"You do the same, if you know how." Knox gave them a last unfriendly glance and walked away.

Ross drained his champagne as well. "This was a short party. Not very hospitable."

Willie caught a last glimpse of one of the Hondurans following the mermaid into a bedroom. He was making freestyle swimming motions, as if he were chasing her across the sea.

Willie and Ross were headed back down the corridor when the elevator door opened and out stepped someone else Willie recognized.

It was Dinah the Golden Girl, who he had last seen flying across Biscayne Bay in a cigarette boat. She was wearing a short, low-cut black dress, extremely high turquoise heels, and she carried a small matching purse. Willie assumed that the gun mentioned by Red was tucked in the purse.

It wasn't until Dinah was almost on top of them that she recognized Willie and stopped.

"Good of you to come this evening," Willie said.

She put a hand on a hip and gave him a stern look. She had the tough-girl act down cold. "I don't have any more time to talk to you now than I did yesterday."

"You owe me for the dry cleaning. You got me all wet."

"You were already all wet, if you know what I mean."

Willie smiled. He was good at playing the straight man, even with women who might be involved in murder.

She tried to walk around him, but he got in her way. That made her angry.

"Since when do I have to talk to you? You're not a real cop. You're a private investigator. In fact, yesterday you were impersonating an officer."

"And just how do you know I work for myself?"

"That's none of your business."

"Is that right? How about if I tell you my business is phony cigars. How about if I go to every marina and cigar salon in town, flash your picture, ask questions about cigar counterfeiting? I don't think you'd like that."

That made her pause and do a slow burn. She obviously didn't need that kind of trouble. "What is it you want?" she asked finally.

Willie pointed down the hallway. "On your way to see your friend, Mr. Knox?"

"What if I am?"

"Did you know he was once indicted for drug smuggling?"

She took the Fifth on that one and didn't answer.

"Why isn't Carlos Espada with you?" Willie asked.

"You'd have to ask him."

"Where is he?"

"I don't know. I'm not his legal guardian."

"Yesterday you said you'd never heard of him. Next thing I know you're going for a boat ride together."

"That's not against the law, just like going to see Richard Knox isn't. But detaining me against my will is a crime."

She suddenly sounded like an attorney, like her friend Knox.

Willie wondered how on earth a mama's boy like Carlos Espada could ever have become involved with a woman like this. Something really radical had to be going on inside for him to make this drastic a change in his feminine ideal. Willie thought of Victoria Espada, with that cordon of isolation, of solitude that always seemed to surround her no matter who was around; that alienation that came from belonging to a more graceful time and more beautiful place. He thought of Esther Espada in the same way, in that same place. And now he looked at Dinah, who looked like Las Vegas on a bad day.

He studied her face. The toughness seemed shallow, as shallow as her make-up, as phony as the cigars she had an interest in. Willie figured he'd pull her chain, maybe he'd hit the jackpot.

"How about if I tell you he has an old mother who's about to kill herself because he's missing."

For just a moment he thought he saw a glimmer of feeling in her. But it was only his own badly placed belief in common decency. She shook her head.

"I don't know anything about him or his mother."

"Well, I know about you. I've been told that you showed up on the cigar scene here about two months ago and started talking about counterfeit cigars. Shortly afterward people started showing up dead. Yesterday, Cesar Mendoza is murdered, maybe by counterfeiters. Murder is against the law. Perhaps the police would be interested in talking to you right now."

She didn't like being threatened. She showed her teeth, swung her other hip out, put her other hand on it.

"Is that right? Well, then why don't we go see the police right now?"

She turned on a heel and headed back for the elevator. When it came, she, Willie and Ross got in. She pressed L for lobby and stared Willie down as they descended. The elevator stopped, she got out and walked straight toward two cops standing near the front desk, one in uniform and one in plainclothes, both of them big. She marched right up to them.

"Do you see these two guys?" she said, indicating Willie and Ross. "They're harassing me. They're following me and I want them to leave me alone. Can't a woman walk into this place without being hounded?"

Both the cops frowned at Willie and Ross. Willie smiled and held up a hand.

"Now wait a minute, gentlemen. You don't understand . . ."

But the plainclothes guy didn't give Willie time to finish. He got in his face. "This woman says you're harassing her. There's never any excuse for harassing a lady."

"No, you don't understand. I'm Willie Cuesta, former sergeant, Miami PD. And this is Clarence Ross, former . . . "

That got him nowhere fast. Dinah began to head for the door, making her escape. Willie tried to follow her, but the plainclothes cop grabbed him by the coat. The uniformed guy blocked Ross' way.

"Not so fast. The lady said not to bother her."

Willie watched Dinah go out the door. Two minutes later, after a short lecture on possible prosecution, the cops let them go. By the time Willie and Ross got outside, Dinah was gone, swallowed up by the tropical night.

CHAPTER TWENTY-FIVE

Willie drove Ross back to his car, helped him load his cigar booty into the old Volkswagen bug and said he would call him the next day. He watched the old man take off and then started to pull around the corner to his parking space.

Before he could turn, Willie noticed something unusual. Down Calle Ocho, maybe fifteen blocks, a golden glow had appeared in the sky. It could only be a fire.

Old habits die hard, and Willie, an old patrol cop, couldn't resist. He put the car in gear and headed toward that glow. Most good cops never lost that curiosity and most good cops would also clue you in that they were just a bit psychic. Not much, just a bit. Right now, Willie felt a twinge.

He was no more than two blocks away when he saw that his suspicion had been right. Don Ricardo Tirado's business was ablaze. The front of the workshop was not yet burning, but Willie could see flames lapping the roofline at the rear.

He pulled up just as he heard the first sirens sounding in the distance. He ran down the side street and saw that the back of the building was already blazing. He also saw, at the end of the block, the silhouette of a person watching it burn. For a few moments, Willie and the silhouette both stood dead still, as if it were Willie's own shadow. But the moment Willie took a step toward it, the shadow began to run. He turned the corner quickly, maybe a hundred feet ahead of Willie.

Running hard down the middle of the street, Willie reached the corner just in time to have two shots fired at him out of the darkness. He hit the ground, rolled behind a parked car, pulled out his gun and peered around a tire. He saw nothing, but he heard running footsteps again. The shooter wasn't waiting around. Willie got up and saw the silhouette sail around the next corner. Willie cut across the lawns, but it was too late. As he turned the corner, he saw a car peeling out and disappearing from sight.

Willie walked back to Tirado Cigar and arrived just as the first firetrucks pulled up. Firefighters with axes busted the front windows, while others hooked their hose to a hydrant and began to arch a stream of water into the night so that it fell on the roof.

Willie stayed out of the way but maneuvered himself into position to see the action. The fire had started in the big back storage area where Tirado stored his tobacco. Already the night sky was full of the sweet smell. The firefighters had broken through the back windows, too, and Willie could see the tobacco leaves burning, like a big cigar ember.

Anybody who wanted to put the old man out of business, at least temporarily, would accomplish that by torching his tobacco supplies. And if it was arson, police wouldn't have to go far to find a suspect. Just two hours earlier, Tirado had been involved in a short, but bitter argument with Mario Calderón in front of a crowd of convention-eers.

It didn't take long for the firemen to extinguish the blaze. They caught it before it crawled up to the workshop area and Don Ricardo's office. A few sleepy-eyed neighbors had wandered out onto the sidewalk. A couple of patrol units had cordoned off the street, but Willie was already inside the cordon, and they didn't hassle him. A fire captain and other firefighters crouched over a spot in the alley behind the storage room and Willie joined them.

Unnoticed, Willie peeked over the captain's shoulder. He was inspecting the butt of a cigar lying on the macadam. Leading away from it was a charred line that had apparently been gasoline, kerosene or some other accelerant. It wasn't hard to figure out. Someone, probably the silhouetted man, had used the cigar as a fuse, and waited within sight to make sure it did the job.

Willie craned forward to see better. "What kind of cigar is it? What brand?"

The captain turned the cigar over with a pencil point so that they could all see the label. It was a Great American Corona. Cooler's company—and Calderón's too.

Only then did the firefighters notice Willie. The captain, a guy named Fuchs, knew Willie from his days in Patrol.

"What are you doing here?"

"I saw the flames, that's all. And I know the guy who owns it."

"Maybe you should give him a call."

Willie took out his cellphone, but he didn't call Tirado. The old man had already had enough excitement for one night. He would find out soon enough. Instead, Willie called Knox, ringing the hotel and being put through to suite 690. A woman answered over the noise in the background, and it took a couple of minutes to get Knox out of a bedroom.

"Sorry to take you away from your soiree," Willie said. He informed him about the fire. Knox said he would be there as soon as possible.

Willie caught up with Fuchs in the charred back room. What had been bales of tobacco were now smoldering heaps of ash. It looked as if a giant had been smoking an enormous cigar and had flicked ash everywhere.

"Doesn't look good," Willie said.

Fuchs shrugged. "Actually, the guy who owns this was lucky. Either the people who did it didn't know what they were doing, or somebody was just trying to cause limited damage."

"Why's that?"

"Because if they had wanted to destroy the place, it would have been easy. They would have used more accelerant and they would have poured it all the way into the front room. They didn't. It was almost like they wanted us to get here before the whole place burned."

Fuchs led Willie back outside. Knox pulled up a few minutes later in his white stretch limo. He gave Willie a chilly glance.

"One can't go anywhere these days without bumping into you, Mr. Cuesta."

Fuchs told Knox there was no doubt it was arson. Since arson, as often as not, was perpetrated by the owners of buildings so they could collect insurance, Fuchs asked Knox about his whereabouts in the last hour or two. Knox told Fuchs about being at the Hamilton Hotel, although not the details of his activities there. Then he pointed to Willie.

"All you have to do is ask that man. He will not only tell you where I and my partner were tonight, but he can tell you who almost certainly did this."

Fuchs frowned at Willie. "You don't say."

Willie shrugged. "I can't tell you who did this. But I will confirm that Ricardo Tirado, Mr. Knox's partner, got into an argument with another man. Threats were exchanged."

"And who was this man?"

"His name is Mario Calderón. He works for the Great American Tobacco Company."

Fuchs made a face. "Just like the band on that cigar in the alley."

"No question about it."

Fuchs wrote it all down in a small notebook. He wouldn't inspect the case himself. Fire marshals would handle that and there was little doubt where they would start.

Knox stared into the charred shell of his storage area and scowled.

"It could have been worse," Willie told him. He related what Fuchs had said about the lack of accelerant.

Knox sneered. "I don't think these fuckers did us any favors. I think they wanted to burn us down. These people are jackals."

"You don't know it was Calderón."

"Calderón and Nathan Cooler."

Willie shook his head. "I don't think Cooler is the type to try this kind of thing."

"You don't know what has happened to people in this business. Now that they see a chance to be rich, they turn into jackals. I'm telling you."

Willie didn't argue. There were moments when you couldn't tell the jackals without a scorecard. Willie didn't have his scorecard figured out. He decided to go home and sleep on it. He left Richard Knox staring into the smoky rubble.

CHAPTER TWENTY-SIX

The night echoed with the sound of Willie's heels on the sidewalk as he walked from the corner parking lot to his apartment. Apart from that, it was dead quiet. But before he could open his front door someone called his name. He turned around quickly and saw Esther Espada emerge from a car parked across the street. It was past midnight, and they were the only two people in sight.

She walked up to him still dressed as she had been at the dinner, her white shoulders gleaming above her blouse.

"What are you doing here at this hour?" he asked.

She held out an envelope. "I told you I would bring you Carlos' phone bills for the past month."

Willie took it from her. "Yes, but I didn't think you meant tonight."

"Well, I'm here now. Are you going to turn me away?"

She looked at him the way she had the first time they'd met. It was a naked gaze that dared you to say no.

Willie opened the door and led her upstairs. He switched on the ceiling fans, opened the windows and turned on a Jerry Rivera CD. A song came on about falling stars and how they cross paths with the sounds of love that rise into the night sky. Esther glanced at the CD player, then at Willie, looked around the apartment and took a seat without waiting to be asked.

"I know it's late, but I think I'd like a drink," she said.

"Will rum do?"

"On the rocks, please."

Willie brought out a bottle and two glasses with ice. It was never acceptable to have a guest drink alone.

They touched glasses and then Willie opened the envelope. It contained two bills, one for Carlos' home phone and another for his cellular. The bills were pages long, mostly filled with calls inside Florida, but about four weeks earlier Espada had suddenly started calling two numbers in the Dominican Republic. Some days he called only once. Other days it was several times. After about two weeks, the calls had abruptly stopped.

Willie read the whole list and showed the DR calls to Esther. "Do you have any idea why your brother would have called the Dominican Republic? His distribution territory, after all, was up here."

She shook her head. "He's never done any business there."

"Does he have any friends he might call down there?"

She thought about that. "No one except that woman in the photograph. On the back, it said that photo was taken in the Dominican Republic. Before her, there was nobody."

She wasn't any happier discussing Dinah now than she had been before. Willie decided not to tell her about his run-in with the blonde earlier in the evening. Instead, he picked up the phone and dialed the first Dominican number on the list. According to the bill, the number was in Puerto Plata, which Willie knew was a port town on the north coast of the island. It would be the same time there as in Miami.

It rang several times and then a woman answered. "Hotel Tropical, *buenas noches.*"

Willie said nothing. He simply hung up. That number had been called no less than a half dozen times in a matter of days.

He dialed the only other Dominican number. It was in a place called Santiago, which Willie didn't know. This time a man answered, sounding a bit sleepy.

"Hotel Jardín."

Again, Willie hung up. He sipped his rum.

"They're both hotels."

She shrugged. "Where else could he stay with that woman? He has no house down there."

"One is on the coast and that is probably where the photo on the beach was taken. The other hotel is in a town called Santiago. I don't know where that is."

"It is a city in the center of the island where they make cigars," she said.

"You've been there?"

She shook her head. "No, but I've heard of it. Many of the cigar companies have factories there."

"Did your brother ever have business reasons for going there while he worked for Great American?"

"Not that I know."

Willie sipped his rum and for a minute they both fell into silence. Jerry Rivera was still singing about those falling stars and sighs of love. Esther, meanwhile, was making a study of Willie's apartment. She finally broke the silence, speaking to him, but not looking at him.

"You live here alone."

"That's right."

"But you didn't always live here alone."

She was staring at a small round end table with a delicate crimson vase on it, which had become Willie's property after his divorce.

"No. At one time, I lived here with my wife."

"How long were you married?"

"About two years. It ended five years ago."

"And you've lived here alone since?"

"Yes."

"That's a long time to live alone."

Willie sipped. "You've lived alone longer than that."

She frowned. "No. I've never lived alone. I've always lived with my mother and my brother."

Willie looked into her face. "I wasn't talking about family. I meant you've gone a long time without living with a man."

Her eyes narrowed and she sipped her rum. Willie thought she would rebuke him for his unwanted familiarity, but she didn't. Jerry Rivera made it through another stanza and finally she said in a disembodied voice, "People have always whispered about me."

"Is that right? What have they whispered about?"

"The fact that I've never had a husband."

"Does that make any difference to you?"

She met his gaze. "Not really, but some of them also think that I've never had a lover. I'm thirty-five years old and people think that. It isn't true."

For a moment Willie didn't know what to say. Here was this woman who had a reputation for being beautiful but bloodless, an image out of the past. And now, past midnight, sitting over rum, she was suddenly looking him in the eye and, in a fashion that no one could ever call bloodless, revealing to him her love life, or at least the fact that she had one. She didn't give him a chance to respond.

"Because I don't have a husband doesn't mean that I spend all my nights alone," she said looking away from him again. "It's like you. You're not married, but I'm told you spend very few nights by yourself."

Willie shrugged. "As in your case, sometimes the stories aren't quite true."

She stood up and walked to the window overlooking the back garden.

"One gets tired of maintaining an image for so many years. Sometimes I don't even remember how it began. I guess that's because it began even before I was born. But I know I want it to end."

She turned around then. Her gaze was matter-of-fact, nothing steamy or tempestuous. But she kept staring at him until Willie got up and went toward her. The only woman he had slept with in months was Amy. But Amy had told him, for now, they would just be friends. The look in Esther Espada's eyes had nothing to do with friendship.

They stood there for a long time kissing. When he first put his arms around her she asked that he do it tighter. When he started to move his hands over her, she asked him to do it harder. Willie had strong hands and he moved them over the muscles of her back and shoulders and buttocks and thighs and more gently over her breast. Even then she asked him to rub her harder.

Willie had been lovers with women who had gone a long time without men. He knew to go very slowly. One had almost to bring a body back to life with one's hands, make the blood flow, create feeling, sensuality, desire in muscles that had gone too long without the heat of desire. He had to create that heat on the skin and in those muscles and let it sink slowly into her. He had to squeeze all the loneliness out, the doubt. All the while he had to be gentle, too, so that she wouldn't be scared of him. Soft kisses on her face, over her eyes, fingers that just grazed her cheek, whispering to her that it was all right.

With Esther it was like nothing he'd ever encountered. She kept him there a long time. She would kiss him suddenly, crushing her mouth against his, then pull away. There was passion in her eyes but despair as well. They did this again and again and it was as if he were trying to bring a ghost back to life, and she was straining to become real human flesh for him.

After a while she stepped back from him and pulled the blouse down below her breasts. He kissed her breasts and then her stomach and when he reached below her belly she emitted the first sound of pure pleasure that had escaped her. He pulled all her clothing down over her hips until it lay in a pile on the floor. Then he led her to the bedroom, parted the mosquito netting and laid her down. They made love, not gently, not tentatively, but with their hands still roving desperately over each others' bodies. When at last her moment came, her hands stopped moving and dug into his back, as if she were digging for something under his skin, the same something he had reached under *her* skin.

When they had finished, they lay under the netting on their backs side by side, their arms barely touching. She kept her eyes closed. She might have been a dead person except for the slow rise and fall of her breast. On the CD player, Jerry Rivera's song had come up again. The stars were still falling and the sighs rising.

Willie watched her and thought about everything that had happened in the last three days. He wondered what had made this happen tonight. Was it her brother's escape from the nest that had brought this on? From years of police work, Willie had learned that families were nests of fierce emotions, sometimes as bad as they were good, as destructive as they were life-giving. He had investigated murders within families, and he had seen violence passed down through generations. He had seen families that operated like secret societies, hiding sins and crimes for decades from the outside world. He had seen those secrets eventually cause explosions, bloodshed. He knew how much could be concealed by blood ties, how histories

could be so entwined that the innocent felt guilty and the guilty innocent. But only for so long. It was Willie's experience that it all came
out in the end.

Willie watched her. She had decided to step out of that role she
always played and into this love scene. It turned out to be a cameo,
a very brief one. She opened her eyes, got up and dressed, while
Willie watched her through the gauze of the netting. When she was
finished, she looked again like the image on the cigar box. She came
back to the bed, still gazing at him through the cloth.

"Remember this and remember me," she said.

"I'll never forget it."

"I hope so." She said it as if she would hold him to it some day,
a favor she would call in.

Then she leaned in, kissed Willie once on the lips and walked
out quickly, so that he was left only with a hazy image of her that
might have been real and then again, might not.

CHAPTER TWENTY-SEVEN

Willie dragged himself out of his tangled sheets at ten o'clock the next morning. He shrugged on his worn silk robe, microwaved a *café con leche* and went downstairs to fetch the morning paper.

He turned on the CD player and listened to Willy Chirino's "Oxígeno"—"Oxygen"—which was about a woman, but which also got his lungs working in the morning with the proper rhythm.

The story of the blaze at Tirado Cigar had apparently broken too late to make the news. But there was a new story on the killing of Cesar Mendoza. Grand had told a reporter that the murder might be the result of a robbery, but that he was not eliminating the possibility that Cesar's death might be related to the recent killing of two cigar counterfeiters in North Miami.

"It's a business that's been growing for some time and getting more violent," Grand said.

Willie also read a feature story on the cigar show the night before. It didn't mention the counterfeiting issue. The reporter had missed it.

Willie put down the paper and called Ross. The old man answered on the second ring.

"Haylo."

"*Buenos días.*"

It took Ross a moment to translate. "Yes, it is a good mornin', *amigo.* I was just enjoying a breakfast 'ceegar' after a nice plate of grits and bacon."

Willie tried not to picture Ross' arteries. The thought depressed him.

"Well, it's not as good a morning for Ricardo Tirado. His place got torched last night."

Willie recounted for Ross the events that had transpired after they had parted. He also reminded him of the verbal fireworks between Tirado and Calderón.

"Well, that's one thing about you Latins. Often there's not a lot of ponderin' that goes into these things. One moment there's an argument, next moment the fuses come out."

Willie squinted. "Now you're getting offensive, old man."

Ross chuckled and Willie could hear him pull on his cigar. "I'll tell ya what I really think. Right off the bat I think it sounds just a little bit too durned neat."

"Does it?"

"Yes, it does, my friend. We've both seen cases over the years where two guys get into it over a bottle of hooch and one of them ends up in the ER or the morgue. But this time we're talking two businesses, not two drunks in an alley."

Willie thought that over. "Did you read the paper this morning? Sergeant Grand says the killing of Cesar Mendoza might be connected to those murders in North Miami."

"Always way ahead of the game, that Grand."

"One has to wonder if the torching of Tirado's place last night isn't also tied in."

"Time will tell, *amigo*. I'd just go easy and not jump to conclusions."

Willie told Ross he had to get a start on the day, and they agreed to speak later. He hung up, drained his coffee, shaved, dressed, turned off "Oxígeno" and headed for the car.

First, he drove to his mother's for a quick morning snack. He found her serving a customer, an old lady in an apron with cows on it, who was purchasing an aerosol spray that assured peace in your home. The lady was also buying one of Mama's natural medicines, which was wrapped in plain brown paper. She stuck it deep in her large purse, as if Willie might be able to divine what it was.

Mama watched her go. "That woman came in a few minutes ago and told me she was having trouble recently with her husband. I recommended that she buy the 'Peaceful Home Spray.' But then she began to discuss her husband's irritable disposition and how when he was younger and more virile, he maintained a better mood. I realized then that she had come here to purchase some of the sexual potion, but she was embarrassed to ask me. The word has spread in the neighborhood over these last few days that I have developed a potent medicine. I just hope they use it in moderation. I don't want my customers to end up dead."

"Well, I'm here this morning for your breakfast potion," Willie said.

His mother led him into her kitchen and prepared his second *café con leche* of the morning. She also toasted him some fresh Cuban bread and put butter on it. Then she sat down across from him with a look of displeasure.

"You didn't call me to tell me when Cesar Mendoza died."

Willie shook his head. "I figured it would upset you and that you would hear soon enough."

She stared off in the direction of a life-sized statue of Santa Barbara that stood in the corner of the room, which she also used for private spiritual consultations.

"It's sad, but I always knew it would end like this for him. It was just a matter of time. A blind man like him, running a business by himself and the violent world in which we live."

Willie swallowed some of his bread and washed it down with coffee. "Some people, I'm sure, are surprised he lasted as long as he did."

She nodded. "He used to come in here all the time. For many years he was a customer. He would always purchase that love potion that so many are interested in now."

Willie's brows danced. He had been wrong about randy old Cesar. The blind man did need a little pick-me-up. "I always knew Cesar was a lady's man, but I didn't know you were his supplier, his accomplice."

She made a face at him. "I used to tell him to be careful that he didn't try to do too much. He wasn't young anymore. He would always smile at me but say nothing. When I first heard he was dead, I wondered if it wasn't a woman who had done it."

"Had he been in here lately?"

"Just last week. He picked up a new supply of the powder."

"You didn't tell me this before."

She shook her head. "Like a doctor, that information must always be kept private. But now that he's dead, it's different."

"Well, he might have been killed by a lover. I don't think so, but maybe."

His mother shrugged. "It is always one or the other, women or money, that leads men to early deaths. And sometimes both. But Cesar was a good man. I'm praying to the spirits for him every day."

The bell over the front door sounded and she got up. Willie finished his *café* and gave her a kiss good-bye.

"You be careful in these days," she told him. "Anyone who will hurt a blind man will hurt you too."

Willie said he would be careful, then he left, passing another old lady feigning innocence at the counter.

CHAPTER TWENTY-EIGHT

Willie headed west and north toward Hialeah. The night before Rolando Falcón had shined him on. But now with the police looking into the possibility that Cesar Mendoza had been killed in connection with counterfeiting, maybe the kid would decide it was time to come in from the cold.

Willie passed the Hialeah firehouse, turned and spotted the bright blue building. He was still a block away when he saw Falcón hurry out of the apartment complex and head for a motorcycle parked in front. With that crop of bright orange hair, you couldn't miss him. He jumped on the cycle, kick started it, revved his engine loudly and sped off down the street. Wondering why he was in that much of a hurry, Willie fell in about a half block behind him.

They didn't go far. Falcón led Willie a few blocks to a commercial strip in central Hialeah and then he suddenly pulled over and parked his bike in front of an old cigar store that had been there for years, called Tabacos El Paraíso—Paradise Tobaccos. This wasn't a big new fancy locale, like The Humidor on Miami Beach, or a real aficionado's supply depot, like Cesar Mendoza's shop on Calle Ocho. It was a narrow hole-in-the-wall that sold cheap stogies. It featured a service window for sidewalk customers and a few formica tables along one wall where smokers could light up cigars and sip Cuban coffee.

Falcón disappeared inside. Willie parked just down the street and approached on foot. Most of the clientele at the formica tables were old Cuban gentlemen in aged Panama hats and faded *guayaberas,* chewing on dark, evil-looking cigars and sipping from thimble-size, plastic espresso cups. At a couple of tables these men played dominos. They would probably play all day, with maybe a short break for lunch. It seemed to Willie that over the years anytime he passed this place those very same men had been hunched in those very same chairs, chewing those same cigars and slapping down those same dominos with the same epithets and same judgments on the political events of the day. They lived in a pall of cigar smoke as thick as a cloud. If the store was "paradise," these were the gods.

What was different today among the "gods" was the presence of Rolando Falcón, who took the table all the way in the back, and the woman who was sitting with him. Willie saw first the thick black hair and then the white streak and realized it was Victoria Espada. Wearing a dark suit and sunglasses, seated next to the punker with the orange hair, she completed a very strange couple indeed.

Willie stepped quickly away from the doorway so neither she nor Falcón would notice him. He positioned himself on the sidewalk to watch their conversation through the very edge of the window.

Right away he could see that Victoria Espada was upset. She seemed to be pleading with Falcón. He was listening and trying to calm her. But he also shook his head repeatedly, as if she were asking something that he couldn't, or wouldn't, tell her. At one point Willie thought the woman would cry, and at another that she would strike the kid. She did neither. After five minutes the drama ended. Falcón got up and made his exit.

Willie turned away and studied a shop window next door so that Falcón wouldn't see his face. The kid jumped on his bike and streaked away. Willie figured he'd catch up with him later. Right now, he wanted to speak with Victoria Espada.

She was still sitting at the table, a plastic cup before her, staring off into the steam rising from the big chrome espresso maker, as if she were seeing something no one else could see. Willie sat down before she could invite him, or not invite him.

"Interesting company you're keeping lately, Mrs. Espada."

She looked at him and for a moment she couldn't speak. When she did, she was offended. "So now you are following me? You're not paid to do that. You were paid to find my son, which you haven't done."

"If people like you and Mr. Falcón had told me everything they knew from the beginning, I might have found him already."

"I've told you everything I know."

"You didn't tell me you knew Rolando Falcón, a man suspected of working in a counterfeiting ring. A man who just two days ago denied he knew your son and didn't mention that he knew *you*."

Her gaze was full of regal disdain. "I'd never met him before today."

Willie made a face. "And I suppose you just happened to bump into him here."

She shook her head. "No. I called him this morning. Last night at the convention I heard someone talking about him. They said he had been questioned about the counterfeiting of cigars. I know what people are saying about my son, Mr. Cuesta. I'm not as removed from reality as some people think. I will do anything to find him before something happens to him."

"What did he just say to you?"

"He told me just what he told you two days ago. He said he's never met my son. Never heard of him. I don't believe him."

"What else did he say to you?"

"Nothing. He told me he was in a hurry and then he left."

She stared toward the door through which Falcón had disappeared and then she turned back to Willie, the anger gone, replaced by pain.

"I'm very, very worried, Mr. Cuesta. I have been through many tragedies in my life, but I have never been as worried as I am now. The death of Cesar Mendoza has left me so I don't sleep at night. I have nightmares. Believe me, I'm willing to give up my own life just to get my son back."

"I don't think that will be necessary, Mrs. Espada."

"My son is not a hard man," she went on, as if she hadn't heard him. "He has always done what I asked of him. So now, all of a sudden, when he no longer comes to me and I begin to hear malicious rumors, then I fear that something very terrible is going on inside him. That maybe someone has said something to him that has suddenly changed him, turned him against me. Maybe I shouldn't have asked him and his sister to live the way I have, but it was the only way I knew, the only way I could imagine. Now I feel our family is falling apart after we have struggled so hard over the years to survive. That *all* the gods have turned against us."

One of the cigar-chewing gods in a Panama hat glanced at her over his thick-framed glasses, as if he had been referred to personally. A flush-faced man, he squinted blearily through his own smoke, and then turned back and slapped another domino down on the formica.

Victoria Espada touched Willie's hand to bring back his attention. "Please, if you find him before I do, tell him to come to me. That he should not abandon me. That I have always loved him and his sister more than anything. That our love can survive whatever it is that is happening inside him. Whatever it is. And that his father would not have wanted him to do this. Never!"

In their previous meeting, the woman had spoken of her family's tragedies, but she had contained herself, like an actress in a play. Now Willie felt her pain in a way he hadn't before. Maybe she had never before faced the possibility of her son dying before her. But she was also saying that, somehow, she had failed Carlos. Living in the past had not prepared him for the real world and led him into perdition. And the fact was it was true. Willie wanted to tell her not to feel that, but the depth of her feeling was such that he knew better than to argue with her. Suddenly she seemed not so deluded as before and that made her pain more immediate. It was as if she had woken from a dream, a decades-long fantasy, and was now facing the consequences of her choices. There wasn't much anyone could do to lighten that load, except to find her son before something happened to him.

"I'll try and bring him back to you," he said.

She stared at him mutely, hope and resignation battling in her ravaged eyes.

Then he escorted her out, the sound of a domino slapping a table behind them.

CHAPTER TWENTY-NINE

Willie drove to the Hamilton Hotel and parked again in the lot. The place was not as busy as it had been the night before, but about ten taxis were standing outside.

Willie walked down the taxi rank and showed each driver the photo of Dinah. The drivers tended to work long shifts, sometimes twelve hours. The guy who had picked her up the night before might already be back on the job.

Willie was one car from the end of the line when he hit pay dirt. A bug-eyed, chubby Latin guy nodded when Willie showed him the photo.

"Oh, yeah. I have her in my cab last nigh'."

"Do you remember where you took her?"

The cabbie hesitated. He didn't know Willie. So, Willie handed him a business card. He also let the cabbie see the corner of a twenty-dollar bill under the photo.

"I don't want to harass her or arrest her. I just need to talk to her."

The cabbie licked his lips, took the photo and the twenty, handed back the photo without the twenty, then looked down at his log.

"Eleven o'clock last nigh' I go here."

He held up the log with his finger pointing to an entry that said 428 Edgewater Drive, Coral Gables.

"Thank you for your time," Willie said.

He hustled back to the car and headed for the address. Willie had been to a house on Edgewater Drive some ten years back. He had been dragged to a party one night at the home of a television executive. Willie remembered that the neighborhood was jungle-like with vegetation and that the houses were big and pricey, with backyards giving onto a canal that flowed into Biscayne Bay. Another guest that night had told him there was a lot of narcotics money in that neighborhood. "Nouveau rich and beaucoup drugs, *amigo*."

Willie found the address the cabbie had provided and cruised by it slowly. The house was walled, but through the gate he could see it was large and constructed in a Japanese style. A gallery with a peaked roof led from the house to a gazebo, which sat next to the canal in back. The two structures were surrounded by carefully tended flower gardens. A silver Jaguar sedan sat in the driveway. If Dinah was in the cigar counterfeiting business, she was doing very well at it.

On the property next door, construction was in progress. Willie drove by several pickup trucks in that driveway and parked beyond them. He opened his glove compartment, took out a couple of pens and clipped them onto the pocket of his shirt. Then he opened the trunk and picked up an old clipboard he had left over from his days on the Miami PD.

Properly armed, he walked onto the property.

A big guy in an orange hard hat glanced at Willie as he headed around the corner of the house.

"City Building Department," Willie said. "Just here to take a look."

"We pulled all our permits last week. They're posted on the wall over here."

So, Willie obliged him, marching up to a wall next to the front door to study the designated permits for a minute. He nodded officiously.

"Yep, everything seems in order. I don't want to take you away from your work. Thanks."

The other man headed back to his sawhorses. Willie, meanwhile, drifted around the side of the house holding his clipboard, stopping for a moment to direct a professional eye at workmen installing window sashes. He nodded in approval and continued to roam until he reached the very back of the lot. He stood overlooking the canal, right next to the wall that bounded Dinah's property. He poked his head around the end of it and saw, tied to a pylon, the same black cigarette boat on ·which he had spotted Carlos Espada two days before.

Willie pulled his head back, checked to make sure none of the workmen were watching him and stepped right around the end of the wall. He put his foot on a pylon and then stepped onto Dinah's property, ducking behind a stand of oriental palms. From there he could look along the roofed gallery and into the living room.

The interior continued the Japanese motif and even featured big cushions on the floor. The sliding glass doors were open, but he saw nobody in the main room. Willie angled across the lawn slowly and when he reached the glass doors, he peeked in. The morning newspaper was lying in sections on the floor next to the cushions, along with two coffee cups. The Shogun and Dinah had apparently already consumed their *café con leche.*

Willie heard the sound of a radio coming from beyond the living room. He walked silently across that room, pulled his gun from his back holster and peeked through the next doorway, which faced the front of the house. He saw Carlos Espada sitting alone at a long table. He wore a white terry-cloth robe and looked like he hadn't shaved in several days. The life of leisure.

The table before him was piled with loose cigars. Cigar boxes were stacked all around him. They were labeled "Embajador"— "Ambassador"—the ultimate Havanas. On the table behind Espada lay a slew of seals, the kind that genuine Havanas carried on their boxes, hundreds of seals from the looks of it. If you figured they made hundreds, sometimes a few thousand dollars per box, there were enough boxes and seals to pay the rent on this pagoda for a long time.

Willie had never witnessed this kind of operation before. He had assumed that such a factory would be found in a crummy, back alley locale. But if you were making the kind of money Carlos and Dinah were making lately, then you could afford to live it up.

Dinah walked into the room now. She was dressed down this time, in jeans with a white blouse, the tails of which were tied around her taut, tanned stomach. Like Espada, she didn't appear to be armed. She asked Carlos to help her with something, but before they could leave the room, Willie entered behind his gun.

"Hold on a minute," he said.

They both whirled around and just as quickly they saw the .38. Espada's mouth fell open and he looked scared. Dinah bared her nice white teeth and wagged a finger at Willie.

"This time you're in big fucking trouble," she said through those teeth.

"This time there isn't a gullible cop to help you get away."

She didn't drop her finger. "I'm going to tell you this one time only. You don't know who you're messing with."

"I know I'm probably messing with the people who killed Cesar Mendoza. I know he was waiting for your friend, Mr. Espada here, right around the time he died. Nobody ever saw him alive again."

It was Espada who blurted out an answer. "We would never kill Cesar," he began, but Dinah cut him off.

"Don't say anything."

Willie kept his eyes on Espada. His strategy was to divide and conquer. "I saw your mother today. This is just about killing her. She thinks you've turned against her."

Pain flashed in Espada's eyes. Willie had never met Carlos Espada before. But somehow this was exactly as he had pictured him, with that pain in his eyes, the anguish of someone caught in an emotional tug of war between the history of his family and the need to survive in the present, a disjunction that he hadn't handled very well. Just like now. With a gun pointed at him, he was obviously doing a bad job of survival.

Carlos Espada continued to gape at him. "I would never abandon her," he repeated. "She knows that."

"She didn't know that two hours ago. She says you have never had secrets from her the way you do now."

For a moment Carlos Espada's look of pain disappeared. In fact, he even got a curdled smile that reminded Willie of Esther Espada.

"We've always had secrets in our family. It's in our blood."

Willie squinted at him. He didn't understand what Carlos meant by that. He would have asked him, but he didn't have a chance.

Suddenly there was a very loud sound outside. It made all of them flinch. At first Willie thought it was the construction crew next door. But even as he tried to keep the handgun on the other two, out of the corner of his eye Willie saw the big wrought-iron gate at the foot of the driveway suddenly buckle and collapse. A large black

SUV came crashing through the gate and three men jumped out, all carrying small automatic weapons. They took aim at the windows of the front room and wasted no time trying to kill Willie, Carlos and Dinah.

All three of them hit the floor just as the windows shattered over them. Willie looked up to see the three attackers heading for the house. He pulled off two quick shots, which sent the men diving for the ground. From there, they sprayed the house again. Willie ducked but had enough time to see that one of them wore a red cap and had a big moustache. He figured it might be Fuzzy Face, his visitor of two nights before. One of the guys with him was very large, with stringy, long brown hair down to his shoulders. Willie figured that might be the giant who had acted as Fuzzy Face's accomplice. It appeared that this visit would be no more pleasant than the last, maybe worse.

Dinah, meanwhile, had crawled into the next room and returned with her own gun. She stood peeking around the doorway, the gun held expertly in both hands. A moment later the big guy tried to make it from behind a bed of azaleas to the trunk of a palm tree. Before he could get halfway, Dinah pulled off three shots. The big guy was knocked off course by the first and downed by the last two. That sent the other two guys ducking for cover.

Dinah turned to Espada, who was hiding behind the overturned table.

"We're getting out of here now."

Espada crawled to the doorway. Once he was safe he got up and sprinted for the back of the house. Willie started to move in the same direction, but Dinah's gun swung around until it was pointed at him. Half concealed by the doorway, she had the advantage.

"It's just like last time. You're not coming." She held the gun on him another moment and then she was gone.

Just then, more shots hit the house. Willie returned fire, shooting toward the azaleas. Moments later he heard the cigarette boat in the canal roar to life. He rolled toward the doorway and reached the open doors of the living room in time to see Dinah and Espada do their escape act again.

Then he heard another engine start up. He ran back to the front room in time to see Fuzzy Face and his other buddy back their SUV wildly out of the driveway and go screeching down Edgewater Drive.

Willie waited, poked his head out of the front door to make sure no one else was lurking, then walked carefully across the lawn to where the big man lay. One of Dinah's shots had caught him in the left hip and another square in the temple. He was as dead as he was big, which was very.

Willie was crouching over him when he heard the first sirens sounding in the distance. He also heard a closer sound and looked up to see the same construction worker in the orange hard hat peeking over the wall at him.

The man looked amazed. "I thought you were with the Building Department."

CHAPTER THIRTY

It took the first patrol units only a couple of minutes to arrive. Willie gladly handed over his gun and told them they'd better call Lester Grand.

It was an hour later that Grand pulled up. He lumbered over the defunct wrought-iron gate and considered the big corpse for a few minutes, as was his style. Then he walked over to Willie, who was sitting in a lawn chair near the azaleas.

"This is becoming a habit, Willie."

Willie shrugged. "I'm not sure twice constitutes a habit, Lester. But I understand your concern."

"Who is that gentleman lying there?"

Willie shook his head. "I don't know. I've never had the pleasure."

"Did you have the pleasure of shooting him?"

"No. The lady of the house shot him. You just missed her. She left in a cigarette boat."

"And who is that lady?"

"Her name is Dinah. I don't have a last name yet, but I tried to get one of your men to detain her last night at the Hamilton Hotel in connection with the murder of Cesar Mendoza. He didn't have time for it. Now this gentleman here is dead, although I have to admit she shot him in self-defense."

Willie told Grand everything that had happened since he had arrived at the house. He even provided him a brief tour of the counterfeiting operation and then they walked back outside. Grand stepped away to place a call on his cellular. After a brief conversation, he walked back.

"You can go now, Willie."

Willie looked surprised. "Well, this has been quick." He had to wonder who Grand had called.

"If I need to find you, I know where to look."

"When do I get my gun back?"

"When we're sure that your gun didn't kill this big guy."

"A few days."

"About that. In the meantime, I'd like you to do two things. The first is that you not speak to the media at any time about what happened here. We have our reasons for not wanting this out right now."

"No problem. I've never been crazy for the camera."

"The second thing is that you spend as much time as possible on some other case."

"I don't have any other case right now, Lester."

"Find one. We don't need another corpse. Two is enough."

"I'll do what I can to keep breathing so that it doesn't cost you more work."

"There's another reason. This is an open homicide investigation and butting in where you don't belong could get you put in jail for a time. Obstruction of justice."

Willie feigned fear. "How long do you think I would get for trying to find who killed a friend of mine, Lester? Twenty-five years, or would they give me life without parole?"

Grand made a face. "You've never been a fool, Willie. Don't start now."

"You've never tried to strong-arm me, Lester, so don't start now. We're on the same side here. Let's keep it that way."

Willie reclaimed his clipboard from the lawn chair, said good afternoon, clambered over the crushed gate and reached his car. Some construction workers were standing in the street and watched him.

They'd never seen a building department inspector quite like him before and they probably wouldn't ever again.

* * *

Getting shot at made one perspire inordinately and Willie wanted to go home and change. But he wanted to speak to Rolando Falcón even more.

He headed back to Hialeah, which was about halfway across the county, battling rush-hour traffic all the way. It was after six when he got there, and he didn't see the motorcycle out front. He parked, climbed the stairs to Falcón's apartment, heard music inside and knocked. The door opened, but it wasn't Falcón. It was the girl with the purple hair. Behind her on the floor, he saw a couple of suitcases open and clothes piled on a chair, as if she was packing.

"I'm looking for Rolando," Willie said.

She shook her head. "He's not here."

She tried to close the door, but Willie put his foot in it.

"Where is he?"

She seemed to understand from Willie's tone that the interrogation would be different this time. "I don't know. He left an hour ago."

"He didn't tell you where he was going or who he was going to see?"

"He didn't have time to tell me. People came for him and he left."

"Which people?"

"A man and a woman."

"What did they look like?"

She shrugged. "Like anybody."

"Was she blonde? Was the guy Cuban?"

She shrugged again. "Yeah."

"And he didn't tell you anything about where he was going?"

"I don't want to know. I never wanted to know. If he's going to get in trouble again, then I'm going to be someplace else."

"Did you ever see those two individuals before?"

She hesitated.

"Tell me, or I'll call the cops right now and you'll tell them."

She nodded. "They came here about a month ago, right after he got busted. They took him outside and talked to him for a while. The next thing I know he's off rolling cigars somewhere. He told me he wouldn't get mixed up with anybody doing anything wrong, not anymore, and he said this was strictly legal. But now I don't know. Somebody called him this morning and he left in a hurry. He came back and now these people come and he leaves right away like he's running from something."

"Did he pack up, too?"

"No. He said he'd come back to do that. But he told me I should get out of here. Go stay somewhere for a few days. But I'm not coming back at all. I'm just waiting for a call from a friend and I'm going to move in with her. This is all too weird for me."

"I'd say that's a timely decision, *querida*."

Willie thanked her and headed home. When he got there, he showered and served himself some dinner—Cuban-Chinese takeout he'd picked up along the way.

He was just finishing when his doorbell rang. Given the events of the day, he took precautions. He brought out his extra handgun, made sure it was loaded and then descended the stairs. He cracked the curtain while ducking off to one side. Standing on the steps was Jean Philippe Montand. His chauffeured car was at the curb.

Willie opened the door.

"What is it?"

Montand appeared even more rattled than he had at the convention when he'd described being detained by the police.

"I need to talk to you right away," he said.

"About what? I've had a long day already."

"Carlos Espada just came to see me. He threatened me."

Willie poked his head out the door to make sure no one else was waiting around. Then he let Montand in. They climbed the stairs and Willie brought out a bottle of rum and a glass, pouring Montand a healthy shot. He looked like he needed it. The Swiss dandy wrinkled his nose a bit at the brand, but he downed it.

"When was it Espada came to see you?"

"Just in the last hour. I heard a knock on the door of my condo in Key Biscayne and there he was. I remembered what you said about him contacting Cesar Mendoza just before he was killed. I thought I might die any minute."

"Was he alone?"

"When he arrived at my door, yes. But after he left I looked out the window and saw him get in a car with two other people."

"Did you get a good look at those people?"

"Only for moment. One appeared to be a blonde woman and the other person had strange-colored hair."

"Orange hair."

It amazed Montand that Willie knew that, and it frightened him too.

"Yes, that's right."

"Did you see what kind of car they were in? Did you have time to note the license number?"

Montand shook his head. "I don't know American cars." He held out his glass and Willie poured him more rum.

"What did Carlos Espada have to say to you?"

"He didn't say anything. He spent the whole time asking me questions. He was like a crazy person."

"What did he ask you?"

"First he wanted to know about counterfeiting cigars. I told him what I told you last time. I know nothing about such things. But he kept asking me if other men we know are involved in it."

"What other people?"

"He asked me what does Ricardo Tirado have to do with it. Nathan Cooler, Mario Calderón, Richard Knox. All of them. I told him I'd never heard that any of those people had done anything illegal. And then he went really crazy."

"What do you mean crazy?"

"He grabbed me by the shirt and wanted to know who killed his father all those years ago, as if one thing had to do with the other."

Willie frowned. "Killed? But I thought his father committed suicide."

"Exactly, but he no longer seems to believe that."

"And what did you tell him?"

"That his father wasn't killed. But he kept shaking me and asking me. He said all these years no one had told the truth about his father's death. I thought that he would strangle me. I swore to him I didn't know anything. I told him he should go ask Nathan Cooler. Cooler had been very close to the family. Cooler would tell him the truth."

"What did he do then?"

"The car outside started to sound its horn. He suddenly let me go. Then he ran from the condo. That's when I went to the window and saw him get into that car. I'm telling you he's crazy."

"Why would he suddenly begin to think that someone had murdered his father?"

Montand shook his head nervously, as if he were shivering from cold. "I don't know why he thinks that. Anything might have happened back then. Everyone lived on the brink of despair, of destruction. They had all been wiped out and didn't know where they would even live, how they would eat, let alone when they might produce cigars again. It was as if the greatest hurricane had come and not only destroyed their businesses but picked them up and dumped them here. It was crazy and it was desperate. Maybe somebody did kill Ernesto Espada. But I'm telling you I know nothing about it. I never have."

Willie studied the other man, who slurped his rum with a shaky hand. He realized that Montand had come to see him again for the exact same reason he had come the last time—to tell Willie he didn't know anything. Speaking of habits, this was getting to be one.

Montand finished his rum quickly and Willie escorted him downstairs.

"I'm leaving this city in the morning," Montand said. "I must say it won't be soon enough."

"That sounds like a good idea."

Willie watched him speed away.

CHAPTER THIRTY-ONE

Willie finished his Cuban-Chinese dinner and slipped into black pants and a navy blue silk shirt. He topped it off with a white sport jacket.

Then he looked up Nathan Cooler in the phone book. He was listed, but when Willie called he got a lady housekeeper who told him Cooler was still at the factory. It was 10 p.m. Cooler was putting in some long hours.

The lower floor of the factory was dark when Willie arrived five minutes later, but a light was burning in the upstairs offices. Parked in the lot on the side of the building he saw a late-model Lincoln, much like the one he had seen Mario Calderón driving a few days before. He parked next to it, got out and found the side entrance to the building, a security door, half open.

Willie, who had already spent a considerable amount of the day poking his head through doors, did it again. He called out, to see if he could attract the attention of a night security guard but got no answer. On the wall above the door was a plaque naming an alarm company, but apparently the alarm had not been set.

Willie eased his way into the building, calling again for a security guard and again getting no answer. He groped his way down a hallway to the reception room. The light from the second floor filtered down the staircase leading to the executive offices.

Willie called out one more time and then headed up the stairs. The light glowed from a single globe, barely illuminating the hallway leading to Cooler's office. Willie saw the double wooden doors, one of which was slightly open. Willie advanced and pushed it open the rest of the way.

In the darkness, all of Cooler's cigar store Indians were silhouettes. They stood as if at attention, half to one side of the desk, half
to the other. The only light in the room came from a desk lamp,
which had been bent way down close to the surface of the desk. It
took Willie's eyes a moment to adjust and then he realized someone
was seated at that desk. Willie approached slowly.

"Cooler?"

The seated figure didn't answer. Willie got closer, reached for
the bonnet of the lamp and bent it up. The light hit the person at the
desk hard in the face.

Mario Calderón sat in the seat of power. Given Calderón's attitude, Willie figured the little man had always wanted to run things.
But time had run out on him before he had been able to climb the
corporate ladder. Mario Calderón was dead.

Willie kept the lamp on him. It took him a minute to figure out
how Calderón had been killed. Three red pins had been inserted into
Calderón's chest just above the pocket of his pleated, white
guayabera. Willie craned over and saw that beneath those pins
Calderón had also received a gunshot wound in the heart. It appeared
the gun had been held very close to him when the trigger was pulled.
The cotton was scorched. Blood had run down the inside of the shirt.

Willie remembered the old song about the three pins and what
they meant to cigar workers. If you got three red pins you were dismissed. Well, this night someone had dismissed—and dispatched—
Mario Calderón.

Willie put a hand on Calderón's neck. The skin was still warm.
He hadn't been dead long at all.

Suddenly, Willie heard a noise behind him, and he turned. Staring at him from the shadows were the wooden Indians, a small forest
of grim faces. Willie pulled his extra .38.

"Come out."

None of the Indians moved and nobody else did either. Willie
walked toward them, his gun drawn. He stepped behind a very large
chief in a feather bonnet and brushed by another with a bow in his
hands. Then he heard a noise behind him. He turned, but not fast
enough. A carved Indian crashed into him. It knocked him over and
then fell across him. Willie still held his gun but couldn't feel his
right arm.

The person who had pushed the statue stood over him for just a moment and then started for the door. Willie swung his legs so that the man tripped over them, crashed into another carved figure, knocked it over and fell to the floor. Willie rolled out from under his wooden captor, but the other guy was faster. He sprang up and pushed another figure at Willie so that it crashed across his ribs and knocked the wind out of him. Then the man pulled a gun.

Willie stared at the silhouette of the gun that he was sure would kill him. It was pointed at him only moments, but it seemed much longer. Then suddenly the guy turned and ran for the door, disappearing through it before Willie could even try to move his gun hand.

Willie got free of the Indians, struggled to his feet and limped toward the door. He heard the pounding footsteps of the man running out of the building. There was no sense chasing him. Willie could barely walk.

But it didn't matter much. In the light from the desk lamp he had gotten a brief glance at his assailant. It was Carlos Espada.

Willie took one last look at Mario Calderón and then decided to do exactly what Espada had done—get out of there as quickly as possible. The police had already found him with two corpses and, as Grand had said, Willie didn't want to make it a habit. Calderón would be found soon enough. Willie left the dead man in charge behind that big desk and headed for the door.

* * *

He went quickly to his car, drove several blocks, then pulled over and called the Espada house. Esther Espada answered on the third ring.

"I need to talk to you," Willie said.

"It's late."

"I don't care. I need to speak to you and your mother right now."

"My mother's already asleep."

"Then you wait for me. I'll be there in a few minutes."

When he arrived at the property, he passed through the big old, rusted gate and pulled up to the smaller house. A porch light came on before he could reach the door. Esther opened it and ushered him into the cramped living room.

Right away he saw a difference in her from last time. She didn't come close to him. She stood in the middle of the room and her manner was distant, the way it had been during their first meetings. Maybe she somehow sensed what he was going to tell her.

"Your brother killed a man tonight."

She simply stared at him. Maybe her brother had called her to tell her what had happened. Maybe she had known before it happened. But she had been aware of Calderón's death before Willie told her the news. He was sure of that.

"Why would your brother kill Mario Calderón?"

She shook her head. "I've told you before, my brother wouldn't kill anyone."

Willie closed the distance between them until he was inches from her, almost as close as he'd been the night before. "I was there just minutes ago. Calderón was dead with a bullet in his heart. Your brother was there, and he had a gun. He ran."

None of that seemed to phase her. "I want you to leave. We don't want you to find my brother anymore. We don't want you to call here anymore. If you don't leave now, I'll call the police."

"The police? They'll be interested to know what your brother did tonight."

"You do what you please. It has no importance to us anymore. Just leave right now."

Willie stared into her eyes for moments. The woman who had been with him the night before had vanished behind that dark insolent stare. He left her standing there, sinking back into her life of isolation.

CHAPTER THIRTY-TWO

Willie sat outside the Espada house for several minutes. It was past 11 p.m. If Esther Espada knew where her brother and Dinah were, she wasn't going to tell Willie any time soon.

Espada had been at the factory alone. Willie had no idea where to search for Dinah. In three days, he hadn't even discovered her last name, let alone an address—besides the Edgewater cigar factory. The only person whose address he did have who might be able to help him was Rolando Falcón. If he wasn't with Carlos Espada maybe he had gone back to his apartment in Hialeah.

Willie drove back to Hialeah, moving quickly over the nearly empty highways and streets. He pulled up to the bright blue building and right away noticed the vehicle parked in front. It was the same black SUV that had broken through the gate at the Edgewater house that afternoon. The heavy-duty front bumper was dented and the very top corner of the windshield was starred, probably by a stray gunshot.

Willie turned the corner and parked. He walked back to the SUV and made sure nobody was in it. There wasn't. He walked in through the arched front entranceway and gazed around the two-story courtyard. All the apartments were dark, except for Number Eight, Rolando Falcón's place. Willie could see a faint light shining through the porthole window next to the door.

He pulled out his spare .38 again and climbed the stairs slowly and silently. He edged his way to the door. From inside he could hear a muffled voice. He peeked in through the porthole.

Sitting in a hard-back chair not more than ten feet away was Rolando Falcón. His hands were tied behind him and he was bare chested. Standing over him were Fuzzy Face and another man dressed in a black windbreaker who Willie had not seen before. They each held a gun in their hands.

At the back of the room, Willie saw the girl with the purple hair. She hadn't gotten away soon enough. She was facing the wall with her head buried in her lap and her hands pressed over her ears, as if she had been warned not to look or listen.

Fuzzy Face was pressing Falcón for information and apparently the kid wasn't providing the right answers. Fuzzy Face shoved what looked like a sock in the kid's mouth, puffed on a cigar until the ember burned bright orange, like the kid's hair, and then he took it out and pressed it to the kid's pectoral muscle. Immediately Falcón contorted into convulsions of pain, as if he'd been hit with an electric shock. The guy in the windbreaker kept the chair from tipping over. Even with the sock in his mouth Willie could hear Falcón's strangled scream through the glass of the porthole. It sounded like a death rattle. In the corner the girl's body convulsed too, as if she were hooked to Falcón's nervous system and also felt the burning. But she didn't look up.

Fuzzy Face put the cigar back in his mouth, grabbed Falcón by his orange hair, pulled up his head, took out the sock and questioned him again. Willie couldn't make out what he asked.

Willie stood without moving and watched the whole thing happen again. Fuzzy Face said, "Tell me!" The kid looked at him hopelessly and shook his head. The thug shoved the sock back in his mouth and once again used him for an ashtray, this time touching the cigar to his neck.

Willie had to turn away. If he went through the door, it would be two against one. He might not be able to get his shots off in time, and even if he could, he might hit the kid or the girl.

In the end he didn't have to make the decision. Fuzzy Face grabbed the kid by the hair and hauled him to his feet, reached toward the phone and ripped it out of the wall. He said something to the girl that made her bury her face even farther in her hands. Then the two thugs and their prisoner headed for the door, right toward Willie.

He didn't have time to go down the stairs the way he'd come. Instead, he took three quick strides and ducked into a stairwell that led to the back of the building. As he watched, the door opened and they marched out with Rolando Falcón, headed for the front staircase.

Willie took the back stairs two at a time. He knew Rolando Falcón was in cahoots with Carlos Espada and Dinah, but he didn't know exactly what the kid had done wrong. Whatever it was, he couldn't leave him in the hands of Fuzzy Face and his friend, not if he could help it. The kid wouldn't make it out alive.

Willie came around the corner of the building and managed to hide himself behind a car across the street from the SUV. The three men emerged from the main entrance, Fuzzy Face leading the way. He had tucked his gun away. His buddy held Falcón by one arm and pressed a pistol against his head with the other.

They brought the kid to the side of the SUV and were apparently going to shove him in behind the seat. Fuzzy Face opened the door and that was when Willie brought up his gun hand and called to them.

Fuzzy and his buddy both turned quickly, although the second man's gun didn't leave the side of Falcón's head. Willie kept the car between him and them just in case.

"Don't move," he said.

Fuzzy Face didn't move, not at first.

"That isn't you again, is it, Cuesta?"

"Just let the kid go."

Fuzzy Face smiled. Willie could see his white teeth beneath the dark moustache. "And then what?"

"Just give me the kid and you can drive away. I don't care what happens to you. It has nothing to do with me, this little war you guys have going."

"So, all you want is the kid. Nothing else?"

"That's right."

Fuzzy Face was leaning toward the car. Willie couldn't see his right hand and he thought he might be reaching for a gun. But that wasn't it.

"Okay, you can have him," Fuzzy Face said. "I just need to wash him off for you."

Through the darkness Willie could see Fuzzy Face reach into the flat bed of the truck, lift a container and pour some liquid on Falcón, more as if he were baptizing him than washing him. By the time the smell of gasoline reached Willie it was already too late. Fuzzy Face had produced a lighter from his shirt pocket and held it to the kid.

The upper half of Rolando Falcón's body burst into flames with an audible pop. The kid issued a bloodcurdling scream and then came running toward Willie, his mouth gaping in pain. Behind Falcón, the guy in the windbreaker brought his gun down, leveled and fired a shot that sent Willie diving behind a fender. Then he and Fuzzy Face jumped into the SUV. Willie kept one eye on them and the other on the kid, who ran past Willie, burning like a human torch, threw himself on the grass, and began to thrash to put out the fire. As the SUV peeled out, Willie dropped his gun, ripped off his sport jacket and dove onto the kid to smother the flames. His nose filled with the smell of burning flesh. Falcón screamed and Willie closed his eyes and held on.

The night ended three hours later. It had taken only a few minutes for an ambulance to arrive. The kid had suffered burns on his shoulders, upper chest and the sides of his face. His orange hair was completely burned off. But Willie had managed to extinguish the flames before they ate away his eyes or the front of his face. Falcón had howled with pain at first and then lost consciousness while they waited for the ambulance.

The neighbor who called the ambulance had witnessed the whole standoff from a window across the street. He confirmed for the Hialeah police that the assailants had escaped in a black SUV and that Willie had tried to save the kid. Willie told them he hadn't spoken to the kid and didn't know why Falcón had been attacked. Technically, that was true. He never mentioned Lester Grand or Cesar Mendoza or Mario Calderón.

At 3 a.m. they finally let him go.

CHAPTER THIRTY-THREE

It was eleven the next morning when the phone woke Willie. He decided to let the machine pick up and it was a good decision. He heard Lester Grand's baritone on the other end.

"Willie, it's Les Grand. I understand that you didn't take the advice I gave you yesterday. Last night you involved yourself again in the Espada affair. On top of that, a man was just found dead at the Great American Tobacco Company. A Mr. Mario Calderón. We're told that you were at that factory just a couple days ago. So today I need you to come talk to me at my office. I hope you don't make it necessary for me to go and find you."

The last thing Willie wanted to do was talk to Grand. The person he did want to talk to was Rolando Falcón.

Willie got up, got ready and headed for the trauma center at Jackson Memorial Hospital. That was where the ambulance had taken Falcón the night before.

He parked right in the circular driveway in front and went in through the sliding doors. Family and friends of patients who were being operated on or undergoing other emergency procedures had to wait in the general waiting area on the first floor. During his time as a police officer Willie had spent more than a few nights there questioning survivors of violence. Families tended to separate into pods, each with their own grief.

Willie stepped through the front door and made sure neither Lester Grand nor any other homicide detective was in evidence. Then he spotted the girl with the purple hair. She was curled up in a chair at the very back of the waiting room, her head half in her lap, much like the night before.

Willie sat in the chair right next to her. The girl's eyes, which had black rings around them from lack of sleep, went big when she saw him.

"How's Rolando doing?" he asked.

"He's being operated on right now. They're grafting skin onto his face."

"Did you get to talk to him before they started?"

She shook her head. "They had him on drugs to keep him knocked out because of the pain and he's going to be on the drugs after they finish. I don't know when I can talk to him."

"What were those guys asking him last night? Why did they do that to him?"

She made a face. "I already told the police all of this."

"So, tell me."

"They kept asking him about those two people he knows."

"Did they mention names?"

She hesitated. Willie leaned close and whispered.

"Let me guess. It was Dinah and Carlos. Carlos Espada."

Her eyes widened again, and she nodded.

"The two guys, what were they asking about Dinah and Carlos?"

"Where they were. They wanted to find them."

"And Rolando wouldn't tell them?"

"He didn't know where they were right then. He kept telling them that. I guess they had been at some house and now they weren't anymore." She was talking about the roost on Edgewater. "Rolando went out with that Dinah and Carlos yesterday. He came back at night and said we had to leave right away. But before we could, those two guys came through the door. That's when they started to do what they did to him."

"What else did they ask him?"

"Nothing. The whole time that's all they asked over and over. Where they were."

"Do you know what Rolando talked about with Dinah and Carlos?"

She shrugged. "Only what I heard when he took the phone call yesterday. The woman called just before they came to get him. I answered and I handed it to him. That's how I know who it was."

"And what did you hear?"

"They talked about the Dominican Republic."

Willie's eyebrows danced. "What did they say about the Dominican Republic?"

She shook her head. "I just heard him say it, as if somebody was going there. He said something else I didn't understand. Trans Air."

"Trans Air?"

"Yes."

Willie stared and nodded at her, lost in thought. After a minute, he got up.

"Thanks for your help. I'm sorry about what happened last night. I'll be in touch."

She didn't look enthused by that promise. But then nobody in that room looked real enthused.

Willie went back to the car, hauled the yellow pages out of the backseat and turned to Airlines. Trans Air was a local charter service that largely ferried the well-to-do to Caribbean islands and back. The phone was answered by a woman who sounded older rather than younger and southern rather than northern.

"Trans Air. Can I help you today?"

"Yes. I'd like to speak to a friend of mine, Mr. Carlos Espada. He's taking a plane to the Dominican Republic."

"You already missed him, honey. He left at noon."

"Damn! Did his girlfriend, the blonde girl, make it in time for the flight? She was afraid she'd miss it."

"She got here on time. I know she got on that plane."

Willie thanked her for her time. As he drove back to Little Havana, he called the airlines. The soonest he could find a seat to Puerto Plata was that evening. He booked it. Then he went home to pack.

He was still there when the phone rang. It was Amy.

Willie sat down on the bed. "Did you get the roses?"

"Yes."

"When we spoke I was upset."

"I realize that. I read about your friend."

Neither of them said anything for a few moments. What could he say? It was Amy who broke the silence.

"I went back to the guy I told you about. The guy in my office who buys the cigars. I explained to him why I was asking, the killing and all."

"What did he say?"

"When he wants cigars, he calls a number and puts in an order. Then he picks them up."

"Where?"

"It's usually at a restaurant called Enrique's in Little Havana."

"I know it. It's on Flagler." And only a couple of blocks from Great American.

"Who meets him?"

"Most times it's a man with a shaved head and wearing a lot of gold." She was describing Mario Calderón. He told her about the murder of Calderón.

"My God, Willie!"

"What else did that guy tell you?"

"He said one other time he was picking up a large order, which included some extra boxes for clients of ours. About a dozen boxes at seven hundred dollars each. As always, he had to bring it in cash."

"And?"

"And he picked them up on the beach."

"Where?"

"Actually, it was right at the foot of the Forty-first Street Causeway. A guy met him there in a car at the edge of the bay."

"What did the guy look like?"

"He didn't see him. It was a limousine and the only person he saw was the chauffeur. He passed him the money and got the cigars. Somebody else was sitting in back, but he didn't see who it was. It was dark, but he felt somebody watching him. It's a good thing he didn't get killed."

"Thank you for getting all this," Willie said.

"That's all right. I'm sorry about your friend."

"I have to go out of town, to the DR. Will I see you when I get back?"

"Yes, you'll see me, but be careful down there."

Willie said he would, although he knew that might be impossible.

CHAPTER THIRTY-FOUR

Willie arrived at the airport an hour before the seven p.m. flight for the Dominican Republic. He waited in line and watched baggage handlers wrap all kinds of possessions in black plastic—televisions, rocking horses, a mannequin for dressmaking. His fellow passengers then carried them in line, until Willie began to feel that he was part of a peculiar, modern sculpture exhibit.

The lady behind the ticket counter was not wrapped in black plastic. She was tall, dark, Latin and very friendly. She assured him that the flight was on time.

Willie hustled through the terminal, passed the security check, and headed for his gate. All the time he kept an eye out for Lester Grand and any other police who might want to keep him from getting on that plane.

He had hidden out at Ross' house all day and had checked his voice mail several times. Sure enough, Grand was still looking for him. Willie didn't return the calls. Instead, he confirmed his airline reservation for the DR, called the hotels listed on Carlos Espada's phone bills and reserved rooms there for the next two nights. He hid his car in Ross' garage, then watched the TV news reports while Ross tied fishing leaders.

"Watch out down there, bub," Ross said when he dropped Willie off at the terminal. "I know you like to *merengue,* but don't turn your back on nobody."

The plane lifted off into a gray-blue sky about an hour before sunset. Based on the conversations around him, Willie figured about half the passengers were Dominicans and the other half were tourists. Of the latter group, some were American, but many were German. Willie listened to them talking to each other in their native tongue, with Spanish words thrown in. It amounted to an unusual linguistic stew.

Willie also checked as many faces of his fellow travelers as he could. None of them looked familiar or suspicious. No one to worry about.

They were about halfway to the DR when the sun set. From his window seat, Willie watched the swollen orange sun touch the horizon, causing a momentary slick of gorgeous colors to spread across the surface of the Caribbean. When the uppermost tip of the sun finally disappeared, darkness enveloped them. The Germans around him *oohed* and *aahed*. The tropics were working their magic and they hadn't even landed yet.

Another ninety minutes elapsed and then the pilot told them to prepare for landing. The plane made a sharp turn, and Willie peered down and saw a narrow strand of lights tracing the otherwise dark, curving coastline. It was mysterious, exotic, attractive. Then more lights appeared—a small airport—and they floated down for a landing with the black silhouettes of palm trees rising up to meet them.

At the bottom of the gangway a Dominican steward said "auf Wiedersehen" to Willie's neighbors and "hasta luego" to him. The night that closed over them was thick, humid and hot. They had to walk through it a short distance from the plane to the terminal.

The building was painted in bright, tropical colors, a relatively new structure that seemed bigger than it needed to be, especially since Willie and his fellow Miami passengers were the only ones in the airport. It was unreal that way, as if the airport and the attendants were only there to greet that one flight and would disappear from the face of the earth once the passengers were gone. Here and there stood uniformed police, however, with what looked like very old, very real rifles over their shoulders, guarding that illusionary structure. Willie smiled as he went by, but they didn't smile back.

Willie, the other Americans and the Germans were all walked right through the *migración* and customs checkpoints. No hassles for tourists with hard currency. The Dominicans remained behind, all holding their modern, plastic-wrapped sculptures for official inspection.

Of course, Willie wasn't exactly a tourist. This surprised the slim, elderly, black taxi driver in the navy-blue New York Yankees

cap who grabbed Willie's bag the moment he stepped from the terminal. Willie was not going to one of the coastal tourist resorts with
all the other Americans and the Germans, at least not tonight. He was
headed to a hotel right there in Puerto Plata. He had made a reservation over the phone with a clerk who, given her tone, had been equally surprised that an American would be stopping there. It was off the
beaten track.

The cab drive took about twenty minutes along that lonely
coastal road, which Willie had seen from above. It was a two-lane
blacktop that cut through jungle made of banana trees and thick
scrub. Except for one other vehicle about a mile behind them, the cab
was alone on the road. As they made the curves on that narrow highway, the headlights illuminated scatterings of houses, miniature vil-
lages that appeared suddenly and then dissolved again into tropical
darkness. Willie could smell the sea through the open rear window,
but he couldn't see it.

Puerto Plata turned out to be a small seaside city composed of
wooden houses painted bright shades of pink and green and blue,
with balconies rotted by the salt air. These buildings crowded narrow
Spanish Colonial streets that ran down to the docks. Willie liked the
place. He had always liked the port towns of the Caribbean, probably
because he had them in his blood. His parents came from the coast
of Cuba. He had been conceived amid the sea breezes. His mother
said that the slice of green color in one of his brown eyes had been
left there by the color of the sea off the city of Matanzas. Once he
became a young man, she told him that his womanizing ways came
from that port town, too.

Most of the houses were dark, but a few bars were still open.
From one, a jukebox spouted a famous *merengue* about a woman
who gave a man a fever because she refused to be his lover. Willie
had read in a tourist brochure about the town's colorful past. Pirates
and smugglers had used that stretch of coast as a base going back at
least two hundred years. Willie hoped if the pirates were still there,
that they were already asleep. All in all, the place was colorful, ripe
with the legendary lust that men developed at sea.

The Hotel Tropical was right in the middle of the town, a wood-
en place painted bright red with yellow shutters. Several large trucks
were parked on the street outside and the cab driver informed him

that many truck drivers from the capital, Santo Domingo, stayed
there because it was quiet and cheap. Its central courtyard was lined
with big potted plants—palms, banana trees and tropical flowers—
and also with a half dozen large, wooden bird cages. The desk clerk,
the only person in evidence, was a young woman dressed all in
white, who was just putting covers over the cages for the night, as if
she were performing a solemn ritual.

Her name was Esperanza, according to the tag on her chest. She
had skin the color of an old penny and muddy brown eyes, one of
them slightly off center. Willie registered and she stared at his name
strangely for a few silent seconds. Willie broke that silence by asking
her where he could rent a car the next day. She said there was only
one agency in town and offered to contact it first thing in the morning and have a car delivered for him. He thanked her for the service.

Willie told her the hotel had been recommended to him by a
friend and asked her if she remembered the name Carlos Espada.
She didn't, so he pulled a photo of Espada from his suitcase and
asked her if she recognized him. She studied the photo longer than
seemed necessary, the way she had stared at his name on the registration card. Either she was deciding what to tell Willie, or she was
just slow. She finally shook her head.

"No, I don't remember him, but we have many guests."

"Can you look up his name? He would have stayed here a month
ago."

She shook her head slowly, not taking her eyes from him. "I
don't have those records here. Only the owner has those."

"Maybe I could ask him tomorrow."

She was still shaking her head. "He is out of town and won't be
back for some time."

"I see."

With the cast in her eye, she seemed to be studying him from
two directions at the same time. Willie thought she might be talking
from two directions as well. She handed him his key and pointed
toward the back of the hotel. Willie thanked her and headed down a
long, red-tile hallway. He turned once and found her standing at the
end of that passage, staring at him. She ducked out of sight again as
Willie reached his door.

Willie opened the room and flipped on the light. It was painted a bright yellow, like the shutters outside, with a red-tile floor and red curtains over a window that looked out onto a rear alleyway. It was rustic, to say the least. One bare bulb hung in the center of the room. The cord leading to it sagged down from the ceiling like a clothesline. Willie took off his white *guayabera* and hung it on that line. He turned on the rusting metal ceiling fan, then dug into his suitcase. He brought out a small traveling bottle of rum and poured himself a double shot in a plastic glass he found on a wicker dresser. He lay in bed, sipping the rum and listening to the muted *merengue* from down the street. A stain on the ceiling looked vaguely like a black human face.

A month earlier, Carlos Espada had come through this hotel. Willie was sure of that. He was sure the girl was lying to him. The question was who had asked her to lie. It wouldn't be hard to scare her, or to buy her silence if you were a big man in the tobacco game. The question was why.

Willie drained his rum, undressed, killed the light and tried to go to sleep. One of the truck drivers had apparently brought along his wife or girlfriend or found love on the local byways. The sound of lovemaking, sighs rising past the falling stars, echoed in the night. Willie distracted himself by listening to another popular *merengue* coming from the local jukebox, about a world where it rained coffee on savannahs of strawberries.

The humid darkness enveloped him, and Willie fell asleep. It must have been about an hour later that voices woke him. They seemed to be right outside his door. The whispering lasted about a minute and then receded. Willie got out of bed. Opening the door a crack, he saw the clerk, Esperanza, heading away down the hall with a small man in a bright pink silk shirt and a black Panama hat. Willie thought he recognized the shirt from the crowd outside the airport. When the man turned to speak to her Willie saw a large cigar clenched in his teeth.

Willie eased the door shut so they wouldn't see him. Then he lay down in the darkness.

CHAPTER THIRTY-FIVE

Willie was awakened the next morning by the sounds of the caged birds in the courtyard, but also by the heat that descended from the corrugated tin roof.

He showered and shaved with tepid water and then dressed in his long crimson shirt embossed with green parrots. He didn't want to make himself hard to see. His bag packed, he carried it out to the courtyard, where Esperanza was still on duty.

"Your car is waiting for you," she said. It was just 8 a.m., which was very good service indeed. The rental agent had left the paperwork with her, and Willie filled it out quickly as she ran his credit card. He found the car parked right outside the door, a Honda painted a bright lime green. They didn't want him to be hard to see either.

Esperanza told him how to find the cross-country highway, which led to the city of Santiago. She didn't wave as he pulled away.

Willie maneuvered the narrow streets lined with those brightly painted houses. He kept the seafront on his right, found the outdoor market she'd told him about—tables piled high with papayas, watermelons, mangoes, flowers of all kinds—and turned onto a two-lane highway that headed toward some very green hills.

He passed a couple of horse-drawn carts and was out of town and into the foothills before he knew it. At one point he was afraid he had gone too fast, so he slowed down. But in less than a minute he saw the other car, no more than a hundred yards behind him. Willie looked in the rearview mirror and saw that his pursuer had changed his bright pink shirt for a red and white striped number. But Willie recognized the black Panama hat and he thought he could even make out the big cigar.

The farther they drove that curving road into the hills, the greener it became. Some hillsides were covered in banana plants; others were buried under vines. The morning mist was still burning off and it hung in the ravines. The narrow creeks were gorged with muddy run-off water.

A half hour later they came down out of those hills onto a plain and Willie saw the first tobacco plants, row after row of them with glossy, spade-shaped leaves and red and white buds on top. Here and there in those fields stood large tobacco barns and thatched lean-tos, where bunches of harvested, golden-brown tobacco leaves were drying. Tied to horizontal poles, the tobacco looked disturbingly like drying scalps. In strange territory already, being followed by a man he didn't know, Willie didn't feel good about anything that reminded him of scalps.

After miles of tobacco, Willie reached the outskirts of Santiago. Like a lot of Caribbean metropoli, it was dusty and ramshackle on its outskirts. But as Willie penetrated to the center of town, he found attractive Spanish Colonial buildings side by side with some less attractive modern structures crowding narrow streets. From time to time he passed a park where royal palms grew. Willie went slowly to make sure he didn't lose his tail.

In the very center of town, he saw the sign he was looking for atop a multi-story building—Hotel El Jardín—The Garden Hotel. Willie pulled up in front, took his suitcase and gave the car keys to a valet.

The lobby featured a single large potted palm and mirrored walls all around so that Willie, in his parrot shirt, and the palm were multiplied into infinity by the reflections, creating a well-populated jungle.

The clerk was a small man with a black pompadour hairdo, a Day-Glo flowered shirt and a ludicrously large smile, which exuded exaggerated hospitality. He ran Willie's credit card, gave him his room key and pounded a bell on the desk, which brought a red-coated bellboy into the lobby. He was a very large bellboy, especially for a Dominican. At least six-foot four and broad-shouldered, he carried Willie's suitcase as if it were a school lunch box.

Just before they stepped into the elevator, Willie saw the man in the black Panama hat pull up.

The elevator was small, creaky, hot as a sauna, and smelled of disinfectant. The big bellboy had to hunch over to fit in it, like a jack-in-the-box. He stared at Willie; there was no room to stare at anything else.

"You are here for business or pleasure, señor?" he asked.

"I'm here for both," Willie said.

The big man's brows lifted suggestively. "If I can help you in anything, you will let me know." It was the nature of bellboys no matter where you went to be of help in all ways, seemly and unseemly, and Willie would keep him in mind.

The room he opened for Willie was papered in a floral pattern. It, too, was as warm as a hothouse, but the bellboy turned on the air conditioner—a rattling wall unit. He also brought Willie some ice. Willie tipped him well.

When he'd gone, Willie left the door open halfway, sat on the bed facing the door, fanned himself a bit, looked at his nails and waited. Within five minutes, like a mouse to the cheese, the man in the Panama hat was standing there.

Willie motioned him in. "Don't stand there, you're wasting the air-conditioning."

The man hesitated a moment. His eyes darted around the room, then he smiled, revealing a couple of gold caps amid yellowed teeth. He stepped in, easing the door closed behind him.

Willie took a better look at him. He was dark complected with a luxuriously thick moustache. In addition to the hat, he wore his red and white shirt unbuttoned halfway down his chest and checked pants. He held a cigar in one hand and had a couple more lined up in his shirt pocket.

He was still looking around the room in the way he might if he were looking for something to steal. But Willie knew he wasn't there for that. At least not on this visit.

He smiled at Willie. "Just spending a little time walking the halls."

Willie smiled back. "You also spent a little time following me from Puerto Plata."

The man smiled more broadly, exposing one more gold tooth. He waved a finger at Willie, which bore a gaudy gold ring.

"You were checking on me. You're very sharp, *amigo.*"

Willie matched him smile for smile. "Yes, I'm a genius. I'm a business genius and something tells me you want to do business."

"What kind of business are you in?"

Willie pointed at the cigar in Black Hat's hand. "I'm in that business."

The other man brightened. "That's good. I'm in that business, too."

"But my clients only want to buy the very best—or what their customers think is the very best." He made his eyebrows dance suggestively.

"You need special product."

Willie shrugged. "The product doesn't matter. What I need is special packaging, if you understand what I mean?"

The other man beamed. "Oh, yes. I understand. I'm here to please you. But this all has to be done without advertising, *amigo*."

"Of course, but I do need to know who I'm dealing with. And I have to assure myself that your operation will supply me with what I need."

Black Hat thought that over. "Until recently, I've had a client who bought most of what I could supply, but I haven't been contacted by him since he took the last shipment."

Willie nodded. "I know your client. He ran into some financial and legal difficulties. He asked me to take over his end of the operation."

He was speaking of Carlos Espada and the other man seemed to know that. Black Hat looked at his cigar and then at Willie.

"How can I be sure of that?"

"You can call his sister. She will confirm it for you."

The dark man smiled. "Did you take over that part of the partnership too?"

Willie gave him his best smarmy gigolo look. "Now it's your turn. Who are you? Who do you represent, *amigo?*"

The other man shook his head. "You'll excuse me, with all respect, but I won't tell you that yet. You'll have to give me a few hours to make the proper communications. I need to see what we have in stock. I also need to confirm some information."

Willie shrugged. "You do all the confirming you want. I need to arrange for a transfer of money in the meantime."

The other man showed his bad teeth, tipped his black hat and left.

CHAPTER THIRTY-SIX

When the man had gone, Willie hung his clothes, took his extra cash out of his wallet and put it in a lightweight money belt. He took his .38 out of his suitcase, where it had made the journey—along with his special Miami Police Department weapons waiver, which he had never handed in. He returned the gun to his back holster and then took the elevator to the rooftop restaurant for an early lunch. A gray-haired piano player sat at a baby grand in the corner. He played the romantic old standard "Perfidia," filling it with intrigue and romance.

Willie ordered shrimps *al mojo de ajo*. While he waited, he walked to the balustrade and looked out over the city. *Flamboyán* trees were aflame in all directions. Beneath them, motor scooters went flying through the narrow streets in what seemed like a labyrinth road race. As in the port town, the balconies all seemed to be crumbling. Walking under them would be an adventure. The corrugated tin roofs had rusted and many of the stucco walls were stained a reddish color, as if they themselves were rusting, or as if the whole valley had once been underwater as the result of a massive tropical storm. Somewhere out in that rusty city Black Hat was making the contacts he needed to make. Willie wished him luck.

He went back to his table and was just finishing lunch and paying his bill when he saw the large bellboy enter, apparently to fetch a room service order. Willie thought of him not as the bellboy, but the "bell giant." He stopped him in the hallway just outside the door of the restaurant.

He took out a copy of the photo of Carlos Espada and Dinah.

"Do you remember this gentleman? He stayed here at least once about a month ago."

The giant brightened. "Oh, yes, I recall him. A very nice gentleman, very refined."

That probably meant Espada had tipped well.

"Was he here with this lady?"

The bellman looked around to make sure no one was watching and shook his head.

"No. He was by himself. Or at least he was by himself in the hotel."

"And outside the hotel?"

The big man shrugged. "When he arrived here I asked him the same question I asked you, señor: if he was here for business or pleasure. He told me he was here for business, serious business, that is what he said. But he would not object to having some pleasure before that business." The bell giant flared his eyes mischievously.

Willie nodded. "And what did you say?"

"I told him where a man might go to have that pleasure."

"And where was that?"

The bell giant looked around again and back at Willie.

"There's only one place. It's called *La Casa Rosada*. The Pink House."

"Is it close by?"

"It's not far, but you shouldn't walk there, especially not at night. The neighborhood around it is bad, dangerous. You just tell any of these cab drivers where you want to go. They will take you and bring you back."

Willie slipped the bell giant another healthy tip. Then he went back to his room and whiled away the early afternoon waiting for Black Hat to call, which he didn't. Finally, he put a "Do Not Disturb" sign on the door, took off his clothes and tried to make up for the sleep he hadn't gotten the last few nights.

When he woke it was dark. Willie showered, shaved again and dressed in his gray linen suit, black silk shirt and black shoes. He went down in the elevator, through the lobby, which again multiplied him into a convention. He told a cab driver he wanted to go to La Casa Rosada and they wheeled off through the now dark, narrow streets. They drove away from the center of town to areas where the streetlights were planted farther apart, and the streets got darker.

They crossed a rickety trestle bridge that seemed very unsteady and turned into a neighborhood that ran along the river they had just crossed. Like the streams Willie had seen in the hills, the river was muddy with runoff. It exuded an aroma of rotting vegetation. Wooden houses also rotting, flanked the river on either side. They had to slow way down because the streets, if they could be called streets, were so full of holes you couldn't go faster than fifteen miles per hour. The farther they drove, the fewer streetlights worked, and Willie wondered if the potholes hadn't been put in the street by Dominican carjackers waiting to jump them. But he didn't ask the driver. If the guy dared to go into that neighborhood, he either knew what he was doing, or he was crazy. Willie hummed an old Willie Colón number about a moonlit street where homeboys had died.

They rumbled slowly along the river until they stopped in front of a long, pink stucco wall. It was brightly painted and clean, totally unexpected in that waterlogged neighborhood, like a very high-priced call girl who had gotten lost.

The cab driver sounded his horn and an electronically operated gate swung open. They drove in and it slid closed behind them. Willie saw a guard wearing camouflage pants and carrying an AK-47. The cab driver saluted him, and they drove on.

The compound they entered was a two-story, horseshoe-shaped motel, painted bright pink everywhere you looked. Sitting or standing outside many of the hot pink doors were working girls, each dressed in her idea of seduction. Skin-tight vinyl hot pants, which had to be extremely warm in that climate, were particularly popular.

Willie gazed around as the taxi pulled into a parking spot. He spotted another guard with an automatic weapon. Willie was seeing his own obituary. "FORMER MIAMI POLICE DETECTIVE FOUND DEAD IN HOT PINK DOMINICAN WHOREHOUSE!" No, his mother wouldn't like it at all.

The cab driver got out and Willie followed him into a circular pink building in the center of the horseshoe. It turned out to be a discotheque, which was very dark and featured multi-colored laser lights shooting in different directions, threatening to pin you to its pink walls. The latest technology at the service of the world's oldest profession.

A doorman frisked Willie, found the .38 in the back holster and asked for the gun. The driver advised him to give it up, that there was no danger of being shot, at least not in the disco. Willie handed it over and the doorman, a short, square-shouldered guy with a flat top, dropped it into his own pocket, the way you drop a penny into a well.

Willie and the cab driver crossed to the bar. A ballad played in the background, an old Latin favorite about an affair that began with a dance. The center of the room was occupied by a raised dance floor where more women in vinyl hotpants danced with each other. It was surrounded by tables and plush couches where patrons were being coddled, caressed, maybe suffocated by more hostesses. In the spasmodic explosions of the laser lights, you saw the heavily made-up faces of the girls, a bit ghoulish, vampire-like, as they appeared and then suddenly disappeared back into darkness. A high-tech brothel populated by Dominican vampire ladies in the middle of banana groves. It was all a bit strange, even for a well-traveled fellow like Willie.

The cab driver got the attention of the bartender, a big man with what appeared to be a knife or machete scar across one cheek. The driver introduced him as Azúcar—Sugar. Despite the nickname, the man didn't look sweet, but he did look knowledgeable, the way bartenders do.

Willie showed him the photo of Carlos Espada and said he was looking for anyone who might have spoken to him. Willie said he would pay any girl her fee, not in exchange for her usual favors, but for information. He assured Sugar that all such data would remain confidential and that neither Sugar nor the girls would run any risk. Sugar didn't seem too worried about risks.

"So, all you want is to talk with a girl?"

"Yeah. Let's call it verbal sex."

Sugar didn't find Willie all that clever. In fact, he probably thought Willie had something wrong with him. But he left an assistant in charge of the bar and disappeared into the laser-streaked darkness of the club, carrying the photo, like a man setting out on a dangerous reconnaissance mission.

Willie sipped an extremely strong lime daiquiri, which the assistant mixed for him. A couple of vampire girls swooped down on him, batting their eyelashes, exposing their teeth, not getting a bite and disappearing again into the darkness. Then another one swooped by, took Willie by the hand.

"Come dance."

She didn't give him a chance to say no, hauling him onto the dance floor. She was tall for a Dominican girl, with a mane of long thick black hair. Her cheekbones were pronounced, and the hollows of her cheeks were accented with rouge that was dark brown in color. She wore black—a halter top and a long black leather skirt.

An old *merengue* was playing, and she danced it extremely well. This wasn't surprising because the *merengue* had been born in the DR. It was said of the Swiss people that over centuries of culture the only thing they had ever invented was the cuckoo clock. Well, in more than five hundred years the most notable invention attributed to the Dominicans was *merengue*—but that put the DR way ahead of Switzerland.

The girl in his arms put her hips into the basic rocking rhythm of the music but managed to have her lovely rear-end swaying to its own rhythm and her thighs keeping a back beat as they rubbed against his. This was a clever bit of advertising about the pleasures one might experience in one of those pink rooms beyond the disco. Unfortunately, she was wasting her time with Willie. When she proffered the invitation he let her know that she danced beautifully, but advised her that he was there on business. She told him he also danced well, gave him a sad smile and then left him standing by himself on the dance floor. Business was business.

Willie arrived back at the bar just as the scar-faced Sugar emerged from the same darkness with a girl in tow. He put the photo on the bar. "This one says she knows him."

The girl was small, with dyed red hair, dressed in a halter and hot pants, both hot pink, and she was obviously wary of Willie. He wanted to question her there, but Sugar insisted that procedures be followed, and Willie wasn't going to argue with him. He made Willie shell out fifty dollars for the girl and the room. Willie asked for a receipt for his expense account, and Sugar made one out for food and beverage, not for verbal sex. He then dispatched them to a room in the pink horseshoe.

They walked past the big doorman, the armed guard and a couple of the other girls and entered a hot pink tryst room. It was small, just big enough for a tryst, if you didn't get too imaginative. The double bed almost filled it. As for frills, it resembled a surgery theater more than a motel room. The bed was covered in a flowered spread, but a sheet of clear plastic covered the spread, with a ratty half sheet on top of that. That's where you were supposed to make love, not under the covers. An enamel basin, a bar of soap and a hand towel sat on a scarred end table. Very antiseptic. All that was missing was a scalpel on the pillow.

Music was piped into the room through a pink speaker hanging in a corner. At the moment a *bolero* was playing, about "a love without hope," which kind of defined the enterprise at hand.

The girl sat on the plastic-covered bed. In her hot pink outfit she almost faded into the walls. Willie tried to touch nothing. He held up the photo.

"Can you tell me about the last time you saw this man?"

She stared sullenly at Carlos Espada. "I only saw him once."

"When was that?"

She rolled her eyes and said nothing.

"About a month?"

She shrugged. "I guess."

"What did he talk about when he was with you?"

"He wasn't with me."

Willie frowned. "I thought you said he was."

"He was with me the way you're with me. He did nothing except talk. He was too scared."

Willie squinted at her. "Scared about what?"

She looked scared herself. "He said he was mixed up in something very dangerous. That maybe someone wanted to kill him or that maybe he would kill himself. He said he had come here to make love a last time, but he couldn't."

"Did he say who it was who might kill him?"

"No."

"Did he say why he might kill himself?"

She shook her head. "I asked him. All he said was he had problems in his family." She shrugged. "I told him we all have problems in our families." She looked like she'd had more than most. Hookers usually did.

"Did he say anything else?"

She shook her head.

"And you haven't seen him since? Especially in the last two days?"

"No, and I hope he doesn't come back. When they tell you they want to die, it isn't worth the money. You have bad dreams about it." She looked very young just then. Willie left her sitting there, listening to the *bolero* about long nights of embraces without hope.

CHAPTER THIRTY-SEVEN

Willie rode in the backseat of the taxi and said nothing to the driver. He had retrieved his gun from the doorman and now the cab made its way back through the desolate neighborhood to the center of the city. The streets were empty. People had shut themselves in, probably to watch the nighttime soap operas, as they seemed to do everywhere in Latin America once the sun went down. Behind the rotting shutters, citizens were steeped in tragedy, betrayal, violence. Well, Willie was too, except his wasn't on television.

Before Willie knew it, the cab had pulled up to the hotel. He tipped the driver generously and sent him back into the night. Then he stopped in the bar off the lobby and ordered another lime daiquiri, which was not as strong as the one he'd been served at the whorehouse, but good enough. He was trying to decide what to do, but without a tremendous amount of success.

He was in a country he didn't know well. In fact, he knew no one. He was searching for the killer or killers of Cesar Mendoza. He was pretending to be in the same crooked enterprise as Carlos Espada, a business that apparently had made Espada fear for his life. Four people who had been involved in it or come in contact with it were already dead. Willie was as blind as Cesar had been as to where he should step next. This was not very good.

He sipped his daiquiri and gazed down the bar. A black man had appeared there, wearing a bright yellow shirt. Willie wasn't sure, but he thought he had seen the same man at the bar of the bordello. It was not impossible that he had been followed from there. He hadn't looked to see if anyone was trailing him. Why someone would follow him he wasn't sure. Maybe this man simply wanted to rob him and didn't want to try it at La Casa Rosada, where they had all that security. He wore his yellow shirt long and out of his pants so that it was impossible to see if he was packing a gun.

The man looked past him, and Willie turned to see another drinker at the opposite end of the bar. That man also wore a long yellow shirt and kept one hand plunged into his pocket. Willie thought of the old Rubén Blades song about the gangster who always kept both hands hidden in his pockets, so you didn't know which one held the knife. Well, in this case Willie knew, but it didn't make him feel any better.

Their matching yellow shirts should have been cute, but they were worrisome. Very possibly, during his visit to the whorehouse, Willie had asked the wrong questions about the wrong people. Counterfeiters might well be big men at La Casa Rosada, making it a dangerous place to go searching for Carlos. This was an equation that would never have escaped Willie's comprehension in Miami, but had eluded him here in this tropical back-water. He might have to pay for it.

He decided that he would prefer not to pay for it right then and there with those guys in the yellow shirts on either side of him. He would go up to his room where he could put his back against one wall, watch the door and try to figure out who to call.

He settled his tab, giving the bartender a very large tip so he would at least be well remembered. He smiled at each of the men at either end of the bar. He would have to give them his back as far as the elevator, but he could watch them in the lobby mirrors.

They didn't disappoint him. As he crossed the lobby, the two canaries came out, also headed for the elevator. In the mirrors they looked like bright yellow birds flying through the reflected jungle. Willie looked toward the desk clerk, but the man in the pompadour glanced at the two canaries and then disappeared quickly into the back room. He seemed to know what was corning and wasn't waxing friendly anymore.

Willie went to the desk anyway and hit the bell with the palm of his hand. He was hoping the bell giant would emerge, but he didn't. The guys in the yellow shirts kept coming toward him. Willie watched them in the mirrors, not turning to face them, but already planning a balletic leap over the counter, with a half twist and an agile tugging of his gun from his back holster. Movie shit, that's what he was down to. And that was only if he wasn't dead before he moved a muscle.

That was his plan, but he didn't get to launch it, or himself. Before he could spring, the elevator door slid open. Out into the lobby walked the small, dark man with the thick moustache and the black Panama hat. He took in Willie, and then the two canaries. They stopped the moment they saw him, obviously recognizing him. A three-way standoff ensued. There was no doubt the canaries were worried by the little man. Their eyes were pried open, unblinking in his direction, as if he were a black cat.

It was the little man who managed to end the standoff. He walked slowly over to Willie. "We're going to leave here now," he said, loudly enough so that the other two couldn't help but hear.

Without hesitating, Willie fell into step with him and crossed the tropical lobby. Willie kept an eye on the mirrors, but the canaries didn't move. Willie and his escort passed through the glass front doors and descended the stairs. A van wheeled up efficiently and mysteriously out of the shadows. A man sat next to the driver, holding a machine pistol in his hands. Willie smiled at him politely. He and Black Hat hopped in and the van took off, leaving the two canaries perched alone on the hotel steps.

Once they'd turned a couple of corners and left the hotel well behind, Willie turned to his savior to thank him. But he didn't have a chance. His savior had his hand out.

"You'll please give me the gun you carry in the small of your back. And don't hold it by the handle but by the barrel."

Willie was taken aback by the icy tone. He was also surprised that the man in the front seat had the machine pistol pointed in his direction. So, Willie did as he was told, as the taxi headed out of town again. It traveled toward the tobacco fields.

"You wouldn't mind telling me where we're going, would you?" Willie asked.

The little man glared at him. "Didn't you say you wanted to do business?"

"Yes, I did"

"Well, in some industries, business is not done in the daylight, *hermano*. It's done now."

Willie watched him. Gone was the shuffling, good-natured go-between of earlier in the day. He was all business now. Willie was starting to worry about the look of recognition between this man and the murderous canaries. Maybe this individual was another form of bird life. In that black hat, he could be a vulture, and everybody knew what you could expect from vultures.

Within minutes they were out of the city and into the quietude of the tobacco fields. They drove mile after mile, row after row, without a person in sight, without a light in the distant houses that were almost hidden amid the plants and the tropical night.

Willie tried again to ask where they were going, but the little man had little more to say.

"Didn't you say you wanted to see the operation, *amigo?* To see the boss?"

Willie was thinking about throwing open the door and falling out, but they were going too fast and also the man pointing the machine pistol at him never looked away. Willie would end up as little more than roadkill.

A minute later the car slowed, and the driver turned down a dirt road that looked no different than the other roads they had passed. They followed it, crowded on each side by tall tobacco plants, until they reached one of the rustic tobacco barns Willie had seen in the daylight that morning. They climbed out of the car into dead quiet. Not even the sound of bugs, not in precious tobacco fields.

The man with the machine pistol prodded Willie in the back. He followed Black Hat through a narrow, wooden door into the dark, dank drying barn. Someone flipped on a dim light, a small lightbulb hanging in the rafters of the building. It barely illuminated the racks of curing tobacco. Up close some of those leaves still looked like scalps, while other leaves looked like wrinkled human skin. It was spooky.

In the very middle of the barn, they reached an open spot where a cigar maker's table sat. Its surface was empty except for one thing: a cigar cutter's knife.

Willie turned, but the man who had been riding shotgun stood right behind him holding that same weapon. It occurred to Willie that the only reason his current companions had not let the canaries kill him was that they had a better, quieter place and more economical method for killing him. A slit throat would save ammunition.

The little man picked up the knife, walked up to Willie and turned it over in his hand. "Now you're going to tell me something. You're not here for the reasons you say you are, isn't that the truth?"

"I don't know what you mean."

The little man feigned surprise. "You don't? Well, I'll tell you. Isn't it true that you aren't in the cigar trade at all? That you were once a police detective? That you're here searching for Carlos Espada and some people who are counterfeiting cigars?"

Willie froze. Usually if a person knew you had police connections, they would be careful about killing you. But in the middle of nowhere, in the Dominican Republic, in a place that for centuries had been home to smugglers and other gangsters, they might follow different guidelines.

The little man didn't give him time to answer. "Don't bother to *bullsheet* me, *amigo*. I know it's true because my boss told me, the boss of the counterfeiters."

In the darkness behind him, the ember of a cigar glowed suddenly. The person smoking the cigar stepped into the spill of light, wearing a dark blue coverall with the word "Police" stenciled on it.

"I thought you would never show up, Willie." The person smiled at him. It was Dinah, the golden girl.

CHAPTER THIRTY-EIGHT

Minutes later Willie was riding in the back of a new Land Rover, next to Dinah, and they were being chauffeured back to the coast. Willie raised the question of his suitcase and his rental car in Santiago, but he was told by the man in the black Panama that someone had already been sent to fetch them.

Willie thanked him. "If you don't mind my asking, who are you?"

It was Dinah who answered. "This is Johnny Segura. He is chief investigator for the Dominican Department of Exterior Commerce. And he's a prince."

Segura tipped his hat and Willie turned to Dinah. "And how about you, while we're at it?"

"My name is Dinah Keane and I'm an investigator for the US Commerce Department, based in San Juan, Puerto Rico, but currently assigned to the Dominican Republic and Miami."

"And she's a *princesa*," Segura said with a smile.

Willie looked at the *princesa*. "Where is Carlos Espada and what does he have to do with all this?"

She shook her head. "Right now, I don't know where he is. Carlos was working with me on an undercover investigation of the counterfeiting and smuggling trade. I met him at that cigar club on Miami Beach. I knew he worked for Great American Cigar. We had reason to believe people inside Great American were up to no good."

That surprised Willie. "Is that right?"

"Yes, it is. Carlos told me it couldn't be Nathan Cooler and he was willing to help me discover who it was. This was right after those two men were murdered in North Miami Beach. I let it be known I was going into the counterfeiting business and Carlos pretended to be my partner. He started to ask questions. Then the blind man, Mendoza, was killed."

"What did Cesar have to do with it?"

She shook her head again. "Nothing, at least not with anything illegal. But Carlos went to him to find out what he knew. Somebody must have decided that Cesar Mendoza knew too much about who was involved, and they killed him."

"And Calderón?"

"We suspected that Calderón was one of those involved. Carlos said he was sure of it. So, when he was found dead, we could only believe that there had been a falling out among thieves."

"Are you saying that Cooler killed him?"

"What else could I think?"

"You could think that Carlos himself did it. I got there soon after Calderón had been killed. And Carlos was in the room with him."

Dinah was scowling at him, as if it were Willie who had deceived her somehow. "But he had no reason to do anything to Calderón. Carlos wasn't involved in any sort of scam. I know that for sure."

"But how about if he found out something else. Something more personal, to do with his family. Maybe he told you he wanted to help you bust the counterfeiters, but he really had his own motives. Carlos believes somebody killed his father, at least that's what he said to Jean-Philippe Montand."

Dinah wasn't staring at Willie so much as through him. "The night Calderón was killed Carlos came back late. After those guys found us at the house on Edgewater, we moved to a hotel near the airport. We were staying in adjoining rooms, and I know he didn't come in until the middle of the night. He told me he was just out in some bar watching a ball game. But the next morning he was different. He got real quiet. He made some phone calls that he didn't want to tell me about. And as soon as we got here yesterday, he disappeared on me. He was supposed to go to Santiago with me, but when we were ready to go, he was nowhere to be found."

Willie had assumed a deep squint.

"You don't think he could have killed Cesar too, do you?"

Dinah shook her head. "I know he didn't kill Cesar Mendoza. He was with me all the time at that point."

"So, who did?"

She shrugged. "We don't have the answer yet to that million-dollar question, but because of your meddling we might be a little closer." She put an emphasis on the word meddling.

"Just how did I accomplish that?"

"Because the people who were following you, who maybe were hired to kill you, they work for whoever is running that new counterfeiting gang and that is who killed the blind man. I'll bet on that."

She tapped Segura on his Panama.

"Johnny here says the killers come from the coast and we think we know from where they were dispatched."

"Where's that?"

"You'll see soon enough, and I don't think you'll mind being there."

And she was right. When they reached Puerto Plata they turned west along the coast road, again catching the clean scent of the sea. They didn't go all the way to the airport. Instead, about halfway there they turned and passed through an arched entranceway to a resort called Costa Brava.

A curving cobblestoned driveway, lined on either side by palm trees, led them up to a very large Mediterranean-style villa. A valet in a white coat with epaulettes ran out and opened the door for Johnny Segura, who disappeared inside and came back five minutes later. He was holding a large brass key ring with a key attached.

They took off again, driving farther into the compound, passing a golf course, one side of which was marked by beautiful stands of palms. They drove by tennis courts, a horse-riding stable, and as they approached the beach itself, a sign that directed them to a marina, scuba diving, deep-sea fishing and a skeet-shooting range overlooking the sea. Sprinkled all through those attractions were tasteful Mediterranean revival villas in different pastel colors, each looking out on its own landscape with no view of other villas. It was a kind of tropical Tuscany and it made Willie whistle.

"This is quite something."

Dinah nodded. "Nothing's too good for the man everyone wants to kill."

Willie glanced at her. "You mean me?"

"Sí, señor."

The villa reserved for them was white and just off the beach. They pulled in under an arbor of crimson bougainvillea. Johnny Segura and Manuel, the driver, got out, checked the grounds, went inside to insure everything was all right, and then escorted them in.

Yes, everything was quite right. From the Mexican-tiled floor to the mahogany rafters, from a bar stocked with a dozen brands of rum to arched windows that looked out on the Caribbean in one direction and over a lagoon in the other. The walls were hung with Latin-American modern art that appeared to be the real thing.

On the patio out front, which faced the sea, Segura picked up a long bamboo pole with a cloth bag on the end and plucked a ripe coconut off one of the palm tress.

"You want a fresh coco loco, amigo?"

Willie shrugged. "Why not?"

Willie turned to Dinah. "All these places are rented by the rich and famous?"

She shook her head. "No, some of them are owned outright by the rich and famous, including some of the big boys in the tobacco business."

"And one of those honchos employs the gentlemen in yellow who came after me?"

"That's a good bet."

Willie frowned. "You're saying that someone who is big in the cigar business in the United States is also a counterfeiter? That's one of the reasons I was sure Nathan Cooler couldn't be involved in such a thing. I thought these big cigar producers were the ones losing the most from the smuggling of Cuban cigars and from the counterfeiting of Havanas."

"They are, which is why you work both ends of the business, both the legitimate and the illegitimate. You make even more money. You might call it varying your product line."

Willie shook his head in amazement. The creative complexities of greed always impressed him.

* * *

Everyone settled into the villa, although they wouldn't be able to relax or sleep any time soon.

"We want the people who sent those men after you to think we've dropped our guard," said Johnny Segura. "But we know they'll be coming."

For a while they nursed their coco locos on the veranda, staring into the dark sea. Then they played a bit of poker. Johnny was a player, and he talked the others into it.

"A little something to relieve the tension," he said with a wicked smile.

After several hands Willie knew that Johnny was a frequent bluffer. Too frequent. Willie caught him in a hand of five-card draw standing pat with a pair of sixes. The fact that his protector was a maker of bad bets did not reassure Willie.

They were in the middle of a game of seven-card stud when Manuel came in.

"They're coming," he said.

One might have assumed that the attackers would come from the land side, where they would enjoy the cover of dense foliage. But the mists from the hills had moved over the coast and there was no moon or starlight. Given the thick darkness, they came from the sea. Johnny Segura pointed them out to Dinah, and she passed the infrared binoculars to Willie as they stood on the patio overlooking the beach. About three hundred yards to the west Willie saw a vessel that looked like a shrimp boat heading their way, relatively close to the shore.

"They want us to think they're fishermen," Johnny said. "Well, we'll see who catches who."

The boat motored another hundred yards or so and then the fishermen suddenly turned toward the shore and toward the villa. Even without the binoculars Willie could see at least a half dozen men on the boat. It came in very close to the shore in the small surf and the men lowered themselves over the side. As far as Willie could see they weren't carrying fishing equipment. He assumed they were carrying arms.

And he was right. From behind the stucco railing of the patio Willie and Dinah watched those half dozen shadows start up the beach. When they reached the stand of palms and a ficus hedge that bordered the property, a shot rang out and a voice in Spanish sounded, telling them to stop and surrender. They didn't take that option.

Shots erupted in the darkness. Johnny had positioned a platoon of troops in the vegetation and another few men down the sand. The intruders were now caught in a crossfire. Red tracer bullets riddled the beach.

Two of the "fishermen" retreated into the surf, trying to make it back to their boat. Another disappeared into the thick vegetation that bordered on the beach. The others fell to the sand and returned fire. Several rounds hit the villa. One broke a window just above where Willie and Dinah were crouched with their guns out. A wedge of glass fell, hitting Dinah in the leg. It sliced open her coverall and her calf. She yelped a bit and then grimaced at it. Willie looked around, saw nothing made of cloth, then untied the flowered kerchief from around her neck and they fashioned a tourniquet, which stemmed the flow of blood. He dragged her into the house, keeping low to avoid any other shots. When they were safe, he picked her up and carried her toward a room away from the firing.

Dinah, who still held her gun in her hand, didn't like it.

"Don't put me in bed. I'm not dying."

"You're not dying, but you are bleeding. Give it a chance to stop."

The firing had suddenly quieted. Voices could be heard, and Dinah listened hard.

"Okay, put me down and go make sure none of our guys were hurt."

Willie did as he was told. He headed across the patio toward the voices on the dark beach. Before he could get to the sand, he heard a thrashing in the bushes and then suddenly a dark, bare-chested man was pulling himself up over the far end of the railing. He wore a gun tucked in his belt and was obviously just trying to get away. But he had run into Willie.

Willie glanced at his own gun across the patio, but it was too far away. By the time he reached it, this pirate coming over the rail would shoot him. So, Willie went right at him.

The pirate's feet hit the ground and a split-second later Willie plowed into him, driving the small of his back against the railing. The other man let out a gasp, the upper half of his body bending back over the rail. He took a wild swipe over Willie's head just as Willie brought the heel of his hand up toward the man's stomach, catching the grip of the pistol, knocking it loose from the guy's belt and sending it skidding into a corner.

While Willie looked at the gun, the guy's eyes fell on the potted palm next to him. Sticking in the soil was a small machete, probably used for pruning. He decided it would be big enough to prune Willie. The guy grabbed the machete and came at Willie as if he were a stalk of sugarcane. Willie saw a potted palm of his own a few feet away, grabbed it by its leaves, and slung it at the pirate. The other man sidestepped it. But that gave Willie a chance to grab the coconut picker, the long bamboo pole with a canvas bag on the end that Johnny had used earlier for their coco locos.

Willie picked it up and feinted at the man. The pirate started toward Willie, ready to cut the flimsy bamboo into toothpicks. Just then, another burst of gunfire erupted from the beach. A round hit the house just above the balcony, shattering another window and showering the patio in glass.

The pirate looked up. It was only for a moment, but Willie brought the pole up and jabbed at the man's eyes with the wire ring at its end. He caught the pirate in the left eye. The other man yelled out and reached for his face. Then Willie turned the pole over, put the canvas bag over the man's head, and drove him backward toward the palm tree bordering the patio. The pirate hit the railing with the small of his back and this time went over it, his head hitting the trunk of the palm with a sickening crack. Willie let go of the pole and looked over the railing. The pirate wouldn't be getting up again soon. Maybe never.

The firing lasted another couple of minutes and then the last fishermen surrendered. To the residents of the other villas, it all probably sounded like no more than firecrackers.

Willie went back inside to make sure Dinah was all right. The resort kept a doctor on call, and he was summoned to tend to her. He arrived within fifteen minutes. Dinah's bleeding had stopped by then.

Then Willie left her and headed down to the beach looking for Johnny, but also to meet the other fishermen who had tried to kill him.

CHAPTER THIRTY-NINE

He found Johnny and his men standing on the sand near the surf. The bodies of two of the fishermen lay sprawled on the beach, dead. One of them wore a bright yellow shirt, now bearing a large red blot over the chest. Willie recognized one of the two canaries who had tried to corner him at the hotel in Santiago. Well, this canary would never sing again.

Johnny had taken into custody the other one, who was slightly wounded in the leg. The prisoner was staring stoically, angrily, out to sea.

Willie and Johnny crouched down in front of him, blocking his view of the horizon. It was Willie who did the talking.

"It's dark here, but I think you recognize me, don't you, *amigo?* You were following me tonight."

The man tried to make believe he didn't hear. Willie tapped him on the knee. "All I want to know is who paid you to follow me?"

Again, the man didn't answer, staring right through Willie. Johnny pulled Willie to his feet.

"Don't worry, *amigo.* He will talk. Just let us convince him."

He led Willie away while his assistants surrounded the man. Police cars and ambulances began to arrive with their sirens blaring. The surf and the palms were painted red by their spinning roof lights and so were the dead men sprawled on the beach.

Willie was standing by himself, watching the proceedings, when from behind him someone called his name. He turned and saw Carlos Espada. He was dressed in a white shirt and white linen pants, but the wash of the police lights painted him red.

Willie went up to him. "What are you doing here?"

"I'm here to see you."

213

Willie grimaced. "Why do you want to see *me*?"

Espada wore his usual solemn countenance. "Because I'm here to turn myself in and I want to do it to you. I'm tired of running."

"Turn yourself in for what?"

"For murder."

Willie's squint deepened as the red lights continued to paint both of them.

"Just who did you murder?"

"Cesar Mendoza and Mario Calderón."

"Is that right?"

"Yes. You know I killed Calderón. You were there at the offices of Great American before I could get away."

"I know you were there. I also know the blood had already stopped flowing. He was starting to cool off. He'd been dead at least an hour, probably more. Why did you hang around there?"

Espada was thrown by the question.

"What's the difference why I stayed? I was there. I killed him."

"Why did you kill him?"

"Because he knew I had been involved in a counterfeiting ring."

"With who?"

"With him."

"I see. And just why did you murder Cesar Mendoza?"

"Because Cesar knew about it, too. He wasn't involved, but he knew."

"That's funny. He didn't tell me about it."

Espada shook his head "No, he wouldn't tell someone like you. You're an outsider, not part of the business."

"If he wouldn't tell someone who wasn't in the business, then he probably wouldn't have mentioned it to the Miami Police either. So, what reason would you have to kill him?"

Espada stared into Willie's face as if he were trying to read an answer written there. He didn't find it but made up an answer.

"I was afraid that someday he might talk. Maybe to you. Maybe to somebody else."

"I see. And when exactly did you kill him?"

Espada shrugged. "The day before you found him. He was in the store alone and I cut him with the cigar knife."

"Then why is it that the federal agent told me that you couldn't have killed Cesar? Why did she tell me that she was with you all that day and evening and the next day, too?"

That surprised and annoyed Espada. He struggled again to find an answer in Willie's face, but Willie didn't give him a chance.

"I don't believe for a minute that you killed Cesar Mendoza. I don't think you're capable of it and I also don't believe you had a reason to murder him. You were never involved in any counterfeiting scheme. Dinah Keane has confirmed that. Maybe Calderón was, but you weren't his partner."

Espada was fuming at him, as if he had been wrongly accused of innocence.

"You don't know what you're talking about."

"Unfortunately, I do. Now the question is why you're lying to me. Who are you trying to protect? You wouldn't lie to protect a person like Calderón, but you might in order to cover up for Nathan Cooler."

Willie stopped there. Now it was he, Willie, who was trying to decipher answers in Espada's face. At the moment it was a face full of pain, eyes suffused with grief and a mouth open in despair. Willie spoke like a surgeon exploring a wound.

"The only problem with that theory is that it doesn't answer the other large issue here: Who killed your father? I understand you think someone murdered him. Why do you think that? And why would you confess to me if you think his murderer is still on the loose?"

The other man bunched his hands into fists and raised them up toward Willie's face. But it was frustration he was demonstrating, not violence. His voice broke as if he would cry.

"You better stay away from us now. You better not ask any more questions. All you'll do is hurt more people, cause more pain."

"I didn't hurt anybody. But somebody did hurt Cesar Mendoza and I'm going to find out who. Did somebody kill your father?"

Espada stood flat-footed, shaking his head, then suddenly he turned and went running into the underbrush. Willie took off after him, but Espada tore through a thicket full of thorns. He ran like a man possessed and Willie lost him in the darkness.

CHAPTER FORTY

Willie made his way back to the beach. Johnny Segura and his assistants had finally found a way to make the surviving canary sing. It was definitely a Dominican coastal interrogation method and not one taught in the best police training schools.

Three of the officers grabbed the man, while a fourth tied his hands behind him and affixed a large cement weight to his wrists. They then carried him toward the water.

The canary began to twist and cry. When the water reached the thighs of his bearers, he pleaded for mercy. And when it reached their waists, he said he would sing. The cold-blooded assassin disappeared and was replaced by a very freaked fisherman. Johnny ordered them to stop and bring him back. He approached the man, who hung suspended in the arms of his captors.

"Who paid you to do this?"

The canary's eyes opened wide, and he stared out into the water.

"It was the American with the big boat."

He was staring toward a very large yacht anchored at a mooring outside the resort marina, about a hundred yards offshore.

Johnny turned to the other officers present.

"Who owns that yacht?"

One agent turned to another and another until the answer emerged in Spanish from the assembled crowd.

"*Un gringo rubio y rico de Miami.*" A rich, blonde gringo from Miami.

Willie looked from one to the other. "What's his name?"

But none of them knew. Willie squinted out to sea.

"What's the name of the boat?"

Again, the answer came in Spanish.

"*El Niño de Ia Fortuna.*" *Fortune's Child*—the name of Richard Knox's boat.

Two minutes later they were back in the villa. Johnny Segura was working the phone trying to find out where Richard Knox might be housed. Willie was looking over the shoulder of the doctor who had been called to attend to Dinah. He was stitching her and ordered her to stay off her feet.

Meanwhile, Willie was trying to work out everything that had happened that week. He had been convinced that Mario Calderón was involved in the counterfeiting business, and he had assumed that Calderón's boss, Nathan Cooler, was also connected. But Calderón had worked for Tirado Cigar as well, before Ricardo Tirado had fired him, and maybe he had found a more likely partner in Richard Knox, former defender of drug smugglers.

Johnny Segura hung up the phone.

"This Richard Knox is here. He came in this morning on a flight from Miami to meet his boat. He's at a villa he keeps here."

Johnny used his walkie-talkie to move more of his agents to the area of Knox's villa. Willie listened to Johnny give his instructions. He also looked at Dinah and at the beach and wished he could carry her down there and let Johnny take care of Knox. But it wasn't to be, not before he spoke with Knox.

They piled back in the Land Rover, headed the way they had first arrived, and then cut off on a short private road that led them to Knox's place. Painted light blue, it sat on the edge of a pond. White roses were planted all around just like his manse in Miami. And just like those other roses, they were beautiful in the starlight.

Knox answered the door dressed in his purple caftan, a slim cigar clenched between his teeth and what appeared to be a martini in his hand. He was surprised to see Willie and none too pleased. He must have expected Willie to be dead by this juncture, but he kept his composure.

"Mr. Cuesta, you're all over the tropics. Impossible to lose you. To what do I owe the pleasure this time?"

"Why don't you invite us in, and we'll tell you."

Knox complied and led them into the living room. It was all black leather and stainless steel. Knox offered them martinis, which they declined.

Instead, Willie introduced Knox to Johnny and told him who Johnny worked for—the Dominican Department of Exterior Commerce. Knox sipped his martini and smiled a smile that was as dry as any vermouth.

"Well, I wonder why I'm getting all this official notice."

Willie looked around a bit. In particular, he admired a painting on the near wall. It was an original by a well-known Miami Cuban artist, and Willie knew it didn't come cheap.

He found Knox at his elbow.

"Why don't you at least give me a clue why you're here, Mr. Cuesta?"

Willie reluctantly turned away from the painting. "The clue is this: Someone had Cesar Mendoza and Mario Calderón killed. That person also fingered me. We're told that person was you."

Knox's mouth opened in an "o" to match his wide-open eyes. He looked from Willie to Johnny, whose pearl-handled pistol was visibly tucked into his alligator belt. Then he shook his head.

"Whoever told you that has his wires badly crossed, Mr. Cuesta. Anyone trying to link me to those deaths or any attempt to knock you off is lying to you. I had no reason to kill them or you."

"You had reason if you were involved in some illegal enterprise and Cesar found out about it."

"I would never have killed Cesar Mendoza. Why in hell would I have killed anyone?"

"Because you were the one counterfeiting Cuban cigars. You were playing both sides of the fence, legitimate and illegitimate, and you tried to make it seem that one was at war with the other, when you were really running both operations. I think your partner in that business was Mario Calderón. I think Calderón was killed because the feds were closing in and you didn't want him compromising you."

The other man stared at him, thoughts obviously running in various directions behind his eyes, forming that complex network that was the life of Richard Knox. He drew on his cigar and smiled that big smile of his.

"Well, you have it half right. You have the business right, but you have the wrong partner."

He crossed the room to a closed door and opened it.

"Come on out, partner."

A moment later Nathan Cooler stepped into the room. He stood and stared in silence. Willie did the same. The puzzle that he had assembled just moments ago was shattered again and he scrambled to find pieces that fit.

On the surface, Knox and Cooler were serious business rivals. They were competitors to the point that they had gone after each other's tobacco and workers, and in one instance had possibly attacked each other's installations. Of course, if you were really in business together, an illegal business, then maybe what you wanted people to believe was that you were at each other's throats.

Cooler wore an expression of pain. He avoided Willie's stare.

"Is this true?" Willie asked him.

The big man nodded almost imperceptibly. He obviously wasn't proud of it. Knox went to him and put his arm around his shoulders, but Cooler shrugged him off. Knox smiled anyway.

"And we didn't have anybody killed."

"We?" Willie asked.

"Yes, we."

"So there came a point when you gentlemen decided to go into the business together."

Knox smiled broadly. "That's right, my friend. Any smart businessman would have done the same thing. We were both losing business to counterfeiters who were peddling what were supposed to be the finest cigars in the world. What do you do if you have a competitor who's taking a chunk out of your business? Someone you can't undercut because he has a brand name you can't beat?"

Willie shrugged. "You tell me."

Knox beamed. "You shift into corporate takeover mode. You acquire that operation and make it part of your own product line. That's what you do, my friend."

Willie glanced at Cooler and back to Knox. "But the two of you had separate product lines. In fact, you were competitors."

Knox nodded. "Yes, that's true, but the smugglers and counterfeiters were doing us much more harm than we were doing to each other. They were making megabucks with bogus operations. We both realized this. I also realized that if my firm tried to go into the counterfeiting trade and my friend here, Mr. Cooler, found out about it,

the news would be out and the police would show up at my door
before I got to work the next day. We had to go in on it together or
not at all."

"So, you picked up the phone and talked turkey."

Knox shook his head. "No. I used an intermediary. Someone
who had been employed by both companies and was intimate with
both operations."

"Calderón."

"Exactly. I made contact with him, and he went to Mr. Cooler,
who agreed with my plan."

"And did Don Ricardo Tirado go along as well?"

Knox shook his head. "No, Don Ricardo wasn't privy to this
new product line. We didn't think he would approve."

Willie glanced at Cooler, who still stood in the same spot, taking
in the proceedings warily. He didn't look as proud of his business
savvy as Knox did. Willie understood Cooler was a businessman but
had thought him more principled. What Knox was saying made
Willie feel naive, something that didn't happen too often.

Willie looked to Cooler. "Is that what happened? Calderón
brought this deal to your doorstep?"

Cooler barely nodded. "Yes, that was the connection," he said
weakly.

"And you were partners just like that?"

Cooler nodded, but said nothing.

Willie shook his head. "I shouldn't admit it, but that surprises
me. In the case of a voracious maggot like Mr. Knox here, I can
believe it. He lied to his own partner, Ricardo Tirado, risked that
partner's reputation, which the old man had spent a whole life building. You, Mr. Cooler, I expected you would have more respect, even
for your rivals, but I guess I was wrong."

If Knox's feelings were hurt at being called a maggot, he didn't
manifest it.

"Cooler didn't have any choice and he knew it," Knox said. "We
had to go at them, or they would ruin us. And given our superior
knowledge in the fields of production, packaging and marketing, we
drove our smaller competitors from the field."

"You drove them out by killing them."

Knox shook his head. "We didn't kill anyone, Mr. Cuesta, and no one will ever prove that we did."

Willie wondered why Knox was so sure, especially if he had employed Fuzzy Face and his accomplices. Willie wondered if Fuzzy Face could be found and made to talk.

"And then the Commerce Department started nosing around. So, you and Mr. Cooler here decided to put them off the scent. You guys were the victims."

The answer came from Cooler. "I had nothing to do with that, starting fires. That was someone else's doing."

Willie looked to Knox. "You fake an attack, bad blood between the two competitors and that causes confusion. But if someone, let's say the Commerce Department or Carlos Espada, later claims you two are in illegal business together, you can say it's ridiculous because rivals trying to burn each other out don't cut up profits together."

Knox shrugged. "Let's put it this way. If you check the police logs, neither of us has ever filed a complaint against the other and my company hasn't filed an insurance claim. So where is the crime?"

Willie looked at Cooler, who had sat down on the edge of a leather chair. Knox freshened his martini from a silver cocktail shaker.

Willie was looking at him when he spoke. "The police may see it differently, Mr. Knox. They may consider it obstruction of justice. In fact, obstruction of a murder investigation."

Knox pursed his lips. "Except, as I told you, we didn't have the motive, economic or otherwise, to kill Cesar Mendoza or anybody else."

"Calderón knew about your crooked business. Maybe he was blackmailing you."

Knox shook his head. "He wasn't. First of all, he was getting a very nice piece of the proceeds already. Calderón was running the counterfeiting operation. Of course, the rollers didn't know what he did with the cigars they made—how he packaged them or what he called them. Calderón was being paid well for his work and he had no reason to turn against us. That you can check with anyone who worked with him in the production line. In fact, Calderón was with us, Mr. Cooler and me, at my house shortly before he was killed. My servants will testify to that. He left to go back to the Great American Tobacco factory, and someone found him there and shot him."

"Who do you think killed him?"

Knox shrugged. "Let's face it, Calderón was an extremely unpleasant man. He had pissed off lots of people. The list of possible killers is very long. It even includes Don Ricardo Tirado, who hated him. But it didn't include me. I had no reason to kill him."

Knox sipped his martini. "And as for Cesar Mendoza, why on earth would I kill Cesar? He had nothing to do with our operation. You saw me with him the day before he died. Did you see any indication that Cesar was a threat to me or to my wealth?"

Willie met Knox's gaze. The millionaire let Willie stare into his eyes. Knox plucked an olive out of his glass and popped it into his mouth. He said, "I've confessed my sins to you, they don't include murder, and I'm not worried about the rest. I can beat those raps." Maybe he was right. He had beaten drug trafficking and money laundering charges in the past.

And he was probably telling the truth about Calderón and Mendoza. So, the question was, who had killed them?

Willie turned to Cooler. "Have you talked to Carlos since you got here?"

Cooler shook his head.

"Did he ever mention to you that he thought his father had been murdered?" Willie asked.

"No. His father wasn't murdered."

"Well, he seems to think so. He said it to Jean-Philippe Montand and to Cesar Mendoza."

Cooler finally looked him in the eyes. "There are a lot of things you don't understand here. Things that have happened over the past forty years. People have done things to each other."

"What do you mean by that?"

Cooler looked away.

It was Knox who finally spoke up. "Now let me give you a tip, *amigo.* Calderón wasn't blackmailing us, but he might have been trying to blackmail someone else, to make a little more money on the side."

"And who would that be?"

"Mr. Montand. I know Calderón was curious about him, about rumors that Montand was in league with Castro, that he smuggled real Cuban cigars into the US. I'm pretty sure Calderón was leaning on him. And if all that was true, Cesar Mendoza would have known it. Maybe Calderón murdered Mendoza and then Montand killed Calderón. That's what I think."

Cooler was staring at the floor. Willie looked back to Knox.

"Montand told me he was leaving Miami. I assume he went back to Europe."

Knox shook his head. "Not so. He's here in the DR. In fact, he's right here in this resort, *amigo*. He keeps the penthouse in the main villa at the entrance."

CHAPTER FORTY-ONE

They left Cooler slumped where he was and Willie, Knox, Segura and some of Segura's men drove to the Plantation House. They parked out in front, passed through the white-columned portico, by a row of potted elephant ears and across the parquet floor to the front desk. A young man in a beige suit with several pens in his pocket advised them that Mr. Montand had checked in earlier that day.

"He always stays in the Planter's Suite on the top floor," he said. "He likes only the best." The clerk also said that as far as he knew, Montand was up there.

Johnny assigned some of his men to the exits. Everyone else took an elevator up to the top floor. They found a white-coated attendant on duty in the hallway, waiting to serve Mr. Montand's slightest desire. They passed him, went to the double doors of the Planter's Suite, and used the gleaming brass knocker. No one answered, so Johnny knocked again, this time harder. When no one came to the door, Johnny summoned the attendant and flashed his ID.

"Have you seen Mr. Montand come out since he arrived today?"

The attendant shook his head. "Some people came to see him about an hour ago, but they left. He's in there. Maybe he's asleep."

Segura had the attendant open the door. The large living area was empty. So was the bedroom. But French doors led from that bedroom out onto a wide veranda that overlooked the entire compound and the sea beyond. It was there they found Montand. Slumped in a chair, he faced the night sea. Blood had run down from a gash in his throat and saturated his white silk *guayabera*. He had been able to wrap a white cloth napkin around his own throat to stem the blood but had apparently been unable to call out or get up. He was still breathing, each inhalation making a gurgling noise.

They picked him up, carried him into the bedroom and laid him on the bed. Johnny called the front desk and told them to send for the doctor right away. Willie turned to the attendant, who was as pale as his jacket. "You said someone came to see him. Who was it?"

"A woman."

"What woman? Young? Old?"

"It was an older woman with black hair, a white streak in it."

He was describing Victoria Espada.

"When did she come here?"

"She arrived about an hour ago. She went in and then I heard an argument, loud voices, she and Mr. Montand. It ended after a few minutes. Then a young man came, and she left with him."

"How was the young man dressed?"

The other man thought for a moment. "He was all in white." He was speaking of Carlos Espada.

"Do you know what Montand and the woman were arguing about?"

The attendant got sheepish, as if he had just been caught eavesdropping. Johnny got in his face.

"That man is dying. You tell us what you heard."

"Something about her children and their father."

Willie turned back to Montand. The small Swiss man was staring desolately up at Willie, his icy composure totally melted now.

"Who did this to you?"

Montand swallowed and spoke in a rasping whisper. "Victoria Espada."

"Why would she do this?"

Montand struggled to enunciate.

"Because I knew."

Willie grimaced. "Knew what?"

"About her children. About her husband. About Nathan Cooler."

"What about Cooler?"

Willie grimaced. Montand rolled his eyes in exasperation, reached up and weakly hooked one of Willie's shirt buttons with his finger. "Cooler is the father of her children."

Willie's mind was reeling. Montand had let go of his shirt and fallen back on the pillow. Willie leaned toward the wounded man.

"Did Ernesto Espada know he wasn't the father? Did they kill him too? Did Cesar Mendoza know?"

Montand was shaking his head. "I don't know . . . I don't know." Montand stopped as he struggled for breath.

"Do you know where they are?"

It was Knox who answered. "I think I know. Cooler was staying on my yacht."

The same doctor who had attended Dinah was coming through the door. He glanced at Willie and Johnny as if they were the ones causing this rash of bloodshed. Willie left the doctor hunched over Montand, and they headed for the marina.

CHAPTER FORTY-TWO

The marina was dark when they got there. Knox went to the dock looking for the dinghy that served the yacht, but it was gone. They looked out into the black cove and could see the yacht floating there. The dinghy was tied to it.

They found the marina's night watchman, who had fallen asleep in the dockmaster's office. Johnny commandeered the small motorboat owned by the marina. He and Willie left Knox in the custody of Johnny's men and the two of them made for the yacht.

The sound of the small outboard was the only noise as they cut across the cove. The sky and sea were welded together in darkness. On the yacht, Willie could see lights, but no movement. He had a bad feeling about what they would find. It got worse a few seconds later.

They were almost to the yacht when a shot rang out. They both flinched, but apparently the round hadn't been fired at them. It didn't pass near them or hit anything behind them on shore. Not that they could hear. The shot had been fired on the yacht, apparently at something or someone aboard.

Johnny cut the engine and let the skiff coast to the aft starboard side of the boat. Guns in hand, they climbed on board quickly and then hunkered down. Nothing moved on any of the three decks.

The two of them were crouched behind some deck chairs beside a Jacuzzi. Then they heard voices coming from the deck above them.

Willie climbed the ladder as quietly as he could, while Segura went forward. Willie advanced until he could see through the rungs of the ladder onto the second deck. He found himself looking into a luxurious lounge area, appointed in teak, with an ample bar, mirrors, plush sofas lining the bulkheads and a billiard table in the middle, all of it lighted only by a hurricane lamp.

In that dim light he saw Nathan Cooler facing a long, curved couch in the corner. On that couch he could barely make out Carlos Espada. He was dressed as he had been before, but now he held a gun in his hand. It was pointed vaguely at Cooler. But Carlos wasn't looking at Cooler. Further down the couch sat Victoria Espada. She was almost swallowed by the shadows, but Willie could see her well enough to know that she also had a gun. It was pressed to her own head.

Willie had barely made a sound, but Cooler heard him anyway. He turned only his head, glanced at Willie, and then looked back at Victoria, but spoke to Willie.

"Please don't do anything sudden. Come up slowly. I can't talk sense to them. Maybe you can."

Willie slipped his gun into his belt and then pulled himself slowly up onto the deck. He took a step, which brought him next to Cooler, but also provoked Victoria Espada.

"Don't come closer. You've already caused enough trouble. I shouldn't have allowed Cesar to hire you."

"I didn't mean to cause you trouble and I don't want to cause you any now."

She waved her free hand at him. "It isn't your fault. I knew that I wouldn't be able to hide my sins forever."

"Maybe your sins aren't as bad as you're making them."

She shook her head, keeping the gun pressed to it. "When you have children by a man not your husband you can't expect mercy."

Carlos Espada was staring at her in horror. Willie watched him. He remembered their run-in at the Edgewater House. "There are secrets in my family," Carlos had said. Had he suspected something was hidden from him, but not known what? Of course, no one would ever have told him. In the Cuban aristocracy, drawn even closer together by the exile experience, what Victoria Espada had done would certainly have been seen as a betrayal in more ways than one. Willie saw why she had wanted to hide it, even to the point of confining her children to her nest. A single grandchild with Cooler's ice-blue eyes might have undone her.

"You can't blame yourself," Willie said. "You were only a girl when all this began."

Cooler turned to Willie. "That's what I've tried to tell her."

Victoria Espada groaned. "I wasn't a girl at all. I was nineteen years old, old enough to have married Ernesto, old enough to leave my country and come to the United States with him. And when he went away to Spain to try to make a living, I was old enough to get myself in trouble."

Willie glanced at Cooler out of the side of his eye. The big man was shaking his head.

"You didn't get in trouble by yourself, Victoria," he said.

She laughed emptily. "Don't try and blame yourself, Nathan. You've done that for too many years. The truth is you didn't have a chance. I was angry with my husband for having left me alone. I was a spoiled girl, always considered the most beautiful young woman in any room. Men told me they would never leave my side. Of course, it wasn't Ernesto's fault he had to go away. He did it to try to support me and the children we would have. But I expected life to be easy, gay, even if it wasn't easy for any Cuban at that moment. Once I turned my charms on you, Nathan, you didn't stand a chance. You were so handsome with your blond hair and your beautiful blue eyes. I never had so much passion for anyone. By the time I woke from that passion it was too late. I was pregnant with Carlos and Esther."

Willie was watching her and Carlos, listening, but he was also starting to wonder where Segura had gone. Johnny was no longer on the deck below. Maybe he was trying to come up behind them. Willie had to give him a chance; he didn't want Victoria to stop talking.

"You kept it from your husband?"

She shrugged. "I tried to keep it from him, to convince him they were his. He came back to Miami six weeks after I became pregnant. First, I hid my morning sickness from him, or tried to, and I made love to him pretending a passion I didn't feel. When Carlos and Esther were born, I told him they were premature, but of course the doctors and nurses in the hospital knew that wasn't true. For a while he wouldn't admit it to himself. He talked only about problems with business, and he talked about killing himself. But when the children were just three months old, he came home one night and he had been drinking. He never drank before that. We got in a fight. He called me a whore." She hesitated. "Even then he didn't hit me. He never hit me. He was a gentle man, maybe too gentle for me. Instead, he started to drink and that night he told me he would drink himself to death.

But before he did, he was going to tell the world what a whore I was."

Her eyes narrowed. "He went out of the house and finished a bottle of rum sitting on the sand at the edge of the water. Then he passed out. I sat nearby him and watched him as the tide came up and it started to cover him. I expected him to wake up when the water touched his face, but he didn't. I watched him and I watched him and I waited."

Her voice was low and sad. Willie was afraid she would pull the trigger. He spoke up.

"He drank himself unconscious and he drowned. It wasn't your fault."

She shook her head and spoke with a strangely languid tone. "I killed him."

Cooler writhed with a pain felt deep in his heart. "No, you didn't."

Willie put a hand on Cooler to control him. Carlos was frozen with horror.

Victoria went on as if she hadn't heard Cooler and as if no one else were there.

"Life went on. I lived my widowhood. But then Calderón had to destroy everything. Calderón had also worked with my husband in Spain and the Canary Islands, along with Cesar Mendoza and Jean-Philippe Montand. Calderón had always suspected me. He never said anything, but I knew it the first time we met here in Miami. It was the way he looked at me, scandal in his eyes, disrespect, evil. I knew right at that moment that one day there would be a disaster.

"Carlos never cared for Calderón either, maybe because I had always had bad things to say about the man. When Carlos found out about the counterfeiting and that someone at Great American was involved, he was sure Nathan knew nothing about it. He didn't know that Calderón was blackmailing Nathan. Calderón told Nathan he would tell the world about our affair if Nathan didn't turn a blind eye to his crooked business. When Carlos began to ask questions, I knew it would all come out. So, I killed Calderón."

That made Carlos look up at her with that same look of pain he had worn on the beach. His mother continued.

"I had very little problem killing him," she said. "He was an evil man. It was Calderón who killed Cesar Mendoza. Cesar was sometimes consulted by people who bought Havanas and he had told some of them that their cigars were counterfeit. He mentioned to me the day before he died that for some reason Calderón had asked to see him and he suspected it was because Calderón and Nathan were involved in that illegal business. He was worried and thought of going to the police. But I begged him not to. I was afraid that the truth would come out. That night Cesar died. The next day I called Calderón. I told him I needed to talk with him about my son and his knowledge of the counterfeiting. That I was willing to pay him to keep quiet about what he knew. I would sell the last property I owned. He played with me for a couple days and finally told me to come to the offices of Great American at night. I found him sitting behind Nathan's deak."

She paused, staring into the darkness as if Calderón stood before her.

"I sat across from him. I had brought a small pistol with me and as he recounted my sins and reveled in my fall from grace, I took it from my purse and shot him. The red pins were sitting on the desk and I pushed them into his heart."

"And then you called your son?"

"No, I didn't call him. But his sister had overheard my phone conversation and knew where I had gone. And she made him go looking for me. I had left, but he was still there when you arrived. He protected me. He shouldn't have. He should have handed me to the police."

Willie saw her hand flex on the gun. He needed to buy time.

"Why did you try to kill Montand?"

Her face suddenly grew stem. "Montand was a traitor. He called me after Cesar died to tell me that the police had questioned him. He let me know that he, like Calderón, suspected my secret. I decided if he could betray the cause of Cuba by doing business with the communists then he might betray me. I feel no guilt for what I did to him. In fact, the only guilt I feel is for what happened thirty-five years ago."

It was at that moment that Willie spotted Johnny. He had gone around to the bow of the boat, climbed to the third deck and was now at the top of the carpeted stairs leading down into the lounge. Willie made eye contact with him, and Johnny started silently toward him.

Victoria was lost in the past. "All I was trying to do was protect my children from something I had done when I was younger than they are now. I was trying to protect the honor of our family."

"I'm sure they'll forgive you."

"No, not if they have to go through a trial and visit their mother in jail and suffer the scandal. You have to understand, that is exactly what I never wanted to happen."

The angle of her wrist changed only slightly, but Cooler and Carlos were already lunging toward her. Carlos screamed out.

"No!"

But they didn't get there in time and neither did Johnny Segura. The gun went off. Her head rocked to one side, recoiled and then fell to her chest.

CHAPTER FORTY-THREE

Willie returned to Miami and attended two funerals in the next week: for Cesar Mendoza and Victoria Espada. Many of the same mourners attended both, including Carlos and Esther Espada, Nathan Cooler, Ricardo Tirado and Dinah Keane. Both Rolando Falcón and Jean-Philippe Montand were still hospitalized but recovering. Richard Knox was in custody, charged with the murder of the two cigar rollers in North Miami. He led police to Fuzzy Face and his long-haired accomplice, trying to pin the killings on them and the late Mario Calderón, but Grand wasn't buying it. He told Willie that he expected Knox to take the fall.

Most of the attendees, including Willie, accompanied Victoria Espada's body to Woodlawn Cemetery on Calle Ocho. Her children chose to bury her next to her late husband despite what she had divulged that night on the yacht.

Willie was walking to his car afterward when he heard his name called. Esther Espada wore over her shoulders a black mantilla similar to the one her mother had worn during their first meeting.

"I wanted to speak to you," she said. "I want to thank you for trying to help."

"I didn't do quite enough."

She shrugged. "There wasn't much anyone could have done. There never was."

She let him look into her eyes.

"You knew, didn't you?" Willie asked.

She looked across the cemetery to where Cooler was speaking and nodded.

"Yes. I knew from the time I was fifteen years old. You can tell the way two people look at each other. And somehow you can sense in yourself a blood tie to another human being. At least I did."

"But your brother didn't."

"No."

"And that's why you said you had played a role your whole life."

She shrugged. "It's over."

"Is it?"

"Yes. My brother and I are selling the property. Mr. Cooler . . . my father, I should say . . . has promised he'll help us find a buyer. He told me that since the big cigar boom came and he started making more money, he had wanted to do more to help us, but my mother had resisted. By that time the fiction had gone on too long and I think by that time she had decided that there just was no happy ending to it."

"It was generous of Cooler to offer. It sounds like he'll be there for you."

She nodded but was looking at Willie not Cooler. "I don't know exactly where I'll have my studio, where I'll take up my next role, as you might say, and who I will know in it. But I'll let you know where I am."

"Do that."

Willie watched her and her brother drive away. Then he put the tombstones behind him and headed home.

ALSO BY JOHN LANTIGUA